Roman

Vampire's Mate Book One

Grae Bryan

Contents

Prologue

June 18, 1815

Waterloo, Belgium

All Roman knew was pain.

The round shot from the British cannons had torn apart his infantry's formation. He didn't know how many had survived, but it didn't seem to matter anymore.

Roman didn't have much time left himself.

On his back on the hard ground, struggling to breathe, he knew he had been hit somewhere on his lower body, his hip or thigh maybe, but he was too afraid to look down to see the damage. He could feel the blood rapidly leaving his body. He knew he didn't have long.

He was starting to feel very cold. That couldn't be a good sign.

A shadow fell over Roman's face, blocking his view of the clouds. He struggled to focus his gaze. Had a medic found him?

The man looming over him didn't look like a soldier from either side, but his green eyes were nonetheless focused on Roman with unnerving intensity.

"Your leader has fled, I believe." The man's French was accentless, so Roman wasn't sure what he meant by "your leader." Their leader should be the same. Roman said nothing in response.

"Do you want the pain to stop?" The man's voice was low and soft but somehow carried perfectly, even over the groans of the wounded men around them.

Roman shook his head, the man's green eyes looking almost amused at his response. "And why not?"

"With this injury, if the pain stops, it means I am dead," Roman managed to rasp out.

"And you do not wish to die? Even with the pain?"

Roman shook his head again. He wasn't ready. He wanted to see his family again. His sisters, his parents. He didn't want to die in a foreign country, his fellow soldiers lost.

"What if I could stop the pain and still promise you a long, long life?" Soft fingers traced Roman's face.

It sounded too good to be true. A deal with the devil, but Roman was beyond caring. He nodded frantically. "Then yes. Please. Please help." His voice came out gurgled this time, and he could taste the metallic tang of his own blood in his mouth.

The stranger's fingers stilled. "If I help you, what will you do for me?"

"What do you want?" Roman would give him anything.

"Will you promise to stay by my side?"

It was a strange request, to come from a man he'd never met before, but easy enough to answer. "I promise."

The man smiled. Straight white teeth. "Close your eyes."

Roman shut his eyes, hoping his leg wasn't about to be amputated here on the hard ground. Was that what he had just agreed to?

A sharp prick of pain but not at his leg.

On his neck. A bite. The man was...drinking?

Roman opened his eyes, tilting his head to gaze at the face latched at his neck, and the pair of eyes that met his own were no longer green. They were entirely black, no iris or whites showing at all. As if each pupil had expanded over the entire eye.

The man's mouth was smeared red. Smeared with Roman's blood, which was dripping off fangs Roman was sure hadn't been there a moment ago.

A hallucination?

Roman wanted to scream, but he was too tired to manage even a gasp. He'd grown even colder. He was fading.

The last words he heard before the darkness took over: "Remember your promise."

One

Danny

"You goddamn, flipping piece of crap, son of a hot potato!" Danny yelled, shaking his fist at the current bane of his existence. "You were put on this earth to torment me, weren't you, spawn of Satan? Don't even try to deny it."

The copy machine did not, in fact, try to deny it.

"That's what I thought," mumbled Danny, a trifle smugly. Then he remembered he was talking out loud to an inanimate object in the middle of the night, and all smugness was forgotten. He took a quick look around to make sure nobody was nearby. He was generally pretty good when it came to controlling his admittedly dirty mouth while at work, but he wasn't actually quite sure what had come out just now.

The office was abandoned. Chloe, the night-shift charge nurse and his work bestie, had left her computer to go grab coffee and snacks, and he was pretty sure the other emergency room nurses were sneaking naps on some of the gurneys in the lesser-used patient bays.

It was a dead night.

Danny supposed he should be glad about that, since it meant no one was horrifically ill or injured, but it also meant he had time to help out his charge and copy the new schedule, necessitating the use of the copy machine from hell, so his feelings were a little conflicted.

The copy machine that was currently possessed, refusing to copy and also refusing to tell Danny *why*.

"Agh! I give up. You win again, demon."

"Danny Boy, please stop talking to the copier. It's concerning."

Danny jumped at the sound of Chloe's voice. She had appeared in the doorway, coffees in hand, a few bags of chips peeking out of her scrub jacket pocket.

Danny immediately blushed at being caught—he fucking hated that he blushed so easily—but still managed to defend himself. "That beast started it."

"Be a good boy, step away from the copier, and drink your coffee. I appreciate you trying to help me out but not at the risk of your clearly fragile sanity."

He was tempted to stick his tongue out at her, but he was a *professional*, damn it. He took the coffee with a quick grin of thanks.

Danny was nearing the end of his second year working nights in the emergency room, but it was too unpredictable to get used to any sort of routine. Their hospital was in a smaller city, but the mountains around Hyde Park, Colorado, attracted outdoorsy tourists, and that meant that some nights it seemed everyone and their mother needed to be seen and some nights there was not a patient to be found.

It was hard to stay awake on the slower nights, but he knew if he tried to nap like some of the other nurses, he'd just end up throwing off his sleep rhythm. He tried to help out with some of the charge nurse duties when he had time, but sometimes he ended up more hindrance than help.

"I saw Gabe in the cafeteria. He told me to tell you to go see him, if you're not busy."

Danny rolled his eyes before he could stop himself. Of course Gabe had used someone else as a go-between rather than coming to find Danny himself.

"We both have phones. He can text me if he really wants to see me."

Chloe shrugged while scooping her dark curls up into a ponytail. "I figured you'd say that, but I'm not getting in the middle of it—just told him I'd pass the message along." She grinned at him. "I'm an angel that way."

Danny couldn't help his answering grin despite his annoyance with his brother. "You *are* an angel. Thank you. And thanks for the coffee. I'm gonna head back to my station. Call me if you need any help."

"As long as it doesn't involve the copy machine," Chloe teased. "You two are on a time-out from each other."

Danny just raised his coffee in acknowledgment and headed down the hall to the nurses' station, which consisted of a semicircle row of computers facing out toward the patient bays.

Bays that were currently empty.

He sat down in an office chair that had definitely seen better days. To be fair, most of their equipment had seen better days. He took a sip of his coffee—scalding hot and indecently weak, the hospital special—and poked at his book. He wasn't exactly sure why he was reluctant to settle in and read, but he had an itchy, restless feeling that was making it hard to sit still.

A movement at the corner of his eye caught his attention.

"Chloe?" he called out, turning his head to the left. No answer and no one he could see.

He lifted slightly out of his chair and leaned over the counter, trying to peer around the corner. Nothing but empty beige hallway.

He sat back down, giving himself a shake. "All right, Danny, let's stop creating distractions for ourselves. Also, let's stop talking to ourselves. We're embarrassing us."

He picked up his book, leaned back in his chair, and opened up to his most recent page.

"Hello, lovely."

The voice was deep, with a velvety smoothness that sent a little shiver down Danny's spine. He looked up from his book and nearly jumped out of his chair.

There was a man directly in front of him where no one had been just a second before.

And oh Lord, what a man.

He was the kind of handsome one rarely saw in a hospital outside of a soap opera, and dressed in an immaculate, perfectly fitted suit. Cheekbones you could cut yourself on, with sleek black hair swept back, ending just below his chin. And those eyes. A bright, icy blue that seemed to glow underneath the hospital's fluorescents.

Eyes that were focused on Danny with unnerving intensity. But in contrast to the man's greeting, which had sounded warm and even a little sultry, his blue eyes were hard, almost cold.

Danny felt all the hairs on the back of his neck prick up. They could get some really strange people in the middle of the night, but they usually had to get through the entrance desk before ending up back here. Danny hadn't been called about any new patients, and this man didn't have a visitor's badge.

Fuck. Was the night clerk also taking a gurney nap?

Danny mustered up his best patient-friendly voice. "Can I help you, sir? Were you here to be seen? I can show you back to the front desk."

The man's cold stare didn't waver. "I'm not a patient."

"Okay, well." Danny forced himself to keep meeting the man's eyes. "Are you looking for a family member? If you give me their name, I can try to find what floor they're staying on."

"I'm not a visitor."

Danny took in the stranger's immaculate suit again. Was this maybe a new surgeon? That *would* explain the sociopathic stare. Although, he didn't see a badge anywhere. "Are you looking for the doctors' lounge?"

Those icy eyes didn't even blink. "Who were you talking to just now?"

Of course this stranger had heard him talking nonsense to himself.

Danny refused to blush. "Myself."

"I see."

And that seemed to be all that Mr. Handsome Creep intended to say. He just kept staring at Danny, blue eyes stone-cold and eerily bright.

Seeing how this apparently wasn't a patient he had to be nice to, and seeing as how he had just been forced to admit to an *unfairly* good-looking stranger that he had been talking to himself like a loon, Danny felt entitled to funnel his embarrassment into annoyance instead.

He switched to his *stern* patient voice, the one he used when someone seemed like they were about to take his sweet disposition as permission to throw something at him. "Well, this is nice and all, but I need you to tell me what you're doing here so I can point you in the right direction. Because I can guarantee this nurses' station isn't it. So...?"

Danny was almost positive the man hadn't moved—still hadn't even blinked, for that matter—but he was suddenly much, much closer. He was positively looming over the desk, blue eyes now only inches from Danny's own. Danny was never exactly the tallest guy in the room, topping off at just five feet eight, but had he been standing, this man would have towered over him by more than half a foot.

And *oh*. He smelled good. *Really* good. Like warm spices with some strange undertone. Something almost metallic, something that shouldn't smell so good but most certainly *did*.

It would be weird to sniff a stranger, right?

"Who are you?" The man's question came out clipped, almost angry, bringing Danny sharply out of his smell-induced reverie.

"I'm Danny, a nurse here." It was best to keep it simple when dealing with the unhinged. He pointed at his badge.

The man's eyes finally, *finally* moved away from his, moving down to his name badge.

"So you are," he murmured. "Danny No-Last-Name."

"We have a policy not to give our last names out to patients. Don't want any potential *weirdos*"—Danny couldn't help but make that last part a little pointed—"hunting us down after work."

Mr. Handsome Creep's lips tilted up. Nowhere near a full smile, but a little genuine warmth entered those glacial eyes, and Danny felt his breath catch at the sight.

He found himself thinking of nibbling on those lips. How much warmth would enter those eyes then?

No. No, thank you. We are not attracted to Mr. Handsome Creep.

"No, we couldn't have you being hunted, could we?" The man's voice was a purr now. "Lots of big, bad predators out there looking for a snack."

"Um..." Danny wasn't even sure what to feel. The words were teasing, but the tone was not. Was the man threatening him? Playing with him? Very poorly flirting with him?

All it took was another whiff of the man's spiced scent, and Danny thought, *Fuck it*. This guy might be odd, but he looked like a prince and smelled goddamn amazing, and Danny hadn't flirted with anyone in ages. Maybe he could be graduated to Mr. Handsome instead of Mr. Handsome Creep.

Danny smiled his best "get free coffee from the barista" smile. "Well, I've been called a snack before but never in that context." He winked for good measure.

Danny had thought he'd seen warmth in those eyes, but it was nothing to the heat that flared through them at his comment, silly as it was.

Well then, that cleared up where this guy stood on some dude-on-dude flirting, that was for sure. He was definitely into it on some level. Warmth pooled in Danny's stomach.

Danny was just about to see if he could get an actual smile out of the guy, when he heard Chloe calling his name from the other room. "We've got someone coming in. Five minutes out!" she yelled.

It only took a second for Danny to glance down the hallway, but by the time he turned his head back to the front, the stranger was already gone.

Well, that was...unsettling.

Was the guy some kind of ninja? Cat burglar? A literal cat, perhaps? Danny had never known someone to move so quietly.

He knew he should be relieved that he didn't have to deal with the odd, intense stranger anymore, especially with a patient coming in, but he still found himself wishing the man would come back.

At least long enough for Danny to get another sniff.

Oh God, he was thinking about sniffing strangers again. *Who's the creep now?* He put those blue eyes out of his head and got up to help get a bay ready.

It was an appropriate reminder—he didn't have time for guys, strange or otherwise.

Danny was out the hospital door by 6:00 a.m. on the dot, having had no report to give to the oncoming nurse. They'd already gotten their new patient up to a room. He supposed he could have told her about the strange, tall man with piercing blue eyes possibly wandering the halls, but at this point, he wasn't 100 percent sure he hadn't hallucinated the whole thing.

He immediately threw on his sunglasses, almost blinded by the morning sunlight. Once a friend to him and his olive complexion, the sun had become his enemy after he'd started working nights. Too harsh after twelve hours under hospital fluorescents. And while winter mornings were cold in Hyde Park, they still tended to be bright, with the exception of when there was the occasional snowstorm.

Danny chugged the last of his now cold coffee, willing himself to stay awake just a little longer.

What he was desperately craving was to scarf down some cereal and face-plant into bed, but it was not to be. Mornings were her best time of day, and he didn't want to let her down.

He somehow found himself pulling into a familiar parking lot ten minutes later, having driven himself there in practically a fugue state. He wondered for the hundredth time if it was even safe to be driving after a night shift.

Maybe I should start taking the bus after work?

He parked quickly and pulled down the sun visor to catch his reflection on the inside mirror.

It was worse than he thought.

His chocolate-brown hair, the curls left longer than he'd like for no other reason than he always forgot to make an appointment to get it cut, was sticking up all over the place. He licked his fingers and tried to flatten the worst offenders. Normally he'd throw a baseball cap over it all, but in this case—depending on the amount of lucidity waiting for him inside—he was liable to get a scolding for wearing a hat indoors. The shadows under his eyes he could do nothing for, other than turn back time and get significantly more sleep over the past two years.

"All right, stud. Let's go see our girl." And there he was, still talking out loud to himself. At least he was alone in his car, no one lurking around corners to overhear him.

Approaching the front desk, Danny could already hear the sounds of the usual bustle of morning activity filling the carpeted halls.

"Danny! So good to see you, sweetie. You just coming off work?" The receptionist rounding the front desk was one of his favorites. A sweet older woman who always managed to treat him with empathy that somehow never edged into pity.

Danny felt himself grin wide despite his fatigue. "Hey, Mary. I look that terrible, huh?"

"Please, honey, you couldn't look terrible if you tried." She gave him a brief hug. "You've got half the old biddies in this place asking after you every time you leave. You don't want to hear the things they'd try with you if they were only half a century younger," she teased. "It's just that full set of luggage you're carrying under those doe eyes that gave you away."

"Dang it! Knew you'd call me out on those," he laughed, not offended in the slightest.

"Some good sleep and good food would take care of them." Her expression turned serious, and he sensed a lecture coming. "I'm starting to think you need a keeper. I'd feel better if you had someone looking after you. Isn't your brother back in town? Why doesn't he—"

Danny broke in before she could get any further. "He's doing his best, I promise. Residency took a lot out of Gabe. He's just getting his feet back under him. I'm sure you'll start seeing more of him soon." He cleared his throat. "And I don't need anyone looking after me."

He didn't sound convincing even to himself, but Mary was kind enough to drop it. She gave a small sigh and then was back to her cheerful self, smiling warmly at him. "Come on, sweetheart. Let's take you to see her."

He knew the way by heart, but Mary always liked to walk him back like an honored guest. As they approached the familiar door, wide open to the room inside, she gave his arm a squeeze. "Just a warning, she's been calm so far, but it's not her best day overall."

That was all right. They hadn't had a "best day" in he couldn't remember how long.

The woman seated in the armchair in the corner of the room didn't seem to notice his arrival, her eyes on a television playing an old black-and-white western.

"Good morning, Gladys," he called out softly, entering the room. He'd learned long ago that calling her by name could prevent a good day from going bad right off the bat. Otherwise, he would end up sowing confusion and then the inevitable anxiety.

There would be no more "Good morning, Mom." Not for Danny.

His mother turned her head from the TV then, a hesitant smile on her face. She shared his coloring (or used to, before her hair had grayed) and his nose, but the similarities ended there—her chin was sharper, her lips thinner, and her brown eyes smaller, tilted up at the corners, whereas Danny's were round and wide. But still, you could see the relation at a glance—certain expressions and mannerisms they both shared.

She had raised him to be who he was, and that left a certain mark.

"Good morning." She greeted him politely, without a hint of recognition. "Can I help you?"

"I just came for a little visit." He kept his voice light and cheerful, suppressing any hint of disappointment. "If you're not too busy?"

Her expression remained hesitant, but at least she didn't look annoyed or fearful. It could be worse. "Oh no, not too busy. Watching my show though." She pointed at the TV with a trembling finger.

"That's okay. I can just watch with you, if you don't mind." He sat himself down in the chair across from her.

The room was sizable, with a large bed in the corner, an attached bathroom, and then the makeshift living room they were currently making use of, with two armchairs and a television. A decent place to live overall—he'd made sure of it, trusting himself to make it work financially somehow.

He was managing but just barely.

They sat in silence for a long while. Occasionally during commercials, she asked after him in a vague sort of way, the kind of questions you might ask a stranger, or they discussed the weather, what they were watching.

Some days were like this—she would be content with keeping things light, aware maybe that she knew him in some way but not digging to find out how. Other days she thought he was his father and greeted him by that name.

He'd learned to go along with it, to be content with the knowledge that she knew she loved him, even if she couldn't remember exactly who it was she loved.

More important was that *she* knew she was loved, that there were people out there who cared for her.

Danny could tell when the conversation started to take a toll on her, as it was beginning to now. Her questions began to repeat themselves, her responses to his questions grew more sporadic, and her reactions became slightly more awkward.

Mary was right: it wasn't his mom's best day. But also not the worst. The worst could involve fierce mood swings, emotional breakdowns, screaming matches, an unwillingness to get out of bed or brush her teeth.

There'd been less of that since she'd moved into the care home. The scheduled routines, something he hadn't been able to give her at home while working full-time, help calmed down some of the chaos in her mind.

"Okay, Gladys, I think I'm going to head out," he made himself say, pushing up out of his chair. "But it was so nice talking to you. I hope to see you again soon."

She gave a little nod at him but didn't make eye contact. She was reaching her limit with social interaction, clearly. "Nice talking to you too," she mumbled.

He made his way out of the facility, waving at Mary as he passed by. She simply waved back, not pulling him into any conversation, aware he wasn't always up for talking after a visit with his mom.

It felt like every step he took was heavier than the last. He was just so *tired*.

He knew he should be grateful for days like this. Days she wanted to talk with him, even for just a little bit, even not knowing who he was. Days where her mood was good, where she was dressed and out of bed.

But sometimes he just wanted his mom. He wanted her to hug him, to *know* him.

Danny was starting to worry he'd passed the point of her ever recognizing him again. He just wished he'd known the last time had been the very last one.

He would have savored every second of it.

If tears streaked down his cheeks on the drive home, there wasn't anyone around to see them.

Two

Roman

Roman sucked on his pilfered blood bag—*cold, tasteless, garbage-*—and tried to keep himself and his demon from spiraling.

What in God's name had just happened?

He hadn't even meant to stop in this charmless mountain town. He'd meant to keep driving south for hours longer, possibly *days* longer, before pausing even for blood. But he'd passed by that tiny little hospital and felt suddenly that he *had* to stop.

His demon had practically put his foot on the brakes for him.

Roman normally stuck to larger hospitals when he went the blood bag route for his feedings. More people coming in and out, fewer people stopping to notice a new face, fewer to have to compel to forgetfulness. But apparently his rules were out the window. And he'd felt it as soon as he'd stepped inside.

A presence. A scent. Like warm milk with honey.

And, following that scent, he'd found the boy.

A young man somewhere in his early twenties. Practically an infant compared to Roman.

Big brown eyes, messy brown hair, a smattering of freckles across his nose.

Lovely.

Even with the dark shadows under his eyes and his skin a shade or two paler than natural.

The pull Roman had felt had been so strong he'd assumed the boy must be *other*. Not like him, clearly, but surely not just human. He'd been so nonplussed he hadn't even put on his normal, charming human act.

He'd acted like a creep.

But young Danny wasn't anything *other*, was he? He was just a boy. A simple human man. One with a smart mouth and a smile that could take someone's breath away.

Not just boy, his demon snarled at him. *Not* just *anything. Special. Perfect. Ours.*

Right.

There was another word for what this boy could be—for what he could be to Roman, to his demon. But it was a word Roman hadn't believed in for decades.

One he refused to believe in any longer.

This obsession must be just another symptom of his demon becoming more and more unhinged. It had been a trying few years. Every feeding becoming more fraught, his demon constantly restless and demanding *more*. More violence, more fear, more sex. More *anything* to keep it entertained, keep it sated.

Each time, it was harder to stop a feeding from going too far. Harder to keep from killing.

So he'd been sticking to blood bags. But the lack of a hunt just made the demon angrier. And now Roman was afraid to switch back to live bodies. Afraid he'd been depriving his demon for so long that the first taste of fresh blood would lead to a massacre. Afraid that this time, he wouldn't be able to stop.

And, most of all, afraid he wouldn't even care.

It was what happened to their kind in the end, after all. Complete disconnection from their humanity. A feral state. Lord knew how Soren had evaded it all this time. Luc certainly hadn't been so lucky.

Fucking Lucien.

The reason Roman needed to be moving on in the first place. Luc and his trail of bodies had been getting too close. One would think that after seventy goddamn years, he'd have moved on, found someone else to torment. But the miserable bastard was still fixated on Roman.

And for good reason.

Roman pushed aside the familiar guilty thoughts. They didn't help anything. He tossed the finished blood bag onto the passenger seat floor and started his car. He needed to get moving. To leave this town. He didn't have time for lovely boys with smooth skin and freckled noses and big brown puppy-dog eyes.

Who knew what his demon would do to little Danny if Roman let himself get his hands on him?

And yet, somehow, he found himself pulling in front of a hotel he'd marked on his way into town.

Merde.

The woman at the front desk was beautiful in a plastic sort of way. Subtle makeup, smooth blonde hair, a perfectly fitted suit hugging her impressive curves. She smiled at Roman's approach in a way that told him he could easily have the whole package—a hot meal, sexual release—on a platter, no compulsion required. But for once, his demon wasn't interested.

His damn demon was still angry at him for walking out of that hospital without the boy in his arms.

"How can I help you, sir?" the receptionist inquired, voice sultry.

"I find myself in need of a room."

"We have a few vacancies available. Just one guest? Traveling alone?" She gave him an unsubtle perusal, and Roman had to fight to keep his lip from curling. Apparently it wasn't just his demon that didn't have any patience for non-Danny humans right now.

"Just myself. Just for the night," he bit out. Where was his usual cool, his usual charm?

To the receptionist's credit, she immediately took the hint at his lack of interest, and her tone turned to strictly professional. "Certainly, sir. I can book you right now."

"Perfect." Roman reached for his wallet.

Except he found himself pausing as he took out his credit card.

He cleared his throat. "Apologies, I misspoke. Not just a night. A week. I'll be staying a week."

Goddamn it.

———ele———

Roman couldn't stop pacing.

His demon was driving him completely mad. He'd thought the last few years had been bad enough, but they were nothing compared to the intensity of this complete obsession.

Want Danny. Honey. Sweet. Ours. Ours, ours, ours.

Roman rarely resorted to actually talking to his demon—it felt like a step too far in the direction of madness, talking to himself within his own head, but he needed to calm the situation down somehow. He took a breath and focused inward.

Hush. We've barely talked to the boy. You're losing it.

Not losing. Right there. Waiting. Honey sweet. Waiting for us.

Yes, Roman soothed. *Waiting. Not going anywhere. We can go back. But not now, not right this second. We already frightened him, I think. Do you want to scare him off? Have him run away? Never find him again?* His demon gave a loud growl at the thought. Roman continued on, sensing victory. *He's human. Delicate. We need to be careful. Let me handle it. We're staying, okay? So hush.*

His demon gave another growl in response but much softer this time. It was actually listening to reason, for the first time in a very long while.

Roman let out a loud, steady exhale. He was staying in Hyde Park, at least for now. That much was clear. He knew where the boy worked, where to find him. Hopefully lovely Danny would be working again the next night.

He wasn't sure his demon would put up with any more wait than that. If it was impatient enough, it might even try to take over, take control of Roman's consciousness without his permission, and that was the road to a feral state.

So. See Danny again. And then...

Roman was indeed sure they had frightened the boy. Not that one could tell from the sass the young nurse had been spitting out. But Roman had tasted it in the air—not overwhelming but enough to know he hadn't given the best impression. He hadn't exactly been at his most charming.

But he did *know* how to charm. Decades of experience luring willing victims, for food or for play. He just needed to get the boy alone for a minute. Maybe he could compel an answer out of him, some reason for Roman's draw to him.

Roman had heard rumors before of humans with magical abilities: healing, the sight, telepathy, even shapeshifting. He'd never come across one himself, but their blood was supposed to be especially enticing to Roman's kind.

As of now, the only other logical reason Roman could think of was one he didn't want to consider. Not if he was hoping to move on from this town without sending his demon into a spiral.

And if he couldn't get answers, maybe Roman could fuck the boy out of their system. The thought held more than just a little appeal.

He finally stopped his pacing, readjusting his hardening cock, and took a seat on the king-size hotel bed, ignoring his arousal for the moment. He felt better now that he had a plan. Not exactly a *thorough* plan but better than the instinct-driven mindlessness of the past few hours. See Danny, charm Danny, compel some answers from Danny.

Now he just had to worry about Luc. There was at least one person who could help a little with that.

Roman pulled his phone out of his pocket and sent out a text.

Can you keep an eye on Luc's trail for me? I'm in Colorado. Let me know if he starts traveling south.

He received an immediate reply.

Colorado? Thought you'd be clearing out of the States. I was already planning our tropical reunion. The mountains are fucking boring, bad choice.

Roman rolled his eyes. Little shit. *Something came up.*

What came up?

Just tell me if Luc comes close.

Fine. Be mysterious. Knowing you, it's not anything exciting, anyway.

Brat.

Bore.

He was just putting his phone away when it dinged one last time.

You know if your someTHING is a someONE, you can't let Luc catch up to you. Hurry up with whatever you're doing and move on.

Roman wasn't sure how Soren did that. He always seemed to know what wasn't being said. Roman couldn't tell if it was something that came with his greater age, or a skill he'd just always naturally had.

But Soren wasn't wrong. Roman really couldn't linger.

Just a few days, he told himself. *Just to get some answers, and then I'm gone.*

His demon, mercifully quiet, let the lie pass.

Just a few days.

Three

Danny

"Danny, I've got to give you another one. Bay two. Overdosed downtown. He got two doses of Narcan in the ambulance already, stable and holding his own airway."

"Got it." Danny nodded, typing quickly to catch up on his charting.

So much for a night off.

He'd been finishing a late dinner—if you could call stale cereal dinner—when he'd gotten a frantic text from his work asking if he could come in. The staffing center knew he was always up to pick up extra shifts. He was exhausted enough that he had almost said no for once, but then had reminded himself that student loans didn't pay themselves, and he had two nights off in a row coming up if he could just get through this one.

The chaos in the ER was in direct contrast to the night before. Just after midnight and they were already almost full, even if that wasn't saying much considering their small size. It was the normal variety of a not-so-big city: some dehydration from stomach bugs, a few broken bones, now apparently an overdose. He was supposed to have gone on break a half hour ago, but these things weren't guaranteed on busier nights.

He had just gotten his patient assessed and settled in, making sure his vitals were being measured every fifteen minutes in case the Narcan wore off before the drugs left his system, when Chloe stopped by his station.

She crossed her arms and gave him a stern look. "I'm covering your patients. Take your break—I know you're overdue."

Danny gave her a relieved smile, unable to even pretend to put up a fight. "I promise I'll be quick. Just need some fast calories and caffeine."

She shook her head at him. "Full half hour, mister. I've got 'em, I promise."

He was about to protest further, but she cut him off before he could start. "You need to eat some real food, Danny Boy. Not gonna lie—you're looking wrecked. I'll text you if we get slammed. Scout's honor."

Choosing to ignore the less-than-flattering assessment of his appearance, he widened his eyes at her in mock surprise. "Chloe, were you a Girl Scout for real? Tell me there are pictures of a mini you in a Brownie uniform. I need them in my life."

She rolled her eyes at him, but her lips quirked up. "It's a figure of speech, dummy. Go eat."

He gave a huff but got up from his chair, mumbling some choice words about getting a boy's hopes up for embarrassing photos with no intention of follow-through, but she blatantly ignored him.

Ten minutes later, he was sitting in a cafeteria booth, eyes glued to his book as he shoved half of a slightly soggy turkey sandwich—cafeteria pickings were slim in the middle of the night—into his mouth.

A tall figure slid gracefully into the seat across from him. Figuring it was Gabe by the size of him, Danny didn't bother to finish chewing before giving him a friendly, "Fuck off, I'm reading."

"And a good evening to you too."

He knew that voice.

He looked up to find a pair of familiar bright-blue eyes gazing back at him.

And now Danny was choking on his turkey sandwich.

Eyes watering, he covered his mouth with an arm as the coughing fit took him over. When he finally choked the bite down, he managed to get out a strained, "—not who I thought you were."

Mr. Handsome Creep—or was it just Mr. Handsome now?—gave him an even look. "I figured."

Danny waited for his stranger to continue, ideally to explain what he was doing interrupting Danny's sandwich time, but that was it.

Danny raised an eyebrow. "I see we're still saving up all our words for a rainy day."

The man across from him gave a slight smirk but still didn't say anything else. He was wearing a different suit from the night before, just as perfectly fitted. He looked like he should be strutting the streets of Milan or Paris rather than sitting in a dingy hospital cafeteria.

He must be an employee after all, to be here two nights in a row.

There was something different about him tonight. Something less...harsh. He was still clearly prone to staring, but that cold, predatory look was gone. Which was slightly unfortunate, because without the "creep" part, he was just Mr. Handsome, and Danny refused to drool over another hospital employee.

No drama in the workplace for him, thank you very much.

"Okay, I'll go," Danny relented. "How can I help you?"

"That is a dangerous question."

Danny fought a blush at the man's low tone; his voice had that sultry edge again. What was Danny just thinking about not drooling again? This man was *creepy*, damn it. Danny would not be charmed.

"I'll rephrase," Danny said, keeping any hint of flirtation out of his voice. "What are you doing here at my table?"

"Talking to you."

"Yes, but *why*?"

The stranger placed his elbows on the table and leaned slightly forward, toward Danny, and goddamn it, why did he have to smell so good?

"And here I thought I was being so obvious," he purred.

This...this was flirting, right? Honestly, Danny was so out of practice with the act he couldn't quite tell. "*Obvious* is a not a word I would use to describe you. You must still be pretty new here, right? What unit? You're not wearing scrubs. Or a coat. Are you one of those 'cool docs' who think the white coat is too pretentious? Because I gotta tell you, that suit does not send out the chill vibes you think it does."

Danny had entered babbling territory, but Mr. Handsome just quirked his lips and continued to stare at him from across the table.

A sudden, horrifying thought hit Danny. "Are you—are you management? Did they hire someone to supervise on nights or something? Did I tell my new boss to...*eff off?*"

This time, Mr. Handsome's lips lifted high enough to be considered an actual smile, and that simple act upgraded his appeal to deadly levels. Danny shifted in his seat, unnerved that a smile was turning him on. "I'm not management," the man refuted. "I have some passing business here but not for long."

Danny supposed that was the closest to a straight answer he was going to get. For someone who'd just moments before been telling himself a workplace flirtation was out of the question, he found himself strangely disappointed that the man wasn't going to be a permanent fixture.

He pointed at the stranger's chest. "They should really get you a badge. Makes things a little less confusing. And I'd know what to call you. See?" Danny pointed to his own. "Danny."

"I remember. Danny No-Last-Name."

"And you are?"

"Roman. Roman Mourier." He pronounced his last name with a seemingly flawless French accent.

Mr. Handsome, aka Roman, leaned a little further over the table, and Danny got another hint of his scent, that spicy, metallic mix that shouldn't smell nearly as good as it did. What cologne did this guy use, and would he let Danny borrow some to pour on his pillow?

Roman's eyes seemed to darken as he locked them onto Danny's own again. "Now that formalities are out of the way, I think you should let me—"

But whatever Roman wanted Danny to let him do was interrupted by the sudden blare of Danny's phone alarm. His break was over. Perfect timing, since he was slightly worried he would have let this man do whatever he wanted, and that was a completely irrational reaction to a mysterious stranger, wasn't it?

Time to go before he got himself in trouble.

"Shit," Danny swore. "I mean, shoot! Break's up. I gotta go. Nice meeting you and everything. I'll see you arou— Oh."

Roman had risen out of the booth along with Danny and had somehow made his way over to Danny's side in the blink of an eye. The stranger was now standing at what felt like a *very close* distance. His intoxicating scent was even stronger, and Danny was feeling the incredibly inappropriate urge to rub his face against this guy's neck and sniff him properly.

What the fuck was wrong with him?

"I am not so sure I should let you go yet." Nothing in the man's tone suggested he was teasing.

"Um, you have to?" Somehow it ended up coming out more like a question. Danny was feeling almost light-headed, fighting his body's sudden inclination to sway into the man across from him.

Maybe he was more exhausted than he thought.

"I need to get back and do...nurse stuff. Nurse things. You know?" How had his brain suddenly turned to mush?

Roman was lifting a hand, and Danny had the strangest feeling that the other man was about to stroke Danny's face, when a loud "Danny!" cut through his mental fog like a knife.

He glanced to the right to see Gabe walking toward him, somehow looking like a million bucks even though Danny knew for a fact it was his fifth night in a row. No dark under-eye circles for the Golden Boy, thank you very much.

He narrowed his eyes as his brother approached. "I thought I told you to ignore me at work."

"Very funny, kiddo." Gabe threw an arm over Danny's shoulder, completely unfazed by the less-than-welcoming greeting. "Who's your friend?"

Of course Gabe would have no qualms calling Danny "kiddo" in front of a stranger, even in a goddamn *work setting*. No thought to what treating him like a child might do to his professional relationships.

Danny glanced over at Roman to gauge his reaction and gave a little start of surprise. Roman's gaze was trained on Gabe's arm, the one wrapped around Danny's shoulder, and that cold look from the night before was back in his eyes. The one that brought to mind some predator—a jungle cat or possibly, you know, a serial killer.

Danny was suddenly reminded of why he'd felt so nervous the night before.

He took an involuntary step back, but before he could make any introductions, or perhaps ask "Why are you looking at my brother like you want to knife him?," Roman cut him off with a cold, "Just leaving, actually."

He pivoted away and walked off without looking back at them, and was out of their sight before Danny had time to blink.

Gabe's slightly bewildered expression was probably a mirror of Danny's own. "What a jerk. New attending?"

"Not quite sure what he is. Some kind of consultant?"

Gabe gave a shrug and took his arm off Danny to face him. "Weird. Anyway, I went into the ER to check on a patient, but I didn't see you. Your charge told me you were probably on your way back from break. I told her I was gonna steal you for ten minutes."

Danny fought the urge to roll his eyes. Not only was it slightly humiliating for his older brother to go behind his back and "steal him" from his charge, but it was infuriating that Gabe insisted on catching up with him at work instead of just coming over for dinner every now and then like a normal brother.

He sighed. "And why did you need to steal me for ten minutes?"

Gabe paused to look him over critically, and Danny could feel him sizing up each sign of fatigue. For such an oblivious dope, his brother was annoyingly observant.

"You look like hell, Danny Boy. What are you doing working extra shifts when you can barely stay on two feet?"

And there he was again, babying him. As if Danny hadn't been taking care of himself—and not just himself—since he was a teen.

Danny narrowed his eyes at his brother. "I'm fine."

Gabe laughed. "There is no less true statement on this Earth than when someone says the words *I'm fine.*"

Danny hated having to defend his choices, but it was best to get this unnecessary brotherly check-in over with so he could get back to work. "I'm just doing a favor for Chloe, okay?" he lied.

There was no way he would tell Gabe about his financial struggles. Gabe didn't know how their mother's savings were gone already, spent on her doctor's bills and specialist care. Or about the massive loans Danny had taken out for nursing school.

Danny knew Gabe was just starting to pay his own student loans back, finally making money as a doctor, and he wasn't going to have his older brother bankrupt himself trying to fix everything.

Too little, too late, anyway, Danny thought, maybe a bit uncharitably. But where had all this brotherly concern been four years ago?

When Gabe just frowned at him, Danny decided to turn the tables. "I saw Mom this morning."

Gabe wasn't quite successful at controlling his flinch. "And did she recognize you?"

Danny shrugged and went for the throat. "Maybe seeing another familiar face besides just mine would be helpful."

"You know it doesn't work that way." Gabe's voice had gone carefully neutral, all consideration and teasing gone. And then, just like that, he was giving Danny's shoulder a gentle squeeze and walking away.

Danny glanced at his phone. His brother hadn't needed a full ten minutes after all. It had barely been three.

This was why Gabe cornered him for brief moments at the hospital rather than coming over for a proper visit. To feel like he was checking in on Danny while at the same time controlling the interaction, able to walk away at any moment if Danny pushed him in a way he didn't like.

So stop pushing him, he chided himself. *You've been fine on your own for years now. You don't need anyone else to take care of you.*

But Mary hadn't been wrong the other day—even if Danny didn't *need* it, sometimes it would be nice to have someone else to take care of him for a change, even for a moment.

It was four in the morning when Danny finally left the hospital. They'd cleared out the bays, either discharging patients or sending them to rooms on other floors, and Chloe had sent him away with one last grateful, "Thanks for coming in."

He was dead on his feet, barely keeping his eyes open, crossing his arms tight around himself against the winter chill. His house was technically only a five-minute drive from the hospital, but Danny was legitimately concerned about making it there safely.

He was normally hyperaware walking out to his car. The ER could be a sketchy place, with patients getting impatient and emotional or coming off drugs in a bad way and occasionally getting violent. Statistically, it was the most likely place for a hospital employee to get assaulted, and Danny kept that awareness with him until he was safe at home. At least, usually he did.

But he was more exhausted than he'd even realized, and tonight he had his eyes on his feet more than his surroundings. His car was in a darkened corner on the roof of the parking lot, and Danny was almost to the door before he realized the light above it was shattered and that the darkness was intentional.

Before he could backtrack out of there, a wiry arm wrapped around his chest, and a knife was at his throat.

Fuck. Fudge. No, I was right—fuck.

"Give me your wallet," a man snarled.

Annoyance broke through Danny's fear for a brief moment. Really? After all the creeps he'd had to deal with, all the patients he'd been careful not to give his last name out to, when he was finally assaulted, it was for some basic-bitch mugging?

Still, he wasn't going to play the hero. "It's in my back pocket."

Danny felt a hand dig into his pocket and remove the wallet before he was spun around with a rough grip on his arm to face his attacker, the knife still sitting at his throat.

Who even mugged with a knife anymore?

His assailant was wearing a cap pulled low, but even so, Danny could see the guy's pupils were completely blown. He was on something, that was for sure. But the fact that he was letting Danny see up close enough to notice was a little concerning. He could have kept Danny facing the other way.

Why isn't he worried about having a witness?

The man was pressing in with the knife—not enough to draw blood but enough for Danny's fear to go up a notch. He wanted this whole interaction over with. "Um, my phone is here. In my hand. If you want it." Maybe that would move things along.

But his attacker didn't move. He seemed to be waiting for something, which was the opposite of what one should be doing when mugging someone. *Grab, mug, and run, yes? Isn't that the magic formula to not get caught?*

Before Danny could offer up anything else—the keys to his car, perhaps?—a loud roar echoed through the garage, and his attacker was thrown off him with violent force.

Danny winced as the act of getting thrown caused his attacker's knife to slice through Danny's shoulder, but his attention was focused less on the pain and more on the blur of limbs that was suddenly pummeling his mugger. A blur through which he recognized a familiar, immaculate suit.

"Roman?"

The pummeling paused, and an honest-to-God growl sounded. His mugger was crying, letting out a gurgled, "I'm sorry, man! I don't know what I was even doing!" during the break in blows.

Roman's back was still to Danny. He bent further over the mugger, and Danny could just make out his whispered, "Run," as he let go of the now-weeping man.

Roman stood slowly, and the other man quickly scrambled up, limping to the garage stairs as fast as he could. It seemed for a moment that Roman was going to follow for a chase, as if the order to run had just been him toying with the man, but then his shoulders tensed up again, and he turned to face Danny.

Danny barely had time to register the cold fury on the man's face before Roman was there, directly in front of Danny, faster than he had any right to be. His attack on the mugger had taken Roman and the assailant both to the other side of the garage roof—and how he had even thrown the man all the way across the roof was a question in itself—and yet there he was, inches away from Danny's face.

Something was definitely not right.

His sleek black hair was now mussed and wild, and he was panting. But much more alarming, those bright blue eyes—the ones that had been so eerie under the fluorescent lights—were now completely black.

Not darkened by overblown pupils. But actually, fully black, no irises or surrounding whites or anything.

Danny swallowed hard as he registered the last strange detail of Roman's appearance. The most not right thing of all—Roman's teeth were bared, and the man definitely had fangs.

Either Danny was hallucinating for real, or Roman was something other than human.

And Danny was alone with him on the roof of a dark parking garage.

Fuck.

Four

Roman

Roman should really leave. Right now.

He'd been so close to killing that man. Not even biting him, feeding off him, but just beating the life out of him. But Danny's voice had somehow cut through the murderous fog, his demon tuned in to the trembling boy more than the prey directly in front of them.

That in itself was a revelation.

The rational human side of him was aware he was in trouble—that he had his fangs fully out, his demon showing in his eyes—and that at any moment, Danny would start screaming bloody murder and run for the hills.

But his rational human side was definitely not in charge right now.

Sweet. Honey sweet. Ours, ours, ours.

The boy was bleeding, and...that *scent*. It was the rich, coppery, tantalizing smell of fresh blood but also the smell of Danny, that milk-and-honey intoxicating scent. And apparently his demon was just as captivated by Danny's scent as the rest of him. It had barely registered the attacker scuttling away into the darkness, too focused on the boy himself, on having him in its sight.

The boy who was currently staring at Roman, eyes wide, looking a little fearful but mostly in shock.

"What...just happened?" Danny's voice was barely more than a whisper.

Roman said the only thing he could, the only thing that mattered. "He was hurting you."

Before Roman knew what he was doing, he was reaching for the neck of Danny's shirt, pulling the collar down and to the side to reveal the bleeding cut on the boy's shoulder. He couldn't stop the growl that came out of him then, his demon and him both enraged that someone had *hurt* their lovely boy.

He waited again for his demon to demand to chase, to kill, to finish what they'd started with the boy's attacker, or for Danny to scream and push him away. But neither happened. The boy continued to stare at him, wide-eyed, and Roman's demon was focused in on the cut. *Protect, soothe, lick, heal.*

Roman could maybe, just maybe, fight that urge. Step back and let Danny run from them. But he couldn't find it in himself to even want that. He and his demon were in agreement.

He gave in.

Before he knew it, he was leaning in and licking Danny's cut, letting his saliva heal the wound, and the sweetest taste he'd ever known was filling his mouth.

He pulled Danny closer, his demon growling low enough that it was practically purring, pressing the boy against himself as he licked away any traces of blood on his too-pale skin, the shallow wound already healed in moments.

He was able to keep himself from attempting to mouth out the blood that had soaked into Danny's shirt, but just barely.

Roman paused, lips resting against the smooth skin of Danny's shoulder, and waited again for the demon to demand *more*—more blood, biting, tearing—but it continued to simply purr its approval at having Danny so close, the boy's taste in their mouth a reward for having protected him, healed him.

Roman forced himself to lift his head, leaning back slightly to look at Danny, who was tilting his head to peer at his own shoulder. Those big brown eyes grew even wider, if that was possible.

"He sliced me. I felt it."

"Yes," Roman agreed.

"But the cut isn't there anymore."

"No." Unable to keep the pride from his voice, Roman stated simply, "I fixed it."

"With your tongue." There was a rising edge of panic in the boy's voice.

Danny pushed at Roman's shoulders, not nearly strong enough to move him if he didn't want it, but Roman reluctantly stepped back from him anyway. His demon grumbled softly in annoyance but seemed willing to give the boy some space.

For now.

Roman watched as Danny took a deep breath and then closed his eyes. When he opened them again, some of the shock had left them, and he seemed more like the self-assured nurse Roman had met in the hospital earlier.

"This might seem like a stupid question—" Danny paused and eyed Roman's face, the fangs that Roman still hadn't retracted. "—but are you...human?"

Roman did let his fangs retract then, until they once again resembled a human's ordinary canines. "I used to be."

Danny took another deep breath. "I'm going to say a word. A very silly word—a word that can't possibly be true—and just to humor me, you're going to say yes or no."

Roman nodded. He had a feeling he knew where this was going.

"Vampire."

There it was, hanging in the air between them. Roman found himself reluctant to answer, afraid that once Danny received his confirmation, he would run far, far away and never let Roman see him again.

"You could say...," he started. Danny's eyes immediately narrowed, and Roman sighed in annoyance, realizing he needed to give him a straight answer or the boy would keep pressing him. Or even worse, leave. "Yes."

He wasn't sure what reaction he was expecting, but Danny just nodded and mumbled something that sounded suspiciously like "Mr. Handsome *Vampire* Creep" to himself.

"Can I see them again?"

No question what *them* Danny was referring to. Roman let his fangs descend again, baring his teeth slightly to give him the full effect. *In for a penny...*

He was surprised when Danny leaned in slightly, until his face was mere inches from the sharp fangs, eyeing them curiously. Then his gaze lifted to Roman's. "And the eyes? Is that a vampire thing too?"

Roman nodded, finding himself speechless, enchanted with this boy who was letting his curiosity rather than his fear lead him.

"When will they change back?" Danny questioned.

"When I force the demon back again." Roman was so intent on Danny—and Danny's study of him—that he wasn't paying attention to his own words.

Danny leaned his head back sharply. "*Demon*? You're, what, a *possessed* vampire?"

Was that where this curious boy drew the limit?

"That is simply what I call the...nonhuman...part of me," Roman reassured him. "The part of me that awoke when I turned. The part that craves blood and...other things. My demon. I have heard others like me call it different names."

"You're like...two separate beings? Or the same person?"

Roman shrugged slightly. "Sometimes it feels like just another side of me; sometimes it feels like a completely different entity. I never received a handbook on any of it."

Danny tilted his head slightly, as if sizing Roman up. "And why is it—he?—still...out right now? Are you planning on biting me?"

Despite his question, Danny hadn't taken any further steps away from Roman. He shook his head gently at the boy in response, pushing his demon back and allowing his eyes to return to their natural blue state.

"I don't know which version unsettles me more." Danny's eyes narrowed. "You don't actually work at the hospital, do you?"

"I do not."

Danny gave a small, tired smile, then glanced around as if suddenly remembering where they were. "I need to go home now."

"I will take you," Roman blurted out. He prepared himself for the arguments against it, but once again, Danny didn't react the way Roman would expect him to.

"Okay," was all the boy said. "But I don't want to leave my car here, so you'll have to drive it. I'm that one." He pointed to a dark-blue Toyota that had seen better days.

"You are...not afraid I am going to bite you in the car?"

"You just said you wouldn't. And to be honest, Mr. Handsome Vampire Creep, I am too fucking tired to care. I think I have a higher chance of survival just having you drive instead of my exhausted ass. We can take the rest as it comes."

Roman looked at the boy—really *looked* at him. He took in the pale complexion, the dark bruises showing under his eyes, and realized how exhausted the young man must really be.

Danny looked tired, not in the way of someone who'd just had a long night, but in the way of someone who had been working too hard for too long with no one to take care of him.

And that, Roman decided, just would not do.

Ours, his demon rumbled.

Ours, he agreed.

"It's here, on the left. The yellow one."

Roman pulled into the driveway of a small yellow house near the end of a cul-de-sac. All the houses on the road backed onto what looked to be forest lands, and Roman could see the tops of pines behind Danny's home.

It had only been a short drive from the hospital, and they'd driven in silence, other than Danny's few soft-spoken directions.

As they approached the front door, he held up the key ring for Danny to pick out the house key, biting back a grin as Danny just pointed to the correct one, allowing Roman to unlock the door for them.

He'd been preparing himself for a "thank you for the ride, now go away forever, you blood-sucking monster," but apparently he was being allowed inside the house.

"You live here alone?" Roman questioned.

Danny nodded as he shrugged off his jacket, hanging it on a coatrack in the entryway. "I grew up here. It's the family house, but Gabe wanted his own apartment and my mom is living...elsewhere...right now."

Roman found himself stuck on one part of that statement: *Gabe wanted his own apartment.*

His demon went on alert as well. Who was *Gabe*? A boyfriend? Maybe that handsome, cocky doctor that had felt so comfortable putting his arm around Danny earlier that night?

Roman's demon had wanted to rip the man's arm off, and Roman suddenly wished he had let it.

He cleared his throat, forcing his voice to remain calm. "Gabe?"

"My brother," Danny replied, tossing his wallet and keys on a side table. "You saw him earlier, at the hospital. He's a doctor there."

Ah. Roman and his demon both settled. A brother.

"So that's one myth debunked."

He turned to look at Danny, who was giving him a small, cheeky grin. Roman raised an eyebrow in question.

The boy smirked at him. "I didn't need to invite you in."

Roman gave a startled laugh. So their entry had been a test? "No, no formal invitation necessary. Although, for politeness's sake, I do try to make sure I am welcome before entering someone else's home."

"Mm-hmm." Danny looked skeptical.

Roman stalked closer to the boy, unable to keep his distance. Danny tensed slightly as Roman leaned in, but didn't back away. Roman breathed in, ignoring the way his cock twitched at the boy's scent—there was no smell of fear. "You're not afraid of me."

It wasn't a question, but Danny answered anyway. "No."

Roman tried not to be pleased at the answer. "You are entirely too trusting of strange men," he warned.

Would this boy let just anyone into his house? Did he know what a monster he'd just allowed to waltz into his home?

"I'm really not though," Danny said, tilting his head thoughtfully. "Just with you. Isn't that funny?" But Danny wasn't laughing, only peering at Roman with that direct, no-nonsense look he seemed to specialize in. Then the boy shrugged, breaking his gaze. "Anyway, I need a shower. I always want one after a shift, but I especially need one now—I've got gross mugger germs all over me."

Would Danny ask him to leave, then? Roman wanted to stay. He *needed* to stay. "I'll make you some food," he offered.

Danny raised his eyebrows at him. "You can cook? Why? Do you even eat human food?"

Roman was already heading toward what he thought looked like the kitchen. "I do not need to, but I can. Besides, I am French. I would be a traitor to my nation if I did not know how to cook."

No laugh at that. He waited to be told to leave, but all he heard was the sound of Danny heading up the stairs.

The boy's pantry was a disgrace, same with the fridge. There was hardly any fresh food of any real substance stocked. Someone had *not* been taking care of himself properly. Roman found mostly an assortment of packaged meals in the freezer—*horrible*—and some sugary cereal—*disgusting*—but at least there were a few eggs and a loaf of bread.

Eggs and toast it would be, then.

He was plating the scrambled eggs and just starting to worry that Danny had fallen asleep in the shower, when he heard the soft patter of feet coming down the stairs.

Roman turned toward the entryway into the kitchen and barely kept in his demon's low growl at the sight that appeared in front of him.

Danny looked simply *delicious*, and not as something to eat. His hair was damp and sticking out adorably every which way, the boy apparently too exhausted to bother with combing it. He was wearing soft-looking pajama bottoms and a thin T-shirt, barely holding his tired eyes open.

Something about the open vulnerability of it all had Roman's cock hardening.

He really was a predator.

He wanted to tackle the boy, lick him everywhere, rub his own scent all over Danny's body.

Roman wanted to *claim* him.

But taking care of him needed to come first. Roman didn't let himself think about why he felt that way. The boy needed to eat, and he needed to sleep.

He set the plate of eggs and toast in front of Danny as the boy sat down at the kitchen counter. Danny gave him a grateful smile and a soft thank-you before focusing on his food, letting out an appreciative hum at the first bite.

After a few minutes with nothing but the sound of chewing, Danny broke the silence, eyes still on his plate. "You're staring," he whispered.

"Am I?" He was.

"You're always staring at me." There was no anger or fear in Danny's voice. He simply seemed to be stating a fact.

"Well," Roman answered, unable to keep himself from leaning in closer, "you are always looking delectable."

Danny looked up at that. "Delectable as in...vampire food? Or..." He trailed off.

"Or," Roman replied. He watched in fascination as a blush stole over the boy's pale cheeks, spreading all the way down his neck. Roman was suddenly desperate to know how far down that blush went.

Danny cleared his throat, pushing his now empty plate away. "Speaking of vampire food, how often do you need to *eat*?"

Roman had been expecting something along this line of questioning. The boy had too much of a curious nature to let things lie. "You mean feed on blood? About once a week. If I go any longer than that, it starts to get...testy."

"'It' as in...your demon?"

Roman nodded.

Danny hummed, eyes on the wall behind Roman's shoulder. He seemed to stare off into space when he needed to focus. "You healed my shoulder just by licking it."

"I did. Our saliva has healing properties, up to a certain point. I cannot do anything about large injuries, but I can heal shallow wounds like yours. I think of it as an evolutionary mechanism. So we can feed regularly without leaving victims walking around with suspicious holes in their necks."

Roman couldn't remember the last time he'd shared so much about what he was with someone. Possibly he never had. Why was he just telling the boy everything he wanted to know?

"Walking around?" Danny questioned. "So you don't have to kill to feed?"

"I do not. Neither do the few vampires in my acquaintance. We do not require all that much blood to survive, really. But I cannot speak for everyone. Not all vampires hold on to their humanity as well as others. We may not *need* a lot, but need is different from want, wouldn't you agree?"

Danny gave another thoughtful hum. "I knew you weren't a killer."

Roman shook his head. This boy was entirely too trusting. "Do not convince yourself I am not dangerous. My demon may not want to *eat* you, but it has other feelings toward you. Very...*possessive* feelings." Roman leaned in even closer, delighting in the way the boy's breath hitched at his proximity. "You might run in the other direction if you could hear some of the things it thinks about you."

Danny waved a hand in dismissal, as if a vampire's inner demon wanting to own him was inconsequential. "You fought off my attacker—*without* killing him, by the way—healed me, and then fed me dinner/breakfast. If that's your demon being possessive of me, I think I can handle it. Being a nurse has taught me to trust my instincts, and my instincts tell me to trust you."

Danny nodded sharply as if that was the end of that, but then gave a little start as if he had just realized something. "Unless...that's a vampire thing too? Is it some compulsion thing? The way I'm drawn to you? Is that why you smell so good?"

Roman was momentarily stunned. Danny was drawn to him the same way Roman was drawn to Danny? Maybe the boy wasn't overly trusting and naive; maybe he just knew somewhere inside him already that he belonged to Roman.

Roman no longer suspected the boy of any magical inclinations, hadn't really since their second meeting. Danny was too clearly...too *achingly* mortal, ordinary.

His demon was smug as all hell at the thought. *Knew it.* Knew it. *Ours, ours, ours.*

Roman understood exactly where his demon was going with this, but he wasn't ready to go there in his mind. Not yet.

He focused back on Danny. "We can do something like that. We can draw humans in, make ourselves alluring, and fog their minds. But that is a conscious effort. Something we do on purpose in specific instances. And I have not been doing that with you. *Could not* continue for this long, not without bringing my demon forth."

Danny nodded, seeming again to easily trust what Roman was telling him. "Then why? Why aren't I more afraid of you?" he asked.

"I have a theory," Roman hedged. "But I would rather discuss it when you are feeling a little less exhausted."

Danny gave him a frown, about to argue, but then relented when a giant yawn took over his face.

"Time for bed," Roman urged, eager to end the conversation.

Danny nodded. "Are you staying?"

"Do you want me to?" If his demon had anything to say about it, they were never leaving this boy's side again.

"I think so. Isn't that weird?" Danny gave a small laugh, amazingly unconcerned at the whole situation. Was it possibly his exhaustion was making him so compliant?

Roman followed Danny up the stairs to the boy's bedroom. He stood to the side, waiting in the corner as Danny slid under the covers of his bed.

How close would the boy let him get?

Danny eyed him from the bed. "Do you sleep?"

"Yes, I sleep. Although, my kind do not need as much as you do."

"And will you burst into flames if the curtains are open in the morning?"

Roman gave a small laugh. "No, that is another myth. Sunlight does not harm me. It is only slightly irritating to my demon."

"All right then." Danny patted the bed. "You can crash here with me. Keep the other baddies away. Just no biting."

His demon was offended at the implication, that it would hurt this boy it had decided to claim, a fact Roman found almost hilarious considering its recent bloodthirsty inclinations.

He crossed the room and lay down on top of the covers, forcing himself to keep a few inches' distance between their bodies. He was worried if he started touching Danny, he wouldn't be able to stop.

And he wasn't going to let himself scare this boy away.

Not even an hour later, Danny had inched himself not just next to Roman but all the way on top of him, arm thrown over Roman's chest, leg thrown over his hip. As if the boy hadn't been able to resist the pull between them in his sleep.

Roman's cock was achingly hard at Danny's proximity, the boy's delicious scent surrounding him, but he was able to ignore his own arousal after all, soothed by the boy's unconscious trust in him.

Roman tightened his arms around Danny's back, and his demon let out a contented purr as he allowed himself to close his eyes.

And then his demon said what they had both been edging around, voicing it whether Roman was ready for it or not.

Mate, it purred. *Our mate.*

Goddamn it.

Five

Danny

Danny moaned. Something smelled *so good*.

It was that delicious Mr. Handsome scent surrounding him—had he let Danny borrow his cologne to douse his pillow after all?

He turned his face into his pillow and took a deep breath in. *Heaven*. The scent made him feel safe, and cozy, and...turned on?

Yep. Definite yep. His morning wood twitched as he inhaled again. Except...

"Not pillow," Danny mumbled, his voice garbled by cloth and...chest. That was definitely a hard male chest his head was resting on—one that was starting to shake as its owner let out a soft laugh, all gloriously smooth and deep and rumbly. Oh no. That was definitely not helping Danny's morning wood situation at all.

He lifted his head and found himself gazing into familiar bright-blue eyes. Had Danny thought they were cold and predatory before? Now they were warm and soft, with a heat building in them that had Danny's toes curling.

"Awake already, lovely? It has only been a few hours." That smooth, deep voice sent a shiver down Danny's spine.

He let out a grumble-snort that was supposed to translate into, "Awake is a relative term." Hopefully Roman got the gist. Mornings were not Danny's thing, even at the best of times.

As the sleep fog slowly left his brain, he realized with some amount of mortification that he was wrapped around Roman like some kind of horny octopus. At some point in his sleep, Danny had apparently kicked off the covers and decided the man—the *vampire*—was his personal life-size teddy bear.

Which—double mortification—meant Danny's hard-on was currently pressed right into Roman's hip.

He let out an embarrassed groan and tried to untangle his limbs from Roman's body. "I'm so sorry, I—"

He was cut off by a low growl as Roman's arms tightened around him, keeping Danny firmly in place, without an inch of space between them.

Danny took a moment to relish the feel of the vampire's embrace. He would have thought vampires were cold, but Roman's body gave off a delicious heat. "Um...," Danny mumbled into Roman's chest. "I didn't mean to sleep-accost you."

"It was not unwelcome." There was a hint of laughter in Roman's voice.

Well, there's a ringing endorsement. "I'm serious. I didn't realize I was such a cuddler. I would've warned a guy."

"I would have done the same from the beginning had I known it would be acceptable."

That was surprising. "You would have...cuddled me?"

Danny felt Roman rub his stubbled cheek against the top of his head, like he was some kind of big cat. He hummed into Danny's hair. "I would have touched you, held you—yes."

That thought took a moment to process in Danny's brain. He blinked at the incongruity of his fierce vampire-demon protector wanting to play big spoon, little spoon with him. "Oh. And you don't mind...um...you know...?"

Roman chuckled softly. "I don't *know*, but if you mean this"—he rubbed his hip against Danny's hard cock, causing heat to spread from Danny's groin through his whole body—"I do not."

Oh my Lord. Danny buried his face into Roman's chest, cheeks flushed with embarrassment and...other things.

That deep, smooth voice sounded even more amused, if a little husky. "You might even have noticed I'm in the same predicament."

He said what now?

And then Danny did feel, against the leg he currently had draped over Roman's midsection—Jesus, he really had engulfed the man—that the vampire had his own little situation going on.

Except...not little. At all. A big situation. A big, hard situation. A big, hard situation that Danny would very much like to—*ahem*——handle for him.

Danny hadn't even realized he'd started squirming against Roman again until he felt a large, firm hand on his lower back. "Settle, lovely boy. My restraint is stretched thin as it is."

Danny stilled instantly. What in the goddamn goodness was wrong with him right now? He felt the need to clarify. "I'm not...usually like this. Definitely not with men I've just met. Definitely, *definitely* not with vampires I've just met."

That soft chuckle again, which Danny felt more than heard. "Neither am I."

Danny lifted his head to narrow his eyes at his bedmate. "You're telling me that you—looking like you do—don't have many casual hookups? One-night stands? Rolls in the hay?"

Danny doubted it. Majorly.

"And how do I look to you?" The damned vampire was smirking at him now, looking a trifle too smug for his own good.

Danny just raised an eyebrow.

Roman's face turned serious. "I have had countless one-night stands, lovely Danny. Never do they actually last the night. Never do I hold someone until morning."

Danny wasn't sure whether to be horrified by that "countless" or warmed to the bone by the rest of it.

So he decided to change the subject.

"So you were right. You didn't burst into flames with the dawn or anything."

Roman's smirk was back. "How perceptive you are."

Danny had a million questions and barely knew where to start. "So why is that a myth then? What started all those nasty 'daylight equals death' rumors?"

Roman hummed a little, seeming to gather his thoughts. "Our demons do *prefer* the night, it is true. We seem to be more or less nocturnal by nature. It has always made sense to me, seeing as how many of our...predilections...are more conducive to the dark."

That added up. "You mean chomping on people's necks?"

Roman huffed a laugh. "The biting, yes. But also more than that." He pressed his erection up into Danny again, sending a pool of warmth into Danny's stomach. "Blood and sex, Danny. That is what our demons crave. What *I* crave."

Well, holy shit. That should not be so hot. That should be terrifying, not arousing. Danny forced himself to focus. He felt they were building to something, clinging to each other the way they were, but no jumping the vampire's bones until he had some more answers.

There was one thing he definitely wanted to know.

"Last night you said there might be a reason. A reason I feel this...drawn to you."

Roman gave a sigh, settling his hips back down into the bed.

Danny tried not to mourn the loss.

"I did say that."

"Care to share with the class?"

Roman stayed silent for so long Danny began to think he was refusing to answer the question. Then, with another sigh, he began, "First, keep in mind there is no organized vampire society, no council in charge. In general, vampires—as far as I know—are relatively solitary creatures. Generally if you move into an area and realize it has been established as another vampire's territory, you leave. Otherwise, it can be seen as a challenge. Our demons can get restless, aggressive with each other. There are exceptions, of course. The one who turned me—we traveled as a pair for over a century."

Danny wasn't sure where this was going, but it was fascinating to hear about. He had a million questions, and normally he might not be able to keep his mouth shut. But with Roman's large hand now rubbing circles on his lower back and his deep voice rumbling in that hard chest under Danny's ear, he was content to just listen.

"Sometimes, when two unacquainted vampires are both traveling through an unclaimed territory, they might meet and swap stories or news about the wider supernatural world. It is part of how we learn about what we are, what traits band us together as a species."

Roman paused then, and Danny gave a small nod against Roman's chest to let him know he was still listening. "One of the things I have heard of is the idea of...mates. Vampires whose demons recognize each other. Belong to each other. They become bonded permanently. Soothe and calm each other, prevent the descent into a feral state that our kind succumb to."

"Feral state?" Danny did not like the sound of that.

Roman tensed slightly beneath him. "The older a vampire is, the more they tend to lose touch with their humanity. The demon inside takes more control and gets wilder, more violent. Many of those vampires end up dying at the hands of our kind. Put down before they can expose us all."

Danny had a hard time imagining the man currently rubbing his back so gently as some sort of feral demon-beast. "And at what point does this happen?" he asked tentatively. "How old does a vampire have to be?"

He felt Roman shrug underneath him. "It differs depending on the individual. Some hold on to their humanity better than others. In theory, we all succumb eventually. But apparently a mate can prevent the descent."

Danny felt like he had more questions than answers. "I still don't understand your demon. Is it a separate creature? A separate...soul...living inside of you?"

"It just...is. When I awoke after I was turned, it was there, inside me. I cannot tell you if it is a part of ourselves that gets awakened or a separate soul that...infests us. But it is part of me now. There are times over the years when it has been more dormant and times when it has been a little more...communicative. When my eyes turn black, when my fangs pop out, that is when the demon is at the forefront of my consciousness."

Danny's brain felt fuzzy trying to comprehend this entire new world he was learning about. He felt like he should switch to a simpler line of questioning. "How old are you, Roman?"

"I have lived over two centuries. But as a human, I was thirty years old when I was turned."

Holy shit. He was cuddling with someone over two hundred years old?

"Oh. Wow. Um...wow. Wow, wow, wow." Danny wasn't sure why—when all this was pretty goddamn bonkers to begin with—it was the knowledge of Roman's age that had finally broken his brain. Maybe it was the realization that this was a man—*vampire, man, whatever*—with not just decades of life experience over him but *centuries*.

Danny suddenly felt small and young and a little foolish. What was it Roman had called him? *Lovely boy.* He really *was* a boy when compared to him.

Roman's hand stopped its soothing circles. "Is this too much? Should I stop now?"

"No!" Despite it all, Danny didn't want Roman to stop talking to him, to stop touching him. "No. Just...processing." He breathed deep. "Tell me more about mates. How do mates even find each other if vampires are so rare and solitary?"

Roman shifted under Danny, his muscles tense again. "From what I have heard, mates are not necessarily found in other vampires. A demon senses his mate even...before...they are turned."

Danny felt a shiver go through him. "You mean, a mate can be a human?"

"Yes." Roman's hand had stilled. "A human who, when turned, will be bonded fully with their mate. Their demons will recognize each other as partners and tether each other to their humanity."

Danny felt hesitant asking this next part, but he needed to know. "And your point was...you think I'm that for you? A mate?"

Roman was silent for a very long moment before answering. The pause was making Danny anxious, but he wasn't sure what he was expecting. For Roman to be all, *Yes, human I just met. I am 100 percent certain you are my pre-vampire-demon soulmate who I will be with forever and ever*? That would be *insane*. Right?

Then why was Danny feeling so invested in the answer?

Roman's voice was quiet when he finally answered. "I had stopped believing in the concept years ago. I have never met a mated pair. Have only heard stories. And I have seen for myself when a vampire was...mistaken about finding his. But I know I have never felt this draw before. Not to a vampire or human. My demon knew right away it wanted you. *I* want you."

Danny pressed himself a little closer to Roman at those words. Not a definitive answer, but it was an ego boost, at least. To be wanted by this insanely gorgeous, protective, magical—actually, literally *magical*—being.

Roman let out an exasperated chuckle. "You should not be moving closer, lovely. You should be running in the other direction."

Danny sighed, doing the exact opposite and pressing his face into Roman's chest. He smelled so fucking good. "I know that logically. But I can't help it. That pull you talk about...I feel it too. Like I want to trust you. Like I feel safe with you. And—and you did save me, you know."

Roman sighed. Danny seemed to have that effect on him. "I told you: do not let that fool you into thinking I am a good man. A good man would leave you now. Give you space to process. Or better yet, leave completely. Let you live your human life. A good man would want to do the selfless thing."

Danny felt a small tug of hope in chest at the direction this seemed to be going. "But you...*don't* want to do that? Leave completely?"

"No." It was more a growl than a word.

Then Roman was turning them both, rolling Danny underneath him, pressing their bodies together chest to chest, groin to groin. "What I want to do, lovely boy," he crooned, running his nose along the length of Danny's chin, "is put my hands all over you. Mark your body with my teeth. Find out what sounds I can coax out of you with my hands. My tongue. My cock."

Danny found it suddenly very hard to breathe and not just from the weight of Roman pressing him into the mattress. He knew somewhere inside him that Roman was right. That the smart option was to take some space and process this entirely unreal situation.

But there was no part of Danny that wanted to be smart right now. He wanted all the things Roman had just said.

He wanted Roman.

"Yes. Yes, that," he said, unable to keep the eagerness out of his voice. "Option B."

And then Roman's lips were on Danny's, kissing him with savage desperation. Despite how gentle Roman had been with him up until this point—the soothing touches, the respectful distance the night before—his kiss was aggressive, dominating. He claimed Danny's mouth like he owned him, hot tongue thrusting, teeth nipping.

Danny whimpered, melting under the kiss, and let himself be devoured. His cock, which had softened during their conversation, hardened in an instant.

Roman let out another growl at his compliance—fuck, why was that so hot?—and moved his lips to Danny's neck, pressing warm, wet kisses along every inch of available skin. He nipped at the junction between Danny's neck and shoulder with blunt, playful teeth—no sharp fangs to tear through the skin.

Danny knew he should feel some apprehension at having a creature that fed off human blood nibbling around on his neck, but all he felt was a heady desire that left him breathless and dizzy.

"More," he urged. "More. Please."

Roman brought his mouth back to Danny's, silencing his pleas, and Danny heard the clinking of a belt buckle being undone. Right. Roman was still wearing real pants. Well, Danny didn't have that inconvenience. He shimmied his pajama bottoms down, taking his underwear with them, groaning with relief when his aching cock was freed. He was rock-hard and leaking precum, but before he could get his hand on himself to get some real relief, Roman was knocking it away and pressing his own freed cock down against Danny's, wrapping his large hand around them both.

Oh, fuck yes.

Danny moaned into Roman's mouth, rutting into the vampire's fist as he stroked them both, reveling in the feel of the satiny-smooth, hot skin of Roman's cock rubbing against his own. Roman was longer and thicker than Danny, proportionate in all ways, and Danny felt a frisson of apprehension break through his pleasure at the thought of such a big cock entering him—his sexual experience was anything but expansive—but not enough to detract from the pure pleasure of what Roman was doing to them both.

Roman broke their kiss and nuzzled under Danny's ear, breaths coming out fast and harsh. "Oh fuck. Merde. You feel so good, lovely boy." He sounded wrecked, and Danny couldn't believe *he* was the one causing this sexy-as-fuck, experienced vampire to lose his composure like this.

The thought of it pushed Danny over the edge, and he barely had time to shout, "Fuck! Coming!" before his cock erupted, cum leaking over Roman's fist onto Danny's stomach.

Roman kept stroking them both, the slide of his hand just this side of too much against Danny's oversensitive, spent cock, but the vampire was close behind him, letting out a noise somewhere between a groan and growl, spurting his own hot cum onto Danny's chest.

They lay there for a few minutes, Roman's body still pressing Danny's into the mattress, both of them silent except for their panting breaths, and then Roman moved to raise himself up and off Danny.

"Feeling good, sweet boy?" he murmured in question.

"Mm. So good. So very, very good." Danny had his eyes closed, his orgasm leaving him content but sleepy, and when Roman's weight lifted off him, Danny had a moment of fear that the vampire was leaving already.

But then Danny felt a soothing, warm wetness, and he looked down to see Roman was licking their combined cum off Danny's stomach in gentle strokes.

Well, fuck. Danny let out a weak moan, his spent cock attempting to rally at the thought of Roman tasting their combined essences, and Roman hummed against him in pleasure.

Danny threw his head back on his pillow. He wanted to keep his eyes open to continue watching the erotic sight, but he could feel the exhaustion of the past couple days combined with the power of his release sending him back off to sleep. They were drifting shut against his will.

He forced himself to open his eyes one last time and look down at Roman.

Black eyes were staring up at him.

Danny held his breath as Roman pushed himself up so their faces were only inches apart. Danny expected to feel fear now that he knew what those black eyes represented, knew that Roman's demon was looking at him, but what he saw in those eyes—hunger, desire, possessiveness—only made him feel just as safe and wanted as the rest of Roman.

Safe enough that he was still giving in to the pull of sleep.

Barely holding on to consciousness, Danny lifted his right hand and cupped Roman's face, thumb pressed lightly against one of Roman's fangs. "Hello, demon," he whispered.

And then he drifted off to sleep.

<hr />

Danny woke hours later feeling well rested for the first time in...he couldn't even remember. He blushed, remembering what had prompted his going back to sleep so sated.

Guess the best orgasm in your life can really do the body good.

He grabbed his phone off the bedside table and checked the time: 1:00 p.m.

Roman wasn't in Danny's bed, and Danny couldn't hear him in the house. Had the vampire left? Danny slipped on his pajama pants—they'd somehow ended up on the floor all the way across the room—without bothering with underwear or a shirt and stumbled down the stairs toward the kitchen.

He blinked as he approached his kitchen counter. There was a big bowl with a variety of fresh fruit that definitely hadn't been there before. And...a note: *I took the liberty of filling this kitchen with actual groceries. Please eat some proper food. You were sleeping so soundly I did not want to wake you. I will see you soon, lovely Danny.*

Warmth filled Danny's chest at the thought of Roman going out of his way to buy him groceries. How long had it been since someone else had stepped in to take care of something for Danny? He opened the fridge and saw it was filled with vegetables, a new box of eggs, orange juice, milk—overall, a far cry from the empty cavern of condiments it had been just last night.

Danny used the eggs and milk along with a new loaf of bread he found in the pantry to make himself French toast, slicing up strawberries and bananas to go on top. He knew how to cook the basics—he'd made meals for himself and his mom before she'd had to move to the facility—he just hated grocery shopping, hated going to the store and searching for ingredients for just himself. It felt like a cruel reminder of how alone he really was these days. So he'd been getting by with infrequent trips, stocking up on frozen meals and canned goods that wouldn't go bad.

He took a picture of the finished product, thinking he'd text it to Roman, and then paused.

He didn't have the vampire's phone number.

He glanced at the note again, at the sweet message and promise to see him soon. But that was it. No phone number. No way to contact him. *And when is soon?* Danny thought, a hopeless feeling replacing the warmth in his chest. *Tomorrow? Two weeks from now?*

Eating his breakfast—or really, lunch at this point—Danny couldn't decide what to think about it all. Roman had rescued him, cooked for him, spent the night, and given him the most amazing orgasm of his life.

And he'd called Danny his mate.

Or...*maybe* his mate. He hadn't exactly said for sure that was what Danny was. He'd actually been quite cagey around the subject, now that Danny thought about it. And then he'd gone off without a way for Danny to contact him.

The groceries were sweet and all, but what if Roman just got off, literally, on taking care of helpless little human men and then disappearing into the sunset?

Maybe the mate thing was just a weird pickup line vampires liked to use on unsuspecting humans. *Hey, baby, you so fine. You must be my mate.*

Danny was unsettled by just how much the thought upset him. What did it even matter? He hardly knew the guy, no matter how safe his vampire pheromones or whatever made Danny feel. So why did the thought of Roman leaving after just one night make it suddenly hard to breathe?

He supposed that what he should be freaking out about was the fact that vampires existed at all, not whether one of them wanted to date him.

But even though Danny generally considered himself a man who believed in science—he was in healthcare, after all—he'd also seen plenty of just...weird shit. Unexplainable things happened sometimes in the hospital, and he had always believed there was more to this world than anyone knew. And he had meant what he said to Roman—his time as a nurse had taught him to trust his instincts, to roll with the punches, and to keep his mind and eyes open.

So—vampires existed. And Roman was one. And he possibly, maybe wanted Danny to one day be one as well.

Could Danny do that? Agree to exchange his humanity for eternal (or at least, he assumed eternal) life and a chance at some sort of demonic true love? He scoffed at himself as he took his last bite of French toast. *Way to get ahead of yourself, dummy.* Was he really stressing out about whether he would agree to turn into a vampire when Roman had never even asked him to?

Danny had only known him for a day and didn't even have his phone number, for fuck's sake.

He could already tell he was going to be turning endless anxious circles in his own brain unless he got some distraction. Or a new perspective.

He couldn't tell anyone *everything* about what was going on, but he could tell someone *some* things.

He grabbed his phone and called Chloe.

"Danny Boy!"

"Hey, Chlo. This isn't too early, is it?" He knew she'd worked the full shift last night, but he also knew she didn't like to sleep in too late on the days when she had a night off.

"Not at all, baby boy. I've even had my coffee and everything. Is everything okay? A phone call instead of a text makes me think someone died."

"No, everything's okay. Just don't have the patience to type everything out. I...um...met someone?"

The shriek that crossed the phone line was just a decibel below deafening. "Oh! My! God! This is huge. Who is he? Where did you meet him? What dirty things has he done to your virgin body?"

Danny couldn't help but laugh. "Chloe, honey, you know I'm not a virgin."

"I'm sorry," she said, not sounding sorry at all. "But I'm pretty sure you qualify as some type of born-again bearer of a V-card, I'm afraid. You definitely haven't hooked up with anyone in the time I've known you, and I have been keeping my eyes *peeled* for that shit."

Danny huffed into the phone. "Maybe I have and I just didn't tell you."

"Please. Like you could keep that from me. You've had a case of what I've secretly diagnosed as stress-induced chastity."

"Nurses aren't allowed to diagnose," he retorted in a know-it-all voice. "You're going beyond your scope of practice."

"Bite me," she replied evenly. "Now tell me more about this someone."

The thing was, Chloe wasn't exactly wrong. Danny *wasn't* a virgin—he'd crossed that bridge in nursing school, with a sweet guy he'd shared a bed with a few times but no real connection—but he hadn't exactly been getting any regular action. Before nursing school, he'd had a few awkward, mostly clandestine high school hookups. And really nothing since.

His life since adulthood had been work and taking care of his mom, and while her moving to the facility had freed up his time, the cost of it meant he had to work more hours to make ends meet. He hadn't had time to meet someone outside of the hospital, and he hadn't been interested in meeting anyone *inside* the hospital.

And then Roman had walked in, all delicious and broody and saving-him-from-muggers-y.

He tried to figure out how to tell a sanitized, vamp-free version of the story to Chloe. "He came into the hospital the other night. Not as a patient. Just visiting. But then last night, someone tried to mug me—"

He heard Chloe gasp on the other end of the line. "Oh my God, Danny, are you okay?"

"I'm fine," he reassured her. "He stepped in, fought them off. He's fine too."

Now that she was comforted in knowing Danny was unharmed, Chloe's voice took on a teasing tone. "Exactly how *fine* is he?"

Danny gave an exaggerated sigh. "I can't even tell you, Chlo. He's the definition of tall, dark, and handsome. Throw in these piercing blue eyes and a fantastic smell and freaking amazing body."

Chloe gave a little squeal of delight. "And how up close and personal with this amazing body has my Danny Boy been?"

Danny blushed, grateful she wasn't there in person to tease him over it. "I...took him home. After the mugging. He stayed the night last night."

Chloe gave an actual whoop. "Yes! Yesss. Good work. Tell me more."

"He made me food. We fell asleep. This morning we hooked up, and it was...mind-blowing, but when I woke up again this afternoon, he was gone. No phone number."

She made a sympathetic sound. "Oof. That's not ideal. You sure he didn't put his number in your phone while you were sleeping or something?"

"No, he didn't. I checked. And it wasn't in the note."

"So he left a note?"

"Yeah, he left a note to explain the groceries? He, um, he got me groceries."

There was a pause on the other end, then, "I'm sorry. Hold up. The man got you *groceries*? While you were sleeping?"

"He...um...seemed to think I wasn't taking care of myself with quote, unquote, 'proper food.'"

"No argument from me. I've never known anyone who was so good at taking care of others and so bad at taking care of himself."

Danny made a noncommittal noise at that statement, not willing to jump into this familiar argument.

"Okay." Chloe moved on. "Let me run this all together. You met a dreamy man at work. He rescues you from a mugger. Makes you postmugging dinner. Spends the night. Participates in a—mind-blowing, I believe you said?—hookup, buys you groceries, and leaves with a note but no number. I got it all?"

Well, clearly not all of it, but that was all Danny could share. "Yep, that's the gist."

"I don't know, Danny. All signs point to a guy that's super into you. You met him at the hospital. Maybe he's expecting to see you again there?"

"But I don't even work the next two nights." Danny could hear the petulant whine in his voice, but he couldn't help it.

"Ohhh." Chloe sounded delighted. "I hear it. You've got a *crush*."

"Mmph." Maybe this phone call was a mistake.

"This is just such a lovely mix of heartwarming and pathetic." Chloe laughed. "All right, solution time. I've got you. The key is distraction. I'm coming over tonight with trash movies and trash junk food. Then tomorrow night you're coming out with me. It's Marcus's birthday celebration, and I know he would be both shocked and delighted if you actually came out. We'll distract you until work, and if you see him, you see him, and if you don't, we throw an 'all men are trash' pity party."

"You can't say all men are trash when you have a perfect husband, Chloe."

"I can, and I will. Marcus would even bake us cookies for it." Marcus was Chloe's incredibly sweet, incredibly loving husband. He probably would too.

Okay. Distraction. That would work, right? He couldn't obsess over unreachable vampire lovers if he was being sociable for once in his life.

After they had the details sorted, he ended the call, feeling unbearably appreciative of his friendship with Chloe. He knew he could be an absentee friend, not around enough to hang out regularly or be a consistent presence—a fact that had prevented him from befriending the majority of his coworkers in any meaningful way—but Chloe met him where he was at, rejoicing when he was available and being incredibly understanding when he wasn't.

Spending the next two nights with her would be the perfect distraction.

Now he just had to make it through the next five hours without obsessing over a certain vampire. He could handle that, right?

Six

Roman

Roman was obsessing.

He'd forced himself to stay away from Danny for one night. To give the boy time to think, time to process everything he'd found out. Time to process *Roman*, really. It was torture, but he knew it was the right thing to do for Danny.

Roman's demon had raged at the distance, insisting they be close to their mate. One taste of Danny, and its obsession had only grown.

They had compromised by stalking the boy.

He'd watched Danny's house the night before, seen another nurse from the hospital come over with what looked like bags of junk food. A female nurse, luckily—Roman wasn't sure his demon would have stood by on the sidelines while another male was alone with their mate. Especially considering the other nurse hadn't left until morning.

But he had reminded the demon—and himself—that it was a good thing Danny had friends, had support. They were not going to be jealous brutes who resented their mate having close ties beyond themselves.

And Danny *was* their mate.

He was sure of it now, after the morning before. Touching the boy, hearing his moans, tasting his release—Roman had never experienced anything like it in his two centuries of living. His cock hardened at just remembering the look on Danny's face when the boy came, cheeks flushed with pleasure.

And then there was the moment right before Danny had fallen back asleep, when he had seen the demon in Roman's eyes and not only tolerated it but *reached for it*. Greeted it with warm, sated eyes and a sweet smile.

In that moment, Roman had felt something in his demon release—a tension that had been present since the moment he had turned, suddenly gone.

He had been planning to show himself again tonight (one night away seemed to be his limit at the moment). But then he'd been surprised to see Danny leave the house, looking beyond delicious in tight black jeans and a baby-blue hoodie under a long dark coat. Roman had been tempted to intercept him at the doorway, push him up against the wall, and have his wicked way with the boy.

But that would probably not be in the spirit of "giving space," so instead, he had followed discreetly as Danny made his way to a bar in town. Roman hadn't thought his mate the type to go out much—he had that look of exhaustion about himself that stemmed from overwork, not overpartying—but then again, he didn't actually know much about the boy he and his demon were obsessing over.

That thought raised his demon's hackles immediately. *Know enough. Know he's sweet, soft, ours, ours, ours.*

He brushed his demon off. *Yes, I get it, you're hooked. Now hush.*

It grumbled some more at him but ultimately backed down. It seemed to trust now that Roman wasn't going to run off and leave Danny behind. Trust that he was just as addicted to the boy as it was.

Roman grew impatient lurking in the parking lot of the bar. What was he even doing? Not for the first time, he chided himself for not giving Danny his phone number. Such a simple, obvious step he'd forgotten. But the thing was, he hadn't really ever, in all his decades, tried to date anyone—to *keep* anyone. He had never needed to leave his contact information with a lover, because he'd never intended to return to one.

He spotted a coffee shop across the street from the bar, one that apparently stayed open late. Perfect.

He ordered himself a coffee from the bored-looking barista at the counter and grabbed a table by the window, one where he could easily spot Danny if he left the bar.

Roman had been sitting there over an hour, staring out the window as if the force of his gaze would cause his boy to appear, when someone slipped into the seat across from him. He was about to tell them, without so much as looking over, to find a table elsewhere, when he smelled a familiar scent—cold ocean air and frozen pine.

Soren.

Roman immediately broke his gaze from the window and ran his eyes over his longtime friend, suddenly here in Colorado. Svelte and graceful as a cat, with a head of golden hair he always kept artfully tousled, he looked incongruous at this casual coffee shop, wearing a fucking brown fur coat over his cream sweater, because of course he was.

He was also looking ridiculously pleased with himself.

"Hello, Roman, dearest," he said, pale eyes glinting. "Surprised to see me?"

"I suppose I shouldn't be." Soren loved to show up without warning. And it wasn't any use asking how he had found Roman—the older vampire had always had a knack for tracking people. It was the reason Roman had asked Soren to keep an eye on Luc's whereabouts to begin with.

His blond friend gave him a positively evil grin. "How's the *something* that's been keeping you in this boring-ass town, Rome?"

Roman sighed. "Is there any use lying to you about it?"

Soren's grin only grew. "Nope," he replied, popping the *p* dramatically. "I'm afraid I've already been following you while you've been following *him*. A real cutie-pie you found there. You should really watch your back though. I was getting really sloppy there, and you didn't even notice me."

Roman grew defensive at the truth in those words. He hadn't had his guard up like he should have, too focused on his fascination with his newfound mate. "It wasn't *me* you were supposed to be keeping an eye on," he groused.

Soren's grin dropped in an instant, his expression turning serious. "I know. But I lost Luc's trail a few days north of here. I'm thinking he either noticed me following him or he found *you* and realized he needed to lay low. He could be on his way. Or here already."

Fuck.

Roman's demon took notice, all coiled tension now. It was just as wary of Luc as Roman was, and with their mate in the vicinity...

His demon leaped to the forefront before Roman could stop it. He let out a low growl, one soft enough that hopefully the surrounding tables couldn't hear it. Soren took notice of his black eyes and leaned back slightly, his own eyes wide. "Holy shit, Rome. You must really like this human."

Roman didn't reply, too focused on pushing his demon back before he flipped the table, busted into the bar, and threw Danny over his shoulder like some sort of ogre.

"Never thought I'd see the day," Soren mused. "Figured you were eternal-loner material since the Luc thing."

"Danny's different." Roman hated how pathetic that sounded.

"And clearly your demon thinks so too." Soren leaned in, narrowing his eyes. "Why, Roman, have you stumbled upon your mate?"

Roman shrugged, wary in verbalizing to another vampire what he'd only just confirmed himself.

"I didn't think you believed in them." Soren was tapping his finger against his lips, trying to hide a bratty smile.

Roman shrugged again, still defensive. "I might have changed my mind."

For the briefest blink of an eye, Roman thought he saw a look of sadness pass through Soren's eyes, but before he could fully register it, it was gone, and the bratty grin was back in place. "Well, congrats, then." Soren pressed a hand to his chest, giving a dramatic sigh. "My little baby's all grown up."

His friend loved nothing more than to point out Roman's relative youth. Despite Soren's own youthful appearance (he couldn't have been older than his early twenties when he'd been turned), he'd become a vampire in his homeland of Denmark sometime in the seventeenth century, making him almost a full century older than Roman.

Roman wasn't entirely sure how Soren had avoided going feral all this time. He thought it might have something to do with his friend's love of excess—be it fashion, clubs, parties—that kept him so immersed in the human world. He didn't skirt around on the edges of humanity like Roman did—he embraced all it had to offer.

And, of the other few vampires Roman had known, Soren seemed to fight with his demon the least. Roman sometimes wondered if that acceptance of his nature was its own defense against losing his control.

Soren leaned forward again, interrupting his reflections. "We should really go get your human, Rome. Luc's good at not being found when he doesn't want to be. Just because I haven't seen him here doesn't mean he's not nearby."

Roman had a moment of hesitation. He knew there was strength in numbers, but both he and his demon balked for an instant at the thought of letting another vampire near Danny, even a friend.

Soren's eyes softened the slightest bit. He placed his slender hand on Roman's arm. "Hey. I promise I'm not going to touch what's yours. You can trust me, Rome. Just let me help while I'm here."

And there it was. Despite his tendency toward debauchery, Soren was incredibly loyal to those he decided deserved it. It was a loyalty he'd proven more than once over the decades since Roman had met him.

"Besides," Soren went on, pushing his chair back from the table, "with Luc's whereabouts unknown, you really shouldn't be letting the boy out of your sight."

Roman knew he was right. And as they rose to leave, he was disturbed by just how much he liked the idea of always having eyes on Danny, of never letting the boy leave his side.

His demon purred its agreement at that image.

We're fucked, Roman thought.

ℓℓℓ

The bar they entered was just a step above a dive, with a long L-shaped bar, some scattered high tables, and a small dance floor where a surprisingly lively group was dancing together to some pop princess or another. Roman thought he spotted some of the staff he had seen when he was lurking around Danny at the hospital. Was this a work gathering, then?

Roman's gaze left the dance floor and immediately landed on Danny, as if Roman had an internal homing beacon just for the boy. He was sitting at the bar and chatting with his friend from the night before, the short brunette, cocktails in front of each of them. He was laughing at something she was saying, but the smile wasn't quite reaching his eyes.

Merde.

His mate was upset about something. The thought disturbed Roman, and he racked his brain to think of what it could be—nothing had seemed to come up in the time that Roman had been watching him. Had something happened tonight while Roman had been distracted at the coffee shop?

He approached the bar with long strides, Soren two steps behind him, settling in to stand at Danny's left, where there was an empty space. Danny's gaze left the woman at his side and landed on Roman, eyes going wide at his unexpected appearance at the bar.

Looking to see what had grabbed Danny's attention, the petite woman eyed Roman, muttering quietly to Danny—but not quietly enough for Roman's vampire hearing to miss it—"You weren't exaggerating in the looks department."

Roman suppressed a satisfied smirk as Danny blushed. So his lovely mate had been talking about him.

"Danny," Roman purred, leaning closer to catch a whiff of his mate's delicious scent.

Danny leaned back stiffly. "How'd you know I was here?" he asked, tone flat. It was only then that Roman noticed the look in the boy's dark eyes was less than welcoming.

Before Roman could answer, Danny glanced behind him, eyes landing on Soren, golden-haired and chic and no doubt grinning like a loon. His mate's face fell immediately. "Oh. You...you *didn't* know I was here. I shouldn't have assumed." The muscle in Danny's cheek jumped as he clenched his jaw. "Well, don't let me interrupt," he finished, turning back to his friend.

The friend who was now shooting daggers at Roman with her eyes.

Was Danny jealous? Roman was almost pleased at the thought, but it was tempered by his displeasure at having Danny ignore him.

Oh no. This would not do.

Roman tapped Danny's shoulder, and the boy turned back to him, a look of such haughty disdain on his face that Roman would have been delighted at his pluck had that disdain not been directed at himself.

"Danny, this is an old *friend* of mine, Soren Iversen," he explained, tone pointed.

Danny's expression didn't change.

"An old, *old* friend," Roman hinted. "We used to...hunt together. Back in the day."

Danny's eyes widened slightly as the message seemed to sink in. A light blush stole over his cheeks, and the haughty expression dropped. He sent a small, apologetic smile to Soren. "Oh. Hello."

Sweet boy.

"Adorable," Soren whispered, softly enough that only Roman could hear him. To Danny, he said, "Nice to meet you. Roman's told me *so much* about you." Roman could only imagine the manic grin Soren must be directing at Danny, but Roman kept his eyes firmly on his mate.

Danny ducked his head in embarrassment, and his nurse friend gave him a small pat on the back, her death glare at Roman finally dropping.

"And I'm Chloe," she chimed in. "Nice to meet both of you." She gave Danny's cheek a kiss and stood up from the bar. "I'm gonna join the birthday boy on the dance floor."

"And I'm going to grab a drink. Let you two chat," Soren added. At Roman's raised eyebrow, he gave a wink and murmured, "What? We don't need to leave immediately. We're both here. Nothing's going to get to him. Handle your business. I myself have spotted several promising specimens." With that, he turned and strutted over to the other end of the bar, where a tall blue-haired bartender with a nose ring started to take his order.

Roman moved closer to Danny, who was frowning at his drink. Was the boy still feeling unsure about Soren's presence?

"I meant what I said," Roman reassured him. "He's just a friend. He's...like me."

Danny rolled his eyes but still didn't quite meet Roman's gaze. "I know. I got it. Real subtle with the 'hunting' reference."

Okay, so not jealous anymore. Clearly something was wrong though. Roman just wasn't sure what. "Then why do you look so upset?" he asked.

"Didn't leave your number," Danny mumbled, under his breath enough that, even with his superior hearing, Roman almost didn't catch it.

Oh. *Oh.*

"I apologize. That was foolish of me. I am not used to—" Roman started, but Danny interrupted.

"You knew how to reach me. Where I work, where I live. And I didn't even have your *phone number.*" His voice was growing steadily louder, and Roman began to suspect this was perhaps not his first cocktail. "You tell me what you told me and then just disappear? That's some...some messed up power dynamics! And I'm not here for it."

Roman was torn between distress that he had so clearly hurt Danny with his inconsiderate actions and overwhelming delight that the boy had clearly missed him.

Danny *wanted* him.

Fix it. Soothe, protect, ours, ours, ours, his demon hissed at him.

Right. First things first. Reassure and comfort their mate. But before he could start to explain himself, a familiar dark-haired figure interrupted them, swooping in over Danny at the spot

Chloe had vacated. "Is everything all right here?" he asked, eyes on Roman, tone accusatory.

Gabe. The brother.

Roman kept his own eyes firmly on Danny, who was rolling his own at his brother. His mate got a little bratty when he was drunk, apparently.

The bartender appeared suddenly. "King," she said, voice throaty. "I've been wondering when you would show up." She gestured at Danny with her chin. "It's just been Little King sitting here for hours."

"Little King?" Roman mouthed at Danny, brow raised in question.

Still scowling, Danny muttered so that only Roman could hear, "Our last name. It's Kingman. Golden boy over there got the nickname King in high school, and then when I showed up four years later..." He shrugged. "Only a few people still use it. Generally"—he sent a pointed look to the bartender, who was leaning over the bar in front of Gabe now, cleavage on impressive display—"when they're trying to get into *someone's* pants."

Roman leaned in so his shoulders were brushing Danny's, ready to finish their conversation now that the elder Kingman brother was seemingly occupied.

"I am very sorry, my *little king*," he murmured, watching as the most delicious blush spread from Danny's cheeks down his throat at the use of his nickname.

How delightful.

"I am...unaccustomed to modern dating," he continued. "Or to any dating, really. I am used to staying in the shadows. I did not think to leave my number. And I wanted to give you at least the semblance of space, should you have needed it."

Danny, too quick by half, picked up on his wording. "*Semblance* of space? Have you been...watching me?"

Roman winced at the slip. "Would that upset you?"

"Not exactly." Danny slowly shook his head. "I know it should, but—"

"It definitely should," Gabe cut in harshly. The elder brother was apparently no longer occupied, the bartender having stepped away to serve someone else a drink. "Who the hell is this guy, Danny? He's been—what—following you around?"

Danny shot a surprisingly vicious look over at his brother. "Butt out, Gabriel."

"I'm not going to butt out when some creep—"

"I would be careful who you call a creep, *Your Highness*," Soren crooned, having materialized a few steps behind Danny's brother.

Gabe peered over his shoulder at the blond vampire, who—despite the challenging tone of his words—was grinning maniacally at Danny's brother. Jesus. This was becoming pure chaos.

"Now who the hell is this guy?" Gabe demanded, tone hostile as ever.

Soren's grin didn't falter. "I'm new in town. Be nice." He stepped in closer to Gabe, breathing in subtly as he went, seeming to inhale the brother's scent. Roman really hoped it was just an intimidation tactic, because having Soren fixated on Danny's older brother was just asking for trouble. "I'm actually in need of a big, strong man to accompany me outside for a smoke," Soren continued. "King Gabriel, was it? I think you'll fit the bill."

That surprisingly seemed to take the wind out of Gabe's sails. Roman watched as he stared, gobsmacked, at the blond man in front of him. "It's just—it's just Gabe. And I'm a doctor. I don't smoke?" It came out like a question. He was looking into Soren's eyes like he was hypnotized. "You shouldn't either. It's, um, bad for you."

"I know." Soren's pale eyes glinted dangerously. "That's why I like it."

And with that, he grabbed Danny's brother's hand, pulling him to the back door of the bar.

Pleased that the distraction was handled, Roman turned to Danny. The boy was looking slightly stunned to see his older brother led away so easily. "Um, your friend isn't going to...eat him, is he?"

"A dainty nibble at the most," Roman teased. He could possibly be more concerned with the fact that Soren had latched onto his mate's brother, but Roman knew his friend wouldn't seriously injure the man, and he was frankly tired of all these other people taking up so much of his lovely mate's time and attention.

Danny was his.

"That's not actually reassur—" Danny started.

"You forgive me?" Roman interrupted. "For the thoughtlessness and the—as your brother would put it—'creepy following'?"

"I guess so." Danny tilted his head to study him. "The phone number part is what it is. And the following...I know it *should* bother me, but...I've never had anyone watching out for me before. Not since I was a kid, at least. It's...kind of nice?"

"I would watch out for you always, if you would let me." Roman meant every word.

Danny pointed at him accusingly then, his hand a little unsteady. "See, that's the part that feels a little unreal to me. You barely know me. You've lived over two hundred years, seen so many places and things, and I'm just...me. I've barely done anything, or seen anything. I'm just Danny."

Before Roman could counter and explain to Danny just how special he found the boy—his obvious kindness and caring, his sweetness mixed with strength—they were once again interrupted.

Roman just barely kept his demon from roaring out its frustration for everyone to hear.

Soren, no longer grinning, was leading a very pale Gabe back to the bar. "Rome, buddy, we've got a problem."

Oh merde. "Did you...?" Roman's eyes darted to Gabe. Maybe his friend was more careless than he had thought?

Soren glanced over at the man's white face. "Oh...no. Jesus. Time and place, Rome. We found something outside. Doctor Highness is in a little bit of shock."

"What did you find?" Danny asked, jumping off his barstool to look his brother over.

"A body," Soren replied. "A very...messy...body."

Roman knew what that meant, if only from the look on Soren's face.

Luc was here.

Goddamn it.

Seven

Danny

Danny once again found himself at his kitchen counter, Roman placing food in front of him. Plain toast this time.

"Eat," Roman urged. "It will soak up the alcohol. Settle your stomach."

Danny didn't feel like he needed anything to soak up the alcohol—turned out surprise murder did wonders in sobering a person up—but it was true his stomach was roiling at thinking of the mutilated body Soren had shown them. It wasn't the gore itself—Danny had seen plenty bad enough at the hospital—but the fact that the corpse's face had been familiar.

His would-be mugger.

When the police came, Roman had urged him not to mention his connection to the body. "No one but us knows what happened the other night. No need to get yourself further involved for no reason," he'd counseled.

So Danny—along with Soren, Gabe, and Roman—had answered their questions about his role in finding the body honestly but had offered up nothing else about his history with the dead man.

Still, Danny had to ask, as Roman drove his car back to his house, if Roman had anything to do with the man's death. Roman, expression bank, seemingly unsurprised and unfazed by the question, had looked him in his eyes and said he hadn't killed the man. That he'd never even tried to track him down after that night.

And Danny had believed him. Just like that.

Did that make him stupid? Putting so much trust in a man—-a vampire—he'd just met? Probably. And that should almost definitely worry him. But for whatever reason, it didn't. *Just further proof you're a dummy, dummy.*

Gabe had almost insisted on coming home with them, catching on quickly that there was more to the situation than anyone was telling him, but when he'd seemed about to argue with Danny's refusal, Soren—Roman's stupidly handsome vampire friend—had stepped in.

"I agree. You *should* come," he'd purred, eyes glinting, lips stretched in that maniacal smile he seemed to have permanently etched on his face. "I might get scared just remembering the whole grisly experience and need someone to hold me in the night."

Gabe had immediately backed down, mumbling about everyone going home and getting some sleep. Danny had never seen him so easily intimidated by anyone. He'd seen his brother hold his own with men built like linebackers, yet this svelte blond supermodel of a vampire seemed to scare the living daylights out of him with no effort at all.

Was it petty of Danny to find that hilarious?

In the end, Soren hadn't come back with him and Roman either. He'd said he'd needed to feed, whispering to Roman something about searching for someone as he made his way out.

Roman set a steaming mug in front of Danny, bringing his mind back to the present.

"I didn't even know I *had* tea." Danny's voice sounded hollow to his own ears.

"I purchased some for you." Roman was eyeing him with concern, as if he would break at any moment.

Well, Danny was made of tougher stuff than that. He gave himself a shake and smiled genuinely at Roman.

"Thank you for the groceries. I didn't get a chance to say it, with my whole 'drunk ranting about phone numbers' thing. It was very sweet of you to do that for me."

Roman just nodded once, watching Danny with the same intensity he always did. "I like doing things for you. It...soothes me. Soothes my demon too. To take care of you."

Danny felt a lump forming in his throat at Roman's admission. How long had it been since someone had wanted to take care of him? He suddenly seemed on the verge of tears.

For fuck's sake, when had he become such a sap?

He decided to blame the stress of the night and change the subject back to more pressing issues. He cleared his throat. "Tell me why you and Soren seemed so freaked out. About the dead man. If it wasn't either of you who killed him."

Roman raised an eyebrow at him.

"I believe you," Danny insisted. "I really do. But I know there's more going on than what you've told me."

Roman gave a deep sigh. Voice full of resignation, he started explaining. "There is a reason I move around so much, even for a vampire. A reason beyond avoiding drawing attention to my lack of aging. I know I told you vampires tend to stick to themselves, other than rumors of mated pairs."

Danny nodded in acknowledgment. He remembered every word of what Roman had told him about vampires.

"There was another vampire I used to spend a good deal of my time with, besides Soren. All my time, once."

Danny's throat tightened a bit at the thought of where this might be heading. "He was your...partner?"

Roman's eyes flashed to his in surprise. "You mean romantically? No, nothing like that. He was my friend. My...brother, really. Lucien. Luc."

Danny couldn't help the little sigh of relief that escaped him. He already felt like a bumbling baby in contrast to Roman with his vast life experience. There was no way he could mentally compete with some centuries-old vampire romance.

Roman continued on, oblivious to Danny's battle with jealousy. "Luc was the one who turned me. I was dying, a wounded soldier, and he...saved me, in his way."

Danny's gut clenched at the thought of Roman at death's door. Already he didn't like to think of a world without Roman in it.

"Luc's own sire had left him shortly after turning him. Luc himself had only been a vampire for a decade at that point. Practically a baby. But he still knew more than me. He helped me adjust to this new...presence...inside of me. All he asked in return was that I stay by his side. I think he had been...very lonely."

The presence inside Roman. His demon. The other side of this man, the one Danny had met so far only in brief snatches. Black eyes, fangs, and an aura of fierce protectiveness—protectiveness over Danny.

Roman's eyes had gone a little unfocused, for once not drilling into Danny, as Roman became lost in the memories he was describing. "It was in the 1940s when things changed. We were staying in New York City. By that time, we had known Soren for a few decades, had heard about fated mates. Luc met a woman there. He was certain, so certain, she was his mate."

Did Roman feel certain Danny was his mate? He hadn't sounded convinced when he'd explained it to Danny.

"He was happy for a time," Roman went on. "She was remarkably unfazed by what we were. She was...adventurous. Tempestuous. Selfish, really. Loved our power and our wealth and what Luc could provide for her. They had a sort of...game...going. Luc would try to convince her to turn. She would deny him. He seemed to think of it as an extended flirtation, certain that after she came into her own a bit more as a human, she would give in."

Roman picked up Danny's empty plate, then turned his back to place it in the sink. He didn't turn back around. "One day, Luc was out hunting. Victoria and I were out together driving. She liked to drive fast. At least, as fast as cars could go in those days. There was an accident. I, being what I am, was fine, but she was losing blood so quickly. Clearly dying. There was not time to get her help. I knew what I had to do, but when I went to turn her, she...begged me."

Roman turned and looked at Danny then, eyes no longer unfocused but instead so full of regret that all Danny wanted to do was throw his arms around his vampire and tell him he didn't have to keep going.

But Danny needed to know what they were up against. He gave Roman an encouraging nod instead.

"She begged me not to turn her," Roman explained. "She told me she had never intended to become one of us, to turn into a killer. Never wanted this *thing* inside of her. So I just held her as she passed. I let her die. When Luc found out...he came close to killing me that night. I would have let him. She was my friend too. I had failed both of them. Denied him his chance at salvation from descent into a feral state. But my demon wouldn't go down without a fight."

Poor Roman. Poor Victoria. Poor Luc. The whole situation sounded so awful it broke Danny's heart.

"He attacked me once more, a few weeks later. I fought him off again but only barely. And then he left. Disappeared for a few decades. One day, he just...reappeared. Showed up in the city I was living. His eyes were now...always black. Like he had given up and let his demon take over. He killed when he fed, something he had never done before. Left a trail of bodies, chasing me out of my city. I fled. He chased. It has been like that ever since. I never stay anywhere long. I do not make human connections. I fear what he would do to them, what revenge he would try to take."

"You've never...tried to take him out? You said your kind do that, when one of you is lost." Danny was hesitant in asking the question. It felt wrong to suggest Roman murder a former friend, but was his friend even still there if the demon was running the show?

Roman shook his head. "For one, it is...incredibly hard to kill one of our kind. Complete beheading or death by fire—those are the only true deaths. But more...I could not bring myself to. It is my fault he has become what he has. It was me who took away his chance at stability, at a future."

Danny found himself shaking his head, getting up from his chair, and reaching for Roman, but Roman took a step back, eyes pained. "There is more, Danny. More to it. I did not...care...about the humans he was killing. Not really. I hated that it ran the risk of outing me, I hated that he would not leave me in peace, but beyond that...I let a woman dear to someone I loved die, and then I ignored the consequences of my actions. Happy to run away from my troubles. I told you. Even beyond the demon inside me...I am not a good man."

A sound of distress left Danny's throat, and he reached for Roman again. This time, Roman let him. Danny stepped forward and plastered his body to Roman's front, hugging him hard. "I can't condemn you for your reaction to Luc's killings. I don't know what living as long as you have does to your perspective of human life, but I expect—" Danny struggled to find the words. "I expect it makes it hard to empathize with life being cut short, when human life seems so short to you already."

When Roman seemed poised to object, Danny just hugged him harder, cutting him off. "But I *can* speak to what you did for Victoria. You honored a choice. That was *her* choice. Not yours, and not Luc's. Just because he's been murderously guilt-tripping you for decades doesn't mean he's right."

Danny looked up at Roman to see him shaking his head at him in disbelief. "Why are you not scared of me?" the vampire ground out. "You have seen what one of my kind can do, back in the alley. You know now that being with me puts you in danger. You should *hate me* for walking into your life."

Danny narrowed his eyes. "I refuse to be scared of you just because of what you are. I work in the ER. I've seen stab wounds, gunshots, domestic abuse—all done by *humans*. Vampires don't have the patent on violent acts. A human partner wouldn't necessarily mean a safe partner." He kissed Roman's chest, a brief peck over his shirt. "*You* make me feel safe, weird as that is. I know, somehow, that you and your demon wouldn't hurt me. And I know you'd protect me from Luc if he came for me. I can *feel* that."

Roman smiled at him then, so gently and sweetly that Danny's breath caught in his throat. Then the vampire bent down to brush his lips over Danny's, the gentle kiss soon turning hungry. He growled and pulled Danny even harder against him, and Danny could feel Roman's cock hardening against his stomach.

"Sweet boy. Gentle, sweet human mate," Roman purred in his ear after breaking the kiss, trailing his lips down along Danny's neck.

Danny shivered, feeling himself melt at the touch of Roman's lips on his skin. How did this vampire have such an effect on him?

But when Roman went to place another kiss on his lips, Danny pulled his head back.

Roman's muscles immediately tensed. He peered down at Danny, blue eyes searching Danny's for some sign. He sighed. "You still worry over something."

Danny nodded, feeling hesitant to voice his concerns. "I'm not afraid *of* you. But there are still things about this whole...situation...that freak me out."

"Luc," Roman hissed.

"Not Luc. Your *reaction* to Luc. That you'll—that you'll leave."

Roman opened his mouth, but Danny continued on before he could voice his protest. "You say that you move around constantly. And I get why now. But I can't just up and leave. I have responsibilities here. My mom. You haven't met her yet. You don't know, but...Gabe can't handle it on his own. He just can't. He's in denial. She won't have anybody if I'm gone."

Roman was shaking his head, his fingers stroking softly against Danny's cheek. "I won't leave you, Danny. You are my *mate*. I know it. I have known it in some way since the first moment I saw you."

"You mean your demon knew," Danny felt the need to clarify.

Roman cocked his head, eyeing Danny as if he was a puzzle he could solve. "And that distinction...bothers you?"

"You said Luc was certain that Victoria was his mate. But it sounded like you don't agree..."

Roman grunted. "Ah. Yes. I was never a true believer, I suppose. And there were...inconsistencies. A mate is supposed to calm your demon, but Victoria seemed to simply...intensify Luc's. He was more labile, on edge, around her. And her unwillingness to turn..." He sighed. "But I could not tell if that was simply me attempting to lessen my own guilt."

"But if Luc was wrong, you could be wrong too. I could be just another Victoria. Just because your demon likes me doesn't mean—"

Roman stopped Danny with another kiss. "Do you really think it is solely my demon that likes you, my little king?" Oh God. What was it about Roman's low voice saying Danny's once-hated nickname that made his cock immediately harden? Danny had practically melted the first time he'd said it at the bar. It just wasn't fair.

Roman continued, oblivious to Danny's inner slut starting to take over his brain. "It is not *just* the demon. You are so...lovely. Inside and out. Kind, caring, strong. You have devoted your life to taking care of others. I know there is a reason you work so hard, and I know it is not just for yourself. So determined to be good, in fact, that you neglect yourself." Roman gave him a stern look. "Something that we will be rectifying."

Roman slipped his hands into Danny's curls, cradling his head, and gave him a look that could melt steel. "And for the record...my demon does not just *like* you. It *craves* you. Is *obsessed* with you. Wants to own you and devour you and never let you go. You would run for the hills if you could hear what it thinks about you. What *I* think about you."

The heat in Roman's gaze combined with the heat of his words...that was it. Danny was a goner. No more discussions. No more thinking. He just needed Roman's hands and mouth all over him. Immediately. He reached up and grabbed Roman's hands, tugging them out of his hair, and started to lead his vampire up the stairs.

Enough talking.

—⁓—

As soon as they entered his room, Danny was on Roman, standing on tiptoe to attack the taller man's lips with his own. He wanted him so badly. Had barely gotten even a taste and was already addicted.

Roman groaned as he met Danny's kiss just as fiercely, and Danny felt the harsh bite of Roman's fingers digging into his sides. But Danny liked that bit of pain. It only served to intensify the moment, to heighten his desire.

Danny walked them backward, never letting his lips leave Roman's. Their tongues and teeth were clashing, messy and raw. It was perfect. As he felt the backs of his knees hit his bed, Roman gave Danny a gentle push until he was sitting on the edge, sprawled back on his elbows.

Danny's breath caught in his throat as he watched Roman gracefully bend to his knees, hands reaching for Danny's hips to pull him closer to the edge of the bed.

"I am at your mercy, my little king," Roman purred, long fingers beginning to deftly unbutton Danny's jeans. "You have me on my knees for you. What would you have me do?"

Danny couldn't seem to find the words, just watched wide-eyed as Roman pulled his jeans down over his hips, revealing underwear already damp from his leaking cock.

Roman gave a little groan of delight at the sight, bending his head to nuzzle Danny's cock through his underwear, mouthing at his hard length.

Even through the fabric, Roman's hot mouth felt *so fucking good*. Danny was panting already.

"What do you want from me, mon petit roi?" Roman asked again. "I am yours to command."

I want everything, was all Danny could think. He wanted Roman's mouth on his cock, wanted Roman to fill him and fuck him until he couldn't walk.

But what Danny blurted out was, "I want you to bite me."

Well, shit. Where had that come from?

But it was true. Danny wanted Roman's bite.

Roman stopped his nuzzling and gazed up at Danny, blue eyes wide. Danny felt himself flush as he explained, "I want to know what it feels like. The other night you said—you said blood and sex go hand in hand for you. Show me."

"They often do go hand in hand, lovely. But they do not have to. I would be perfectly satisfied with any sexual act with you, blood or no blood."

Danny felt doubt creep over him. Was he pushing for something Roman wasn't even interested in? "Do you not...want to?" he asked, annoyed at the insecurity in his voice.

Roman gave a low growl, sending a shiver through Danny. "Oh, I want to, little king. My demon has been dying for another taste of you since we healed your shoulder. We both think you have the most delicious blood in all creation."

Oh. Well, that was...nice? How weird was his life now, that he was feeling proud over a vampire he barely knew calling his blood delicious?

"Then I want you to."

Roman's eyes darkened, and then he was peeling Danny's underwear down, revealing his aching cock. Danny whimpered as Roman licked a stripe up the underside before dipping his tongue into the slit to gather the precum building there. If Danny had been standing, his knees would have buckled.

"What—um—what are you doing? Don't you...um...fuck...my neck?" Danny was having trouble finding words.

He looked down again to see Roman giving him a devilish grin, blue eyes sparkling. "Oh, there are many more places than simply your neck to bite, sweet boy."

Danny had a sudden horrifying thought and couldn't help but glance down at his dick. Roman burst out laughing, a deep, rolling sound. "No, not there." He placed a soft kiss at the head, sending another shiver through Danny. Then he pushed Danny's legs open wider and nuzzled at the soft skin where Danny's groin met his thigh.

"Here." He placed another soft kiss over the spot.

When Roman glanced back up, Danny saw his eyes were once again fully black, and his fangs were peeking out from between his lips. But Danny felt no more fear than the last time. When he realized Roman—or Roman's demon?—was waiting for Danny's permission, giving him one more chance to back out, he spread his legs wider and gave a nod.

Roman growled, lips curling up in satisfaction, before ducking his head back down to the tender spot on Danny's skin. Danny held his breath as he felt the sharp sting of Roman's fangs entering him.

Before he could even focus on the pain, the burning had already given way to a tingling sensation, one that was extending from the bite through the rest of his body. Fuck. It was pure, electric pleasure racing along his nerve endings. Danny felt that if Roman even so much as brushed his throbbing cock, he would come immediately.

"Oh God. Oh holy shit. Oh fuck." He couldn't stop the babbling. Nothing had ever felt quite so good. He could feel his cock leaking precum onto his stomach as he faintly registered the sounds of Roman growling and...gulping?

Almost as soon as it had begun, it was over.

Danny felt the soft, wet touch of Roman's tongue licking at the bite, closing the wound. The tingling sensation ebbed, leaving behind a feeling of loose-limbed contentment.

But Danny's cock was still achingly hard, flushed and pulsing against his stomach.

"Sweet. So sweet." Roman was practically purring, but his voice sounded different, harsher and somehow even deeper. As Danny looked down again to meet black eyes, he realized it was the voice of Roman's demon talking to him. Was it really his first time hearing Roman talk in his vampire state?

They both stayed where they were, gazing at each other, and then Danny watched as the demon slowly licked the last trickle of Danny's blood off his lips.

Danny was overcome with the need to show some appreciation. To give something to this demon who apparently wanted him so much, who had brought Roman to Danny's side.

He reached down and grabbed Roman's hand, leaning back on the bed and pulling the vampire on top of him. He lifted his head and brushed Roman's lips with his own. Gentle, hesitant.

He wasn't sure if the demon even liked kissing. Maybe affection wasn't its thing?

He felt Roman's body stiffen briefly only to melt over him. Roman opened his lips, taking control of the kiss, capturing Danny's tongue with his. Danny could taste the copper tang of his own blood, but he couldn't find it in himself to care.

This vampire was *his*.

After a few minutes, he broke the kiss and rested his forehead against Roman's. "Fuck. Why did that feel so good?"

Roman gave a grunt, and Danny watched as his fangs retracted and the black in his eyes receded, leaving that bright blue. "I imagine it as evolutionary. If done right, a human can receive immense pleasure from a vampire bite. It is easier for us if humans enjoy our feeding on them. Less trauma. Easier to fog their minds afterward, to adjust their memories to remember only the pleasure and not the bite."

Um. What the fuck?

"You can do that?" Danny gasped. "Affect memories?"

Roman gave a little sigh and nuzzled Danny's neck. "Our demons can offer...suggestions, hold compulsions. It is not foolproof. Not perfect mind control. But it helps keep people from fearing us. From outing us, if you will."

Danny had to ask. "Have you—do you ever do that with me?"

Roman lifted his head and looked at Danny with soft eyes. "No, lovely Danny. I have never interfered with your thoughts or your emotions. I *would* never, except perhaps to spare you pain, if you were hurting."

"Vampire anesthesia, huh?" Danny gave what was probably an inappropriate giggle at the thought, and Roman huffed a laugh at him. The act caused their lower bodies to brush against each other, and Danny was made aware that he was half-naked and still rock-hard. As was his vampire.

Roman must have seen the change in his expression, because his eyes filled again with heat, and he began tugging Danny's shirt over his head.

Danny melted back against the bed as Roman began raining soft kisses down his body, stopping to give playful licks to Danny's nipples, then his belly button. Danny couldn't help giggling, but it was quickly cut off by a moan as Roman's next stop was to engulf Danny's cock with his mouth in one go.

"Fuck. Yes." Danny's breath grew ragged as Roman gave long, hard pulls on his cock. "Oh my God. Fuck. Rome. Not gonna last."

Roman hummed his approval, sending a shock wave of pleasure through Danny's body, and then released Danny's cock from his mouth with a soft pop. "Good. Let go, little king," he crooned.

Danny clenched the sheets underneath him as Roman resumed his task with enthusiasm, wrapping his tongue around Danny's length as he sucked him mercilessly.

"Fuck, fuck, fuck. Yes. Yes. I'm gonna—" He lifted a hand to tug at Roman's black locks in warning, but Roman ignored him, solely focused on Danny's pleasure.

Danny exploded with a groan, spurting into Roman's mouth.

The vampire looked up at him, once again slowly licking his lips, this time to gather the remains of Danny's cum off them. "Every part of you is delicious," he purred.

He rose from his kneeling position and began unbuttoning his own shirt, staring down at Danny with unnerving focus. Danny could only stare back at him, his body boneless from his orgasm. He had yet to see much of Roman's bare skin, their last encounter having ended with Roman still almost fully clothed. True, he'd *felt* the muscles, but as Roman finished with his shirt, pulling it off his torso, all Danny could think was, *Oh good goddamn.*

His vampire was lean but still well muscled, his body reminding Danny of the Olympic rowers he'd used to drool over on TV when he was first realizing he wanted to kiss other boys.

Danny wondered if the vampirism contributed to that flawless physique or if Roman had been that way even as a human. Either way, he gave a little prayer of thanks to whatever higher power was clearly cosmically rewarding him for being such a good boy.

"You have quite a filthy mouth when you are aroused, lovely Danny," Roman teased, moving on to his belt buckle. He smirked down at Danny as he lowered his pants, revealing that perfect cock to go with the perfect body.

Danny's mouth watered at the sight.

"Shall we give that filthy mouth something else to do?"

Danny moaned like the hussy he was. "Yes. Yes, please."

Eight

Roman

Roman had lived many lives over—more than he deserved—but he had never in all his time seen such a gorgeous sight as his lovely Danny sprawled back on the bed, flushed and panting, eager for a taste of Roman's cock.

He palmed himself idly as he looked over every bare inch of his mate, this sweet man who had kissed Roman's demon so gently, welcoming him—all of him—into his bed.

He'd had lovers turned on by his demon before, but that had been about the thrill of danger, not about Roman himself. And there had always been the underlying scent of fear in every encounter. If Roman was honest, the fear had added to the pleasure for him, like adding an exotic spice to a dish, making the experience all that more delicious. But with Danny, there was no fear, just sweet submission and trust.

The boy had given in to the pleasure of the bite, kissed Roman's demon face with no hesitation, and then positively melted under Roman's ministrations to his cock.

Sweet, lovely mate.

And now there he was, looking positively debauched, limp-limbed and staring at Roman with those big brown eyes full of dazed contentment and desire. It made Roman want to take him fully, to enter him and claim him completely. He knew Danny would let him fuck him senseless, would give Roman more of that sweet compliance and submission.

But now wasn't the time, what with Danny bordering on the edge of exhaustion from alcohol and the general trauma of the night.

Besides, Roman wanted to take his time, to give Danny only pleasure, and he wasn't sure he had the restraint to do so at the moment.

But he could do other things.

He leaned fully over Danny and began prowling slowly up the boy's body, dropping kisses and nipping at bare flesh along the way, feeling every inch the predator but for once not minding.

He gave Danny one last brutal kiss when he reached the boy's mouth, then reared up to kneel over his chest. "I'm going to feed you my cock now, lovely mate."

Danny whimpered but opened his lips wide, and moments later Roman hissed at the feel of his hot mouth on his cock.

Doe eyes gazing directly into his own, Danny moved his head up to take all of him, pushing on despite gagging slightly until his nose was practically pressed to Roman's hip. Roman's eyes rolled to the back of his head as he felt Danny's throat tighten around the head of his cock as he swallowed experimentally.

"Merde. Fuck. So good, lovely Danny."

Danny backed off Roman's cock, releasing it with a soft pop and grinning up at him with watery eyes. "Looks like I'm not the only one with a filthy mouth."

Cheeky little king.

Roman wound his hand into Danny's soft curls, taking pleasure in the small gasp it elicited from his mate's mouth. He made such lovely little sounds. Roman groaned as Danny relaxed and slackened his jaw, giving him tacit permission to fuck his mouth.

He'd never thought he would get to go to heaven, but here it was: his mate's sweet mouth around his cock, taking every punishing thrust with little moans of delight.

Roman wasn't going to last. He'd been rock-hard since the first taste of Danny's blood, him and his demon both bathed in desire, in pure *want* for this boy.

"Going to come, sweet boy."

He waited for Danny to pull against his grip, but the boy just nodded and sucked even harder, sending electricity through every inch of Roman's body as he came hard into his mate's mouth.

Danny eagerly swallowed every drop, eyes never leaving Roman's, until Roman eventually pulled him gently off his now too-sensitive cock.

Perfect, sweet, ours.

Roman slid his knee up and over Danny's torso, moving to lie on his side, facing his mate, making sure as much of their skin was touching as possible. He lifted his hand back into Danny's dark curls, working his fingers through them gently.

His demon was purring in wordless contentment.

"You really do have me at your mercy, little king," Roman whispered. "All of me."

He watched as Danny smiled softly and hummed a little in acknowledgment, seeming to enjoy the gentle petting just as much as he had enjoyed getting his mouth fucked.

Perfect creature.

Roman thought Danny was perhaps drifting off, but after several minutes, the boy[]s eyes opened, and he turned his head to Roman.

"Can I ask a favor?" he asked in a sleepy voice.

"Anything for you, lovely."

"Can you—can you not do that with anyone else?"

Roman couldn't help the flash of anger that ran through him. Did his mate really think he would be fucking anyone else? That he would ever *want* to fuck anyone else? Had he messed up so badly by disappearing the other day?

He needed to set this straight.

"I will not be touching any other person in that way, Danny. Human or vampire," he ground out. "I would hope—I would hope that you would not be either."

There, that was better than *touch anyone else and I'll fucking rip them apart*, wasn't it?

Roman's fearless little mate actually rolled his eyes at him. "I'm not talking about the sex part, grumpy pants. Could you not...bite anyone else? You said you didn't have to feed very often. Could it be just from me? It just felt so...intimate. I don't think I want you doing that with any other humans."

Danny's voice got softer as he went on, alerting Roman to how hard it must have been for the boy to voice the request, cheeky eye roll aside.

His chest warmed at this unexpected display of possessiveness from his mate, and Roman's answer was easy. "I will bite only you, my little king."

"It's really all right?"

"I was drinking from blood bags before this. I did not want to risk biting humans, too fearful of my demon going overboard. I do not fear that with you, however. You soothe him, even in the act of feeding. I will gladly bite only you. And should you need a break, blood bags will tide me over. I will not risk harming you with...overuse."

He didn't complicate things by bringing up what they would do when Danny turned. He still didn't know how to bring up the subject at all.

How did you ask a man so full of humanity to give that humanity up for you?

Danny had devoted his life to humans—caring for his mother, protecting his brother, working for his community as a nurse. He clearly wasn't ready to leave all that, and it could be very difficult for a new vampire to be around their old life.

Roman had tried, and it had...not gone well. He brushed aside memories of familiar voices screaming "demon!" before they could take hold. Now was not the time to turn maudlin, not when he had his perfect mate in his arms.

Roman could wait for his mate to be ready. He *would* wait for his mate to ready.

Danny turned to his side and curled up into Roman's chest, tucking his head under Roman's chin. "Thank you," he whispered.

"Anything. Always," Roman answered.

"One more thing? Will you stay? Be here in the morning?"

"I will stay."

He waited until Danny's breaths had deepened, the boy sleeping soundly, to whisper the rest of his answer.

"Forever."

Roman had been lying awake for a few hours, content to hold Danny and listen to his mate's rhythmic breathing, when he heard the sounds of Soren returning from his hunt.

Roman had texted Soren Danny's address, with the agreement that Soren would return after hunting and stay with them at Danny's house, at least until the Luc situation was resolved.

An extra layer of protection for his all-too-vulnerable mate.

He gently untangled himself from Danny's sleep-laden limbs—his mate really was something of an octopus at night—and padded down the stairs to the living room, where he could hear Soren moving around.

He found Soren standing in front of one of Danny's bookshelves, perusing the titles. He looked up at Roman's entrance.

"You've fed?" Roman asked.

Soren nodded, grinning wide. "I found the most delicious man. Well"—he gave Roman a sly look—"not as delicious as your adorable boy's big brother. Hello, Doctor Muscles, am I right?"

Roman raised an eyebrow at his friend. "Please do not make my life more complicated by pursuing my mate's brother. There are plenty of other men in this town for you to harass."

Soren gave a mock pout. "Not even a little taste? I can easily make him forget it. Little Danny never even needs to know." Soren had always been especially skilled at compulsion.

Roman shook his head. "Just steer clear. Please."

Soren opened his mouth, seeming to be on the verge of arguing, before he closed it again and gave a little shrug. Even that little bit of resistance struck Roman as odd. In the time that Roman had known him, Soren had always found his human partners interchangeable—fixating on them completely in the moment but discarding them from his mind the moment they left his bed (or club, or alley—Soren wasn't particular).

Roman was fairly sure that Soren had had at least one serious relationship in his past, a vampire ex he never spoke about, but it had seemingly put him off commitment completely. Except, of course, Soren had been the one to tell him and Luc about mates in the first place.

His little friend, for all his own flightiness, had always seemed surprisingly fascinated with the concept of eternal love.

Either way, they had bigger things to concern themselves with at the moment.

"Any signs of Lucien?"

Soren smirked. "Other than the thoughtful present he left us at the bar?"

"And we're sure it was him?"

"I know his handiwork, Rome. So do you." Soren gave him a pointed look. "And knowing it was someone you fought to protect Danny from? He loves that psychological mind game shit."

Roman let out a sigh. He knew it had been too much to hope for it to have been a random coincidence, but he'd needed to hear it said out loud.

Soren tilted his head to the side, studying Roman. "Have you told your boy about it all?"

"Yes. He knows now. The whole ugly story."

Soren's face briefly showed his surprise before he hid it behind another smirk. "And? Did he tell you the same thing I always tell you? That you did nothing wrong, that Luc is just an overdramatic psycho whose only answer to eternal boredom is to mess with you?"

Roman gave a mirthless laugh. "Not in so many words, but yes—he agreed with your general feeling."

"And what about you turning him? Has he agreed to that?"

Jesus, right to the heart of things. Soren never pulled his punches.

Roman found himself crossing his arms over his chest. "I have not brought it up."

"You're kidding me." Soren rolled his eyes. "What are you waiting for?"

Roman walked over to the overstuffed couch in the middle of the room. He suddenly felt he needed to be seated for this conversation. "He is not ready."

"Did he tell you that himself?"

"I just know." Who on this earth *would* be ready to willingly turn themselves into a monster when there was any other option?

Soren gave a mocking laugh. "Well, what I know, dear friend, is that your potential mate there is incredibly breakable in his current state. It would take Luc all of two seconds to dispose of him. Permanently."

Roman's demon was pressing up tight against his skin at the thought. Danny bleeding out, Danny lying dead at his feet. Roman took deep, slow breaths, pushing the rage down, fighting to regain control.

Soren pressed on mercilessly. "You know Luc is going to fixate on him. He already has, if he's been watching you long enough to see your fight with the petty criminal. He saw you protect the boy. He knows what that means. If you turn Danny, he'll be so much stronger. He'll stand an actual chance if Luc catches him without you or me there."

Roman growled his frustration. "He's not *ready*."

"So you'll what...take the boy and run?"

Roman shook his head, frustrated. "He won't go. He has...responsibilities here. Something with his mother. I think she's not well."

"Can't Doctor Muscles handle the mother? Isn't that what older brothers are for?"

"It seems not. I do not know all the intricacies of their relationship, but Danny seems to be doing it all on his own."

Soren threw up his hands. "Well, Jesus, Rome, you're not giving yourself a lot of options here." He hesitated, then narrowed his eyes. "Unless..."

Roman knew where this was headed but wasn't ready to say it on his own. He needed Soren to finish the thought for him. "Unless what?"

"Unless you're ready to finally deal with Luc properly. It's the only real way to keep yourself and Danny safe."

And there it was. The only definite, permanent solution to the Luc problem. All it took was Roman murdering his oldest friend, his vampire brother, the man who'd seen something in him and saved his life so long ago on the battlefield.

Except...

"He hasn't killed me yet," Roman murmured. "Even after all this time. Hasn't really tried to in decades, not after the first two incidents."

"No, he hasn't. I guess you both have the same...twisted loyalty." Soren didn't sound too impressed. "But you don't think he's going to be—oh, I don't know—incredibly triggered by you finding your human mate while he's still wiling away in endless misery, all thanks to you?"

Roman huffed a humorless laugh. "I thought you said I did nothing wrong."

"We both know Luc feels differently. And while he may have loyalty to *you*, he has no loyalty to your human."

"He was my brother," Roman insisted.

"Way back when, maybe, yes," Soren conceded. "But is there even anything left of Luc in there, Roman? When was the last time you actually spoke to him? If he's truly gone feral, you'd be doing him a favor."

"And would you do the same to me?" Roman questioned defensively. "If I started inconveniencing your life, would you put me down so easily?"

Soren just laughed. "Easily? He's been tormenting you for decades, Rome." He looked Roman dead in the eyes. "And yes, if you lost yourself, lost all sense of what made you Roman, and started to threaten those I love? I *would* put you down."

"And who is there that you love, Soren?" Roman regretted it as soon as he said it. He knew he was being unfair, turning his anger against Soren instead of himself.

"Careful, Roman," Soren warned, his voice taking on an icy edge. "I would count you among the few, I think. But even then, my patience has limits."

And Roman should be grateful for that patience, was the unspoken threat.

Sometimes Roman forgot how deadly his beautiful friend truly was. He came across as almost dainty, with his petite stature, delicate features, and flair for fashion. But with age came strength, and Soren was much, much older than Roman. "My apologies, old friend. I did not mean anything by it."

Soren sighed lightly and broke eye contact, examining his nails. "You did, but luckily I'm feeling magnanimous. Take me to my room. You can make it up for me in the morning with pancakes."

His friend really did love everything human, even the food.

After showing Soren to the guest room, Roman returned to Danny's room. His mate was still sleeping soundly, hugging one of his pillows to his chest tightly, as if to make up for Roman's absence from his bed. Roman slipped under the covers and curled himself around his mate's back. He inhaled deeply, taking in that unique milk-and-honey scent that was Danny's alone, soothing himself and his demon like a drug.

He didn't understand the feelings this boy stirred in him. How could he feel protective of another creature so quickly? How could he be entertaining putting down someone he had so much history with like a dog, just to ensure the safety of a man he'd met not even a week ago?

And why wasn't he more troubled by it all?

All he knew was that he and his demon both wanted Danny. They wanted to keep him, and they would do anything to ensure the boy stayed safe.

Anything, he promised as Danny gave a little sigh and pressed back against Roman, searching for maximum contact even in his sleep.

Roman tightened his arms around his mate, finally allowing his eyes to close and his brain to quiet.

Roman would not let Luc take this from him.

Nine

Danny

Life was so fucking weird sometimes.

That was the main thought going through Danny's head as he sat at his kitchen counter, drinking his coffee, the smell of pancakes making his stomach growl. Pancakes that were currently being made by his ancient vampire lover. While his ancient vampire lover's even more ancient—because it turned out that despite looking barely old enough to drink, Soren was older than Roman—vampire friend sat on the counter next to the stove, giving imperious orders.

"Don't let them sit too long. You know I like mine a little bit raw," he was demanding.

"And you know I think that is absolutely vile."

"Don't yuck my yum, Rome."

"I do not even know what that means," Roman muttered.

"Big surprise. Good thing you met Danny here when you did. You were way too close to losing complete touch with the human race." Soren threw a wink at Danny, a flirty grin on his face.

Danny found that he liked the odd, petite vampire. He may have come off as a little...unhinged...at the bar, but he seemed to genuinely care for Roman and was staying in town to help keep Danny safe. And his caring for Roman didn't seem to be in any way romantic, a fact that Danny was beyond grateful for. He didn't want to even think about competing for Roman's affections with a fierce, demonic supermodel.

He didn't want to think about competing for Roman's affections at all.

He still wasn't sure what Roman saw in him, besides Danny appealing to his possessive demon. Danny was just...Danny. And Roman was...so many things. He had lived so many lives. Danny had barely been living his own.

Until now.

He had woken up wrapped in Roman's arms as promised, and the morning had only gotten better from there. Danny fought a blush as he remembered Roman working them both to orgasm with his large, capable hands only hours before.

And now Roman was cooking for him again.

"Tell me why you know how to cook again?" Danny asked. "I don't think being French is enough of a reason, when you've had two hundred years of not needing to eat human food under your belt."

Roman glanced back at him over his shoulder with a little smirk that didn't do anything to help Danny's blush. "Maybe I was preparing for the day I had a sweet human mate to feed, little king."

Soren made a fake retching sound, grimacing dramatically. "Blegh, Roman. There's sweet, and then there's saccharine. Spare us, please."

Soren met Danny's eyes then. "The thing about more or less eternal life, cutie pie, is that it can be incredibly boring. Especially when you don't need to sleep much. It's amazing the things you end up teaching yourself. Roman over here"—he gestured with his thumb—"speaks eight languages, cooks an untold variety of cuisines, and—absolute drudge that he is—is a master at chess." He rolled his pale-blue eyes. "Such a cliché."

Danny was at a bit of a loss. "*Eight* languages?" He himself could maybe sort of sometimes speak a little Spanish. *Badly.*

Roman stayed facing the stove, focused on the pancakes, but gave a little shrug. "Soren speaks six."

Soren scoffed. "Don't sell me short. I also play five instruments perfectly, I draw beautiful portraits, and I could crochet Danny a three-piece suit if he wanted me to."

"You...crochet?" Danny fought back a grin but couldn't quite keep the smile out of his voice.

Soren arched a golden eyebrow at him. "What—needlepoint isn't 'creature of the night' enough for you?"

"It's not that. You're just so…" Danny trailed off.

"So *what?*" There was a glint in Soren's eyes now that reminded Danny he was speaking to a deadly predator, even if it came in a beautiful, delicate package.

"Chic," Danny finished lamely. Soren was, after all, at this very moment, wearing a fur coat over what appeared to be a silk pajama set.

The deadly glint in Soren's eyes faded, and he smiled wide. That smile could be a bit unsettling—a big, manic grin paired with ancient eyes that seemed to know more than they should. "Well, aren't you the sweetest? It's true I'm not exactly rocking my homemade creations out to the club, but I like a good knitwear as much as any other boy when I'm cozying up at home. Plus it's…meditative. Keeps the beast at bay, as it were."

That was interesting. "Your demon?" Danny asked.

Soren shot an amused glance at Roman. "Now you've got the boy calling it that too? So dramatic, Rome." He looked back over to Danny. "I meant metaphorically. I don't see the distinction between the two selves as clearly as Roman does. I guess in my head, I just call that little, bloodthirsty voice he's talking about my *inner vamp.*"

"Do you…talk to yours? Like Roman does?" Roman had told Danny he sometimes had brief conversations with his demon.

Soren hummed in thought. "Sort of? But don't we all talk to our own brains sometimes? It's just like any other voice in your head, any other set of urges. Like, a little stronger, a little clearer, maybe. A little more vicious definitely. But I'm not all that sure it's so separate from the rest of myself."

Well, that did sound a little less dire than Roman's choice of words. But that brought up another question for Danny. "Why do you sound so much more, I don't know, modern than Roman?"

Danny watched as Roman flushed slightly while plating their pancakes. Soren's pancake did indeed look to be a paler color than what Roman was serving himself and Danny. "Soren has always been better at blending into human society than I have—rolling with the times, if you will," Roman explained. "If I focus, I can do better, but mostly I am fine just letting people think I am...eccentric." He shrugged. "Or European."

"What about work?" Danny asked. "How are you running about all the time in your fancy suits without any income coming in?" Maybe it was crass to bring up money, but given the annoyingly large role the lack of it played in Danny's life, he was more than a little curious.

Soren spoke before Roman could, seemingly happy to answer any and all Danny's nosy questions. "We work sometimes. When we feel like it."

The blond vampire giggled a little as he poured an ungodly amount of syrup over his pancakes. "I was an acrobat once. That was a lark. Roman over there was an undertaker, the morbid fuck. But mostly we've had time to acquire and expand on some pretty crucial investments." He took a bite and continued around a mouthful of pancake. "Plus, we've got that whole compulsion thing that helps smooth the way out of a lot of situations. You'd be surprised how rarely we have to use money at all, if we don't want to. But anyway, you won't have to worry about working if you don't want to—you've basically got yourself a vampire sugar daddy there, cutie pie."

Danny found himself spluttering a bit. "I wouldn't—that's not—what?"

Roman hadn't taken a bite of his food yet, had just been looking back and forth between Danny and Soren, as if in disbelief of the situation he had found himself in. "Soren," he said now, a little sternly. "You overstep."

Soren gave a huff and rolled his eyes. "Just speaking the truth. You don't always have to dance around every subject, Mr. Mysterious."

Danny felt the need to defend his vampire. "Roman's been pretty open about answering my questions, actually."

"Well, that makes you the first." Soren eyed Danny with a strange look in his eyes. "Opening up is not Rome's forte."

Danny felt his chest warm at the thought. Roman really *was* different with Danny, it seemed. Why did that thought make him feel so good?

Roman cleared his throat, then muttered, "He is correct though. You do not have to work if you do not wish to. As your mate, I will provide for you."

Danny didn't even know how to feel about that statement. "But—I like my work."

"Why?" Soren asked. He didn't sound mocking, only genuinely curious.

Danny shrugged, a little uncomfortable at the scrutiny. It was one thing to have all his questions answered; it was another thing to be questioned himself. And he couldn't tell them the whole truth, the one that involved him thinking, *Because at any moment, you could walk away, and then where would I be?* "I don't know. I just do. I like helping people. I like being there for people at their worst moments, offering comfort where I can."

Soren frowned. "But you can't always fix them. You humans are so...breakable." He threw a look at Roman then, one Danny couldn't quite decipher.

"No," Danny agreed. "We can't always fix them. But we'll always try. That just has to be enough sometimes."

Soren sighed lightly at his pancakes. "All that work for lives that end so quickly anyways. Little blips of existence."

Danny tried his best not to feel offended. He didn't think Soren was trying to bait him on purpose. The blond vampire even sounded a little sad at the thought.

Danny tried to put into words something he barely knew how to express to himself. "That's the thing though. That's part of what makes it beautiful. You know it doesn't last. So you do your best with the time you have. Help who you can, find comfort where you can, love as much as you can. It can hurt definitely. It can really suck sometimes, how quickly things disappear." Danny was embarrassed to find that he was pushing tears back at this point, the discussion bringing up emotions he tried to keep buried around other people.

"But there's beauty in trying anyway," he insisted, voice thick.

Soren's pale eyes softened at Danny's words. "I understand what Roman sees in you, little human."

Danny didn't know how he felt about being called "little" by someone even shorter than himself, but he appreciated the sentiment nonetheless.

He looked across the table at Roman. He was staring at Danny with heat in his eyes, looking proud and possessive and...something else. Something even deeper Danny couldn't bring himself to name yet.

Before silence could settle fully over the table, there was a knock on his front door. Danny frowned. He didn't know anyone who would just come over without warning. The most likely option was Chloe, but she would definitely call first. She wasn't a complete heathen.

Roman caught his frown, muscles tensing. "Not expecting anyone?"

Danny shook his head, and Roman pushed his chair back. "Stay here with Soren. I will answer it. You will run if I tell you," he ordered.

Danny opened his mouth to protest, but Roman cut a fierce look his way. "You *will* run if I tell you." There was steel in his tone. Danny nodded. What use could he be in the case of some feral vampire storming the house anyway?

He was—how had Soren put it?—breakable.

Danny listened closely to the sounds of Roman approaching the front door but kept his gaze on Soren, who was holding his body with stillness that was unnatural. Inhuman.

They heard the door open.

And both immediately relaxed as Gabe's deep voice rung out. "What are *you* doing answering Danny's door?"

Oh Jesus. Gabe never came over. He very obviously couldn't stand being in their family home alone with Danny. But *of course* he would decide to barge in now, when Danny had two supernatural guests over.

Danny forced a neutral expression on his face as the two men entered the kitchen, Gabe still grumbling complaints about Roman under his breath.

"Gabe, what are you doing here?" Danny demanded.

Gabe looked momentarily startled to see Soren seated at the kitchen counter with Danny, but he recovered his composure quickly. "I want to know what the fuck is going on, Danny. Why you three were acting so shady about the dead guy in the alley. I want to know what *you*"—he turned to Roman then—"have my baby brother involved in."

Danny fought the urge to roll his eyes—they were really going to get stuck up there with how often Gabe drove him to it lately.

"It's not some nefarious plot," he reassured his brother. "I recognized the body. He was someone who tried to mug me the other night. Roman fought him off. We were just freaked out that we knew him."

Gabe's eyes widened. "Why didn't you tell the police?"

Danny shrugged, forcing nonchalance. "Cops are assholes. I didn't feel like being questioned for hours about someone I barely knew—someone who clearly wasn't a nice guy."

"And that's all?" Gabe looked at each of them in turn, trying to find answers in their faces.

"That's all," Danny concluded.

Gabe turned quickly to Soren, tone accusatory. "Why would *you* recognize the dead mugger when you weren't even there at the mugging?"

Soren looked back at Gabe, a look of surprisingly convincing wide-eyed innocence on his face. "I didn't recognize him. I was just freaked out by the body. I thought Roman would know what to do."

Roman had meanwhile walked around the counter to Danny and was stroking his side gently in reassurance. Danny breathed in deeply, surrounding himself with the comforting scent of his vampire. It was so strange—so *nice*—to have outside support when dealing with his family.

Gabe turned from Soren and eyed the two of them, clearly unsettled by their closeness.

"Aren't you supposed to be seeing Mom this morning?" he asked Danny, tone sharp.

Calm the fuck down, Gabe. Danny could feel Roman tensing behind him, preparing to go into protective boyfriend mode.

Wait...boyfriend?

Was that what Roman was to Danny now? Danny wasn't sure how they went from strangers to some sort of fated mates situation in the blink of an eye, but surely boyfriends should have been somewhere in between. Right?

"Why?" he retorted, tone just as sharp as his brother's. "Were you actually planning to come with me this time?"

Gabe didn't rise to the bait. "You always see her Sunday mornings," he insisted.

Danny hadn't actually been aware that Gabe was keeping track of his visits to their mom. Interesting.

"I'm still going to see her. We're just running a little behind. I'm taking Roman to meet her."

"*Meet her?*" Gabe huffed. "Danny, she won't even know—"

That was it. *Enough.* Danny was so tired of this fight, tired of Gabe acting like a concerned brother only for the brief moments if and when he felt like it.

"It doesn't matter," he snapped at his brother. "That's not the point. I choose to believe some part of her knows me. She might not know who I am, exactly, but she knows I love her. She *always* knows that much." He pointed at Gabe. "And she probably knows somewhere deep down that someone else she cares for is missing from her life. So if you're just trying to make yourself feel better by saying she doesn't know you're not there, doesn't miss you, just know I think you're wrong."

Roman's hand had moved from Danny's side and was now squeezing his shoulder in support. So this was what it felt like to be backed up by someone. To have someone on his side in a real way. And suddenly Danny felt like he couldn't stop, that years of resentment were about to burst out in a verbal barrage. "And why are you pulling this protective big brother act *at all*, Gabe? You left! You left me with Mom. She-She wasn't well. And I don't even blame you for that. You were in school, then residency, working toward your future. But you never even *noticed*. You barely ever came home, and when you did, you just put your blinders on. I know Dad was your person, I know it broke something in you when he died, but Jesus, Gabe, make a choice. Are you still part of this family or not? You can't have it both ways. Be my brother at work and a stranger the rest of the time. What did you even move back here for?"

Gabe was looking stricken, and Danny lost some steam then, a little ashamed at having berated his brother in front of two witnesses. Soren was watching them both raptly, a contemplative look on his face.

Danny should have saved it for a time when they were alone, when they could really talk it out. *But when the hell would that be?* he thought bitterly. Gabe never let them be in that situation anyway, always using work or the crowds in the local bar as buffers.

Danny softened his voice, looking to his brother. "You should—you should come with me this week. To visit her. Just think about it. Please."

Gabe nodded slowly, avoiding Danny's eyes. "Yeah, okay. I'll...think about it. I should go. I-I interrupted." He walked out of the kitchen without once looking at Danny, and Danny resisted the urge to call him back. Gabe needed time to process, and frankly, Danny needed time to let the resentment simmer down.

The sound of the front door closing echoed moments later.

"Well," Soren said brightly, back to grinning once more. "Aren't humans *fun*, Rome?"

Ten

Roman

Why did humans insist on making certain types of buildings so unpleasant to look at?

The one Roman and Danny were entering was drab in that particular way of hospitals, government offices, and correctional facilities: beige-gray walls on the outside, beige walls on the inside, vomit-colored carpeting throughout. But it otherwise seemed pleasant enough, as far as these places went.

It was clean, the furniture and art were of a certain quality, and the staff looked alert and friendly. Roman couldn't imagine how much money his mate was spending keeping his mother here. He took a mental note to convince Danny as soon as possible to let him foot the bill instead.

Danny had told him after breakfast about his mother. She had a type of dementia called early onset Alzheimer's. She had been diagnosed when Danny was in nursing school.

Roman placed his sunglasses on top of his head—they kept the demon from getting too irritated on sunny days—and looked over at the boy walking next to him, who'd been tense and nervous the entire car ride there. Roman reached out and took his hand, and Danny looked up and gave him a small, appreciative smile.

Roman was so proud of his mate for standing up to his boorish brother. He'd clearly been shouldering too much alone for too long.

Not anymore, Roman vowed. His demon purred in agreement.

A short, stout woman with a cap of brown hair called out a greeting to them as they approached the main desk. Roman saw her do a small double take at the sight of his and Danny's joined hands before giving Danny a wide-eyed look and a big smile.

"And who is this?" she gushed.

"This is Roman," Danny answered shyly. "He's, uh—"

"I'm Danny's boyfriend," Roman cut in. "Boyfriend" felt juvenile compared to his true title: *mate*. But he wanted some sort of recognizable bond out there for the humans.

Roman wanted everyone to know this man belonged to him.

The woman's smile grew bigger, if that was possible. "You didn't tell me you were seeing anybody, Danny," she chided gently.

"It's pretty new," Danny explained. Roman didn't have to look over to know that his mate was blushing but glanced over anyway, just to enjoy the way the pink stole over Danny's freckled cheeks.

Danny cleared his throat. "Roman, this is Mary. She's the backbone of this place."

"Oh, psh." Now Mary was blushing. She turned a mock-stern look to Roman. "You better be good to this one. He's got a lot of people rooting for him."

"Believe me, I am one of them," Roman reassured her.

"Oh, I like you."

"You two can flirt later," Danny huffed, although he was clearly pleased with Mary's approval. "How is she today?"

Mary's face grew more somber. "I'm afraid it isn't the best day. She hasn't been feeling up for a lot these past few days. She's due for a shower this morning, but so far any attempts have made her...unhappy. We've gotten her out of bed, but that's the extent of it."

Roman felt Danny, who'd relaxed a bit at the beginning of the conversation, tense again. Roman had read up a little bit on his mother's condition while Danny was in the shower that morning, to better prepare for the visit. He knew the mood swings that could occur, and he had a feeling "unhappy" was putting it lightly.

Danny looked up at him with worried brown eyes, and Roman could tell by his expression he was thinking of postponing this visit for another day, but that wouldn't do.

Danny had to know that Roman would be there for him in every respect, in any situation, no matter how difficult.

Besides, Roman and his demon had a better idea.

"It will be okay," he reassured his mate. "Let me meet her. We can leave if it is all too much for her."

Danny nodded, gripping Roman's hand tighter, and turned back to Mary. "We'd still like to see her, please."

The look Mary gave Danny was so warm and empathetic that Roman immediately decided she was on his approved list of Danny's associates. She could join Chloe's name there.

Gabe still had yet to prove he could make the cut.

A short walk down a few hallways later, they entered a room where a woman Roman thought to be somewhere in her midfifties was hunched in a recliner, looking not directly at but instead somewhere past a television set in front of her. Another woman, this one young and in scrubs and clearly some kind of nurse or attendant, was sitting beside her.

"Hello, Gladys," Danny greeted softly.

The older woman turned sharply toward them, and Roman could see bits of Danny both in her features and in the fierce expression she shot their way.

"Jack!" she exclaimed, voice harsh. "What am I doing here? This girl here"—she pointed at the younger woman sitting with her—"keeps watching me. Always *watching* me. I don't understand. Who even let her in here?"

Jack. Danny had told Roman that was the name of his father, that sometimes his mother confused him for a younger version of his own father despite the differences in their appearances.

Danny approached his mother, smiling gently. "I know, Gladys. She's just here to help you get ready for the day. Do you want to do that? We could go outside for a walk." He looked over at the younger woman. "We can take it from here, if you want to take a break."

Danny's mother watched the girl in scrubs closely as she left, then looked over to where Roman was standing, clearly unappeased. "Who's that? Someone else to watch me? Like I'm a criminal!"

"This is Roman." Danny was keeping his voice soft and calm. Roman was proud of his patience. "A friend of mine. I wanted him to meet you."

"Why would you do that?" Gladys's voice took on a petulant tone. "I'm not even dressed! I look terrible. Get him out."

Danny turned toward Roman, and the sorrow in his mate's eyes was like a knife to Roman's heart. "Maybe today isn't the best—"

Roman squeezed Danny's hand gently. "I would like to try something first. Would you close the blinds?"

Danny seemed taken aback by the request. "Um. Okay? But this could get much worse very quickly." His mother was looking back and forth between them, eyes full of suspicion. But Danny, his sweet, trusting mate, went over to the blinds and shut them, leaving the room much dimmer.

Just how Roman's demon liked it.

Roman let it out as Danny walked back over to him, trusting now that his demon would always behave itself around Danny, look out for his best interests just as Roman did.

Danny's eyes widened as he watched Roman's eyes turn to pure black. "Are you—are you hungry? *Now*?" he whispered incredulously.

Roman just shook his head, stepping around Danny and closer to Gladys. He leaned down over the woman until their faces were inches apart. He really, really hoped this would work.

And that Danny would trust that he wasn't going to take a bite out of his mother.

"Hello, Gladys," his demon purred. Roman heard Danny give a little gasp. He knew his voice was different when his demon came out to try compulsion—a little softer, a little rougher. Subtle, but of course his quick-witted mate would pick up on it. "I know you're having a bit of a rough morning," he continued, not breaking eye contact with his mate's mother.

"Yes." She still sounded petulant but no longer quite so panicked. Good.

"I want to remind you that you are safe and cared for. I think you know that already. I am a good friend of Danny's here. And I know he loves you very much. I want you to look at him there and think very hard and very deep about Danny. Your son. You remember, I know you do."

"Roman, you can't just—" Danny's voice was anxious, and Roman momentarily regretted not warning the boy what he was going to try. But he hadn't been positive compulsion would work in this case, and he hadn't wanted to get his mate's hopes up.

Roman had used his skills on delirious or panicked humans before, and he knew his demon could help people access certain parts of their brains, including their memories. But he'd never tried it on a person with dementia before, and Danny seemed on the verge of stepping in.

But then they both watched as the tension left Gladys's body. She was looking at Danny, and for the first time Roman could see the woman—the mother—she was underneath the confusion.

"Danny, sweetie." Her voice was soft and bright now. "I'm sorry. I got—I got confused. I didn't realize you were here. I've been getting forgetful again, haven't I?" She gave a small, rueful laugh.

Roman released a sigh of relief and looked over at Danny, whose expression was hopeful and yet also so terrified.

Roman knew that feeling. Hope *was* terrifying.

He turned his black eyes back to Danny's mother. "Now, I believe you were about to take a shower and get ready for a walk with the two of us. Do you think you'd let someone help you? You've been ill. We don't want you falling."

Gladys nodded at him sweetly, and Danny quickly called the attendant back as Roman's demon receded.

A few moments later, as Roman shut the door, leaving the two women to their task, Danny turned to him, grabbing his shoulders and pressing him—none too gently—up against the wall. "What did you do to her? Are you—are you hypnotizing her? Controlling her somehow?"

His sweet, fierce mate.

Roman didn't fight against Danny's hold, just lifted one hand to caress the boy's face. "I am sorry, little king. I did not warn you because I was not sure of the results. I told you we vampires can compel. I have used it before, to cut through a person's confusion or panic. I thought—I thought it would be worth trying. Perhaps not if she were further along. But at this stage—yes, I thought it worth trying."

"Worth. Trying," Danny repeated the words, still looking stunned and a little angry.

Roman had another moment of doubt. Had he truly done wrong? He was so out of touch with this aspect of humanity—families, emotions, love, and loss.

He tried again to explain. "It is not...permanent. From what I know of her disease, that damage to her brain is not reversible. It is not a thing I or my demon can stop. But whatever parts of her memories are still there, that are buried, my demon can help her access them a little better. There is clearly a part of her that still remembers you, even if she cannot access it most of the time."

Roman waited with bated breath as Danny studied him for a long moment without speaking. Then his mate's hands gentled their grip on Roman's shoulders. Danny still looked stunned, but the anger had gone.

"I told myself it was okay if she never recognized me again. But if—if she did, I would savor every moment, knowing this time could be the last time. And now I can. Thank you." His mate's breath hitched, and he leaned his head against Roman's chest, letting his weight fall into him, as they waited for his mother to get ready for the day.

"Thank you," Danny whispered again.

Roman pressed a kiss to the top of his mate's head. "Anything for you."

⸺ℓℓ⸺

Once Gladys emerged from her room, freshly showered and clothed for the day, the attendant led them to the back of the facility and onto the grounds, which were large and grassy, with a walking path that wound around the edges.

She left them to take a walk together. It was clear as they walked that, while Gladys could now remember who her son was, she was not aware of what *time* they were in. She seemed to think Danny was still in high school, asking frequent questions about his classes and people Roman assumed were Danny's friends from that time.

Roman worried for a moment that she would question his own presence there, given that anyone would be hard-pressed to believe him a teenager, but from her offhand comments, she seemed to assume he was a coworker of Danny's from the movie theater where he worked in his teenage years.

His mate didn't seem to mind the altered timeline though. Roman was walking a few steps to the side of Danny and his mother, who had their arms linked together, but he watched his mate closely, soaking in the joy in his face at having this woman be his mother again.

And Roman could see the love that had been there, before the dementia had clouded things. Gladys clearly loved her son just as fiercely as he loved her.

As she should. Her son was perfect.

Perfect mate, his demon agreed. It was feeling very smug about its role in bringing Danny such happiness.

Had there been love like that in Roman's family? He knew there must have been, based on the pain he still felt at losing his family, but he could barely picture any specific memories now. It was all fogged by time and overshadowed by what had become of him. Of them. There were only hints. His mother's smile. His sister's laugh.

It was unfair how the happy memories faded, when he could picture the loss of them so perfectly.

Roman had returned just once, after he had been turned. Luc had warned him not to, but he had at the very least wanted to say goodbye to those he loved. He had thought he was dying out on that battlefield, and all he had wanted was one last chance to say goodbye to his mother, to his sisters.

But Roman had been a newly turned vampire, unable to easily control his new instincts. Unable to keep his eyes from going black or his fangs from coming out.

"Demon," his mother had called him, eyes filled with fear and hatred. "You are not my son. A demon has taken his place."

They had chased him out. And he had let them. In the end, he had wanted to go. Had not been able to bear to see his family so frightened of him. Of his demon.

He did not think Danny's mother—at least, as she had been before her illness—would have chased Danny away in the same situation. There was something to be said for modernity, after all. Less superstition and fear, in some ways.

Or maybe Roman's family simply hadn't loved him enough to combat their own fear.

He pulled himself out of his bitter recollections and focused again on the pair next to him.

"And where is Gabe today?" he heard Gladys ask.

He watched a shadow pass over Danny's eyes for the first time since they had stepped outside. "He's out with friends, Mama."

"That boy. So popular." She gave a fond sigh at the thought. "Do you really think he wants to be a doctor? Maybe he should run for office instead."

Danny gave a little laughing cough. "I think the doctor thing might stick."

"And do you still want to be a nurse, Danny Boy?"

"Yes, Mama."

"Good. I think you'll be so good at it. My tenderhearted boy." She smiled at her son.

Roman watched as Danny suddenly stopped his mother in her tracks and pulled her into a tight hug. He could see the tears welling in his mate's eyes, but Danny blinked them away quickly.

"Oh, that's nice," Danny's mother said, leaning into the hug. "I hope you never grow up too much to give me hugs like this."

"Never, Mama," Danny replied thickly.

They finished their walk leisurely and then brought Gladys back to her room, where Danny pulled in an extra chair so the three of them could watch TV together.

Eventually Gladys became fatigued enough that even Roman's compulsion couldn't keep her present with them, and he and Danny decided wordlessly to leave while things were still good, to not end the day with bad memories.

As they left, the young attendant back at Gladys's side, Mary called out to them, "I heard she had quite a turnaround." She smiled brightly at Roman. "You must be a good-luck charm."

They made it all the way into the car before Danny burst into tears.

Roman pushed his own seat back and pulled the boy out of the passenger seat, over the console, and into his arms. Once he had Danny settled firmly in his lap, he simply let the boy cry, rubbing his back.

His demon grew restless at their mate's distress, but Roman reassured it, *Humans just need to cry sometimes.*

When the tears had finally subsided, Roman had to ask, "Was I wrong to do that? I thought it would be a-a kind of gift. But I fear I hurt you."

"No!" Danny cried, pulling back to look at Roman. His mate's eyes were red and swollen, his face puffy from crying, but he was still the loveliest creature Roman had ever seen. "You didn't hurt me. It's just the whole...situation hurts. Always. It's been so long since I had my mom really...there with me. I didn't think it would ever happen again." He gave a sniff. "I can't believe you did that for me. For us."

He started pressing fervent kisses to Roman's face. "Thank you. Thank you. Thank you."

For the first time, Roman had used his abilities for something...pure. To make someone else happy. He was alarmed by how good it made him feel. Less like the monster stealing the handsome prince away and more like a man with something to actually offer.

After pressing a final kiss to Roman's nose, Danny tucked his head into Roman's shoulder, rubbing his face lightly against his shirt.

"There was a time, after my dad died, when Gabe and I were really close." Danny's voice was slightly muffled, but Roman could still make out the words. "I have memories of following him everywhere and him letting me. But by the time he was in high school, he had pushed me away again, and it was just me and my mom. We'd make each other laugh all the time. She was silly and loving and so smart. She was my best friend, really."

Roman could see it clearly after the visit today. The love and closeness between the two. He hugged Danny even closer as his mate continued.

"I went to nursing school here in town so I could stay close. I worried about leaving her all alone—Gabe rarely even came home from school to visit. I figured after I graduated, I'd get to spread my wings, maybe try travel nursing. She could visit me on my assignments. Then, when I was in nursing school, she started getting forgetful. Little things at first but then enough that I started getting worried. And for the first time, we were fighting—she'd get so frustrated and embarrassed when I pointed out her memory issues, and I didn't know how to get her to take it all seriously. It took me so long to convince her to go to a doctor, and even after we got the diagnosis, she was in denial. She made me wait to tell Gabe. And even when we finally did..." Danny sighed, his hot breath gusting over Roman's chest. "I guess with residency and everything, he had enough going on. It was like it never really registered for him? He did tell me I should let him know if it got worse. But the thing is it was always getting worse. Slowly but surely. I couldn't pinpoint what to tell him, so I just...dealt with it."

Roman's poor mate. Suffering alone for so long. His brother had a lot to answer for, as far as Roman was concerned.

"And then eventually she got bad enough," Danny continued. "She started going out and getting lost, refusing to do basic things like shower. I was working by then, and the doctor told me she needed routine and supervision. More than I could provide. So we decided on Brookstone. I felt so guilty, and then it was so expensive I had to work more to cover the cost, and it felt like all of a sudden she didn't even remember me anymore when I visited."

Danny pulled back to look at Roman, and his heart broke at the despair in his mate's eyes. "If she had stayed with me. If-if I had quit work and taken care of her instead, would she have remembered me longer?"

Roman reached out and cupped Danny's face. "Sweet, lovely boy. You know it does not work in that way. You did what had to be done for her to receive proper care. And you found her a good place. A *caring* place. I can see that. Her memories of you were bound to be lost no matter how close you stayed. It is the sad truth of her condition. You could not change that."

Danny's eyes glistened, but no more tears fell. Perhaps there were none left.

"When Gabe told me he was moving back to do his fellowship here, I thought we'd be brothers again, but he doesn't even want to *see* Mom. I don't think he even really wants to see *me*. I've just been so tired. And so-so alone."

"You are not alone anymore, my little king." Roman stroked his mate's back. "I am here. I will *be* here. You do not have to do it all alone anymore. I promise."

Danny collapsed with his head against Roman's shoulder again, and maybe there were some tears left after all, because Roman could feel his shirt dampening where his mate was pressed against it.

"You're real, right?" Danny asked. "Tell me this is real. Tell me you're not going to just disappear into the dark a week from now. Tell me you're really mine." His hands were gripping Roman's shirt so tightly they were edged with white.

"I am yours," Roman vowed. "Always yours."

And it was true.

Nothing in this world was going to take his mate from him.

Eleven

Danny

Danny relished the hot spray of the shower beating on his back, the feel of it washing away the grime of an emotional day.

My mom remembered me today.

He still couldn't believe it. He hadn't known how to feel at first. His initial reaction, beyond blatant disbelief at what was happening, had been anger at Roman for messing with his mom's mind without even asking Danny for permission first.

But Danny hadn't been able to hold on to that anger for long. How could he when Roman had so clearly wanted to help? And had so clearly succeeded.

My mom remembered me today.

The rest of their time at the care home had felt like a dream. To have his mom smiling at him again. It hadn't been a perfect reset. She hadn't known what year it was, obviously, and hadn't been quite all there, not like she used to be. But still.

She'd *known* him.

He wished he could tell Gabe. His brother could be a thoughtless jerk sometimes, but he deserved to know there was a way for their mother to remember them now. But Danny wasn't quite sure yet how to have the "my boyfriend is a semi-immortal vampire being who can sometimes sort of control minds but not always in a bad way" talk with his brother.

Was he even *allowed* to tell Gabe? Was there some sort of vampire code about humans knowing they existed?

Danny should probably ask about that at some point. Although, there wasn't anyone for him to tell, really, besides Gabe. Chloe, maybe. And that was it. He hadn't realized quite how lonely his life had become until Roman had swept in, and suddenly there was someone else there, someone to hold him while he cried, to kiss his tears away.

It would be so easy for Danny to depend on him. So easy to love him, demon and all. Danny was probably more than halfway there already.

But what if Danny was just a fun diversion for Roman? A little blip of existence, like Soren had said. Roman said he would be there always, but what did that *mean*? Would Roman still want him when Danny grew old and decrepit?

Or...would he want to turn him after all? Would Danny even want that?

Eternal life.

Eternal *health*.

It had been there, in the back of Danny's mind, since his mom had gotten her diagnosis. The thought that maybe it would happen to him. Some early onset Alzheimer's cases were genetic. Not always, but it was possible.

Danny was terrified of waking up one today to find himself losing his memories, without him even having lived a full life to forget.

He would have to leave this town eventually if he turned. He couldn't stay young forever and expect no one to notice. Which would mean leaving Gabe alone.

But Gabe had abandoned Danny first. And moving from town to town didn't sound horrible, not when Danny had never even gotten to travel before.

It sounded wonderful, honestly. To finally be able to see the world.

And he wouldn't be doing it alone. He'd have Roman.

Roman.

Sweet, dangerous, protective.

A man who listened and comforted, a demon who protected and possessed. He was everything Danny had never had the guts to admit he wanted out of a partner.

After the sobfest in the car, Roman had kissed Danny's tears away and taken him to the movie theater, of all places. A tribute to

Danny's mother assuming they worked there together. She must have thought the older vampire was Danny's manager. Danny couldn't really picture his elegant lover working somewhere so mundane, but Roman had assured him he'd had worse jobs over the centuries.

It had been a silly comedy that Danny couldn't help giggling at. How bizarre, to go on such an ordinary date with his demon lover after said lover had compelled his mother's dementia away. Danny was pretty sure Roman had been watching *him* more than the movie, but that hadn't been the worst feeling.

Roman hadn't stopped touching Danny the entire day.

A hand on his back, an arm around his shoulders, a small kiss to the back of his neck. Danny hadn't realized how touch-starved he'd been until he had Roman stroking him all the time like his personal pet.

It should have been weird to go from being barely being touched at all to this sort of constant contact, but it just felt...perfect. Right. To melt into Roman's touch and drown in his scent.

There were a few drawbacks though.

Like being half-hard all day.

But now they were home. And Roman was waiting for Danny in his room. And Danny wanted it all from him. Wanted everything Roman could give him.

He'd honestly wanted to pounce on Roman as soon as they walked in the door. Jump into his arms and climb his vampire like a tree.

But he'd chickened out and run off to shower instead.

Something about being possessed by Roman completely felt...monumental. Like Danny was going to be crossing a line he couldn't come back from.

But he'd been responsible and cautious and lonely for too long.

It was time to take a leap.

Danny turned off the water, grabbed his towel, and started drying himself off quickly.

Time to fuck a vampire.

—ell—

Danny opened the bathroom door leading into his room, his towel wrapped around his hips, to find Roman sitting at the edge of the bed in his underwear. Danny couldn't help letting his eyes wander over every inch of the vampire's body.

Good Lord, that man had muscles.

Sleek and svelte but defined in a way that had Danny wanting to lick him all over. And he *could*. He had the right to.

Lucky, lucky me.

Danny looked up from his perusal to find Roman staring at him with such heat that Danny was surprised he didn't just burst into flames right there.

"Drop the towel, little king," Roman ordered.

His voice was low and deep, but his eyes were still clearly blue, so Danny knew Roman wasn't using compulsion on him, but honestly, he might as well have been. Danny's hands had undone and dropped his towel before his brain had even fully registered the command.

"Come here."

Danny's feet moved without his permission, and he was walking forward until he was standing between Roman's legs. He gasped as Roman's arms encircled him and pulled Danny even closer. The height of the bed had them at eye level for once, instead of Roman towering over him.

Roman leaned forward, and Danny parted his lips, allowing the vampire to take the lead and devour his mouth. Compared to the sweet, gentle, boyfriendish kisses Danny been receiving all day, this kiss was dirty. Raw. Hungry. And Danny couldn't get enough, moaning as Roman sucked on his tongue.

"Sweet boy. Lovely boy," Roman whispered as he broke the kiss, moving to nibble on Danny's ear.

"What-What you said before," Danny moaned. "In the car. Say it again."

"I am yours," Roman purred.

Danny was panting now, his bare, leaking cock pressed against Roman's stomach, and he couldn't help but move his hips, desperate for some friction. One of Roman's hands traveled from Danny's waist to his ass, and then his finger was pressing lightly against Danny's hole.

He whimpered. He couldn't help it.

"Please," he begged.

"Please what, little king?"

"Bite me."

Roman snarled—literally snarled—and the hand not on Danny's ass reached up and grasped the front of Danny's neck, firm but not harsh, Roman clearly conscious of his own strength.

He tilted Danny's head to the side. Danny shivered. Apparently they were going with the classic bite locale this time, and he couldn't wait.

He watched as Roman's eyes went black.

And then Danny's entire body was singing as Roman bit into him. The tingles spread from his neck down to every part of him. He felt his balls tighten and his cock leak even more.

Why did this feel so fucking good?

Danny guessed Roman didn't need much, having already fed on him that week, and it wasn't long before the vampire lifted his head, eyes black and lips bloody.

"Mine," he snarled, black eyes fierce.

"Yes. I'm yours," Danny answered breathlessly. It was true, like it or not. But he *did* like it. Knowing he belonged to this deadly being.

And then Danny was being manhandled onto the bed, Roman lying on top of him. His eyes were blue again, but his pupils were blown, and Danny could just barely tell they weren't vampire black all the way through.

"Mine," Roman repeated, as if to verify that Danny knew he belonged to them both, demon and man.

"Yours," Danny agreed. "Show me. Make me feel it."

And then Roman was smiling at him, and the sight took Danny's breath away. The vampire started kissing down Danny's body, stopping to lave his nipples with his tongue, leaving Danny trembling. Who knew his body was this sensitive?

It had never felt like this before, not with anyone else.

Roman pointedly ignored Danny's flushed, hard cock on his journey down, kissing and licking the insides of Danny's thighs instead.

He tortured Danny that way for what felt like forever before strong hands gripped the backs of Danny's thighs and lifted them, folding him practically in half and pressing him against the mattress.

And then Roman's tongue was at Danny's hole, and he was licking and kissing and sucking him there.

Danny gave a piercing cry, his entire body shaking from Roman's ministrations. "Ohhhh my God. Fuck. Fuck-fuck. Roman. Please."

"Why does every part of you taste so sweet?" Roman growled against him, removing his tongue and pressing the tip of his finger inside Danny's entrance.

"Please, Roman. Please. Fuck me. Please." Danny couldn't find it in himself to be embarrassed by his own begging.

"I intend to," Roman promised. "Where is your lube, little king?"

Danny's brain had shut off completely. "I don't—what? I don't care. Just fuck me."

Danny yelped as Roman swatted his ass lightly. "I am not going to break you out of carelessness, lovely mate. Lube."

Right. No breaking Danny. That was good thinking. "Bedside drawer."

Roman released Danny's thighs and reached up and over Danny to his bedside table. The vampire paused there, looking inside the drawer. "As a vampire, I cannot give you diseases, but if you want, I can still—"

"No," Danny cut in, knowing where this was going. "No condoms. Just you. I need you to fill me. Now. Please."

Roman chuckled. "Impatient mate. So demanding."

"Yes. Demanding. I demand you fuck me."

"As you command, little king."

Roman slid back down gracefully to his former position, using one hand to push Danny's thigh back, and pressed one slick digit inside him. "So tight," he murmured.

Danny groaned. "More. Give me more."

Roman pressed another finger inside him and started to open Danny up, his actions surprisingly gentle considering how ferociously he had been tonguing Danny's hole earlier.

Danny let it go on for what felt like an eternity before he couldn't wait any longer. "It's enough," he panted. "I promise. Please. Fuck me now."

He used his own hands to pull his thighs back, holding himself open for his vampire lover.

That action was enough to snap Roman's restraint. "Merde," he growled.

And then he was slicking up his cock with his lubed hand, pressing the fat head against Danny's entrance.

Roman glided forward slowly but persistently until he was up to the hilt.

"Yes," Danny moaned. He was so full. So fucking full.

"So. Fucking. Tight." Roman paused there, body trembling from the effort of holding himself back, but he gave Danny time to adjust to his size, to the fullness that was on this side of too much.

Almost.

"You can move," Danny whispered, giving an experimental wiggle. "I'm ready."

Roman pulled back until he was almost all the way out and then slammed back in forcefully. He groaned low and deep. "Perfect."

And then he was fucking Danny furiously, and it was wild and more than a little painful, but Roman was right—it was fucking perfect. Danny had never felt so completely owned before.

His limited experience with penetration before had felt good enough—he'd orgasmed and everything—but that was it. It was part of why he hadn't tried harder to find hookups since nursing school. Sex was pleasant but not essential.

But *this*. Fuck.

Roman fucking him was primal, overwhelming, animalistic. Danny keened every time Roman's cock brushed against his prostate. He thought he could probably come untouched.

He didn't have a chance to find out, though, because Roman was suddenly grabbing Danny's cock, jerking him to the same rhythm as his thrusts.

"Fuck!" Danny exclaimed.

"Not going to last much longer," Roman panted. "Come for me. Sweet boy. Lovely boy. Come."

And Danny did as he was told, coming so hard and so intensely that he just barely registered the rhythm of Roman's hips faltering, the vampire's deep groan as he pressed Danny down against the bed and filled him with his cum.

When Danny came back to his senses, Roman was still on top of him, still inside him, licking the sweat off Danny's neck, murmuring seemingly to himself. "Sweet mate. Perfect mate. Lovely mate."

"Mmm," was all Danny could say in response.

Roman gently pulled out of Danny and propped himself up on his elbows, peering down at him, concern etched into his features. "Did I hurt you? I know I was—I was too rough. I am sorry. I just—"

Danny found the energy to lift his hand and stroked the side of Roman's face. "Shh. No, you weren't too rough. I-I liked it. I like it when it hurts a little bit. I didn't really know that about myself before you, but it's true. The pain makes it feel more real, I guess."

Roman nuzzled into his hand. "That is because you were made for me. And I for you."

Well, fuck.

What was Danny supposed to do with that? He was so far gone for every part of this man, this demon.

The violent possessiveness, the animalistic desire, the sweet concern.

Maybe this would all implode. Maybe Danny would find out he was just a diversion after all. But he was going all in anyway. This wouldn't fizzle away for lack of trying on his part.

He had meant what he said.

He belonged to this vampire, and he could only hope this vampire belonged to him.

For as long as Roman would have him, Danny was his.

Twelve

Danny

"After I gave her the Zofran, she stopped vomiting everywhere, but she did throw her purse at me when I wouldn't let her eat anything yet. We had to move all her belongings out of her reach."

"Well that's a...real lovely report. Thanks, Danny."

The sarcasm was heavy with this one. "Sorry to pass a rough one onto you."

The nurse on the other end of the line gave an exaggerated sigh. "Just my tragic lot in life. Really, I get it. Luck of the draw. Send her up when you're ready. I'll see if the doctor on call will give her a diet order so she can eat something."

"She'll love you forever," Danny responded brightly. "Have a good night."

Danny secured a transporter for his patient, then sat back in his chair with a heavy sigh. He loved his job, but some nights could take it out of a guy. Luckily this night seemed to be slowing down.

It didn't help that he had somewhere else he'd really, really rather be.

Or, some*one* else he'd rather be *with*.

His vampire. His...mate?

His vampire mate who'd been treating him like a precious object all day. Danny had woken up with a warm, wet mouth around his cock. Already a gold star start to the day, in his book.

Roman had teased him to the point where he'd been begging to be fucked, but had then insisted—quite evilly—that Danny would be too sore after the night before. The downsides of a fragile human body, Danny supposed. Roman had swallowed him down instead, driving him to orgasm with hard, furious sucking that had left Danny reeling.

Then he'd made Danny breakfast.

Really, a guy could get used to it.

Soren had even joined them for breakfast again, this time uninterrupted by Gabe. Danny hadn't heard from his brother at all since their confrontation the morning before, and he wasn't sure he was ready to yet. He'd been suffering some guilt for the way they'd left things but not as much as he might've thought. After all, it was Gabe who had pushed their relationship to this point.

For a slightly unhinged ancient vampire, Soren was a surprisingly pleasant roommate. He even did the dishes after breakfast. Danny wasn't exactly sure where Roman's friend went at night. Hunting for Luc? Hunting for blood? Hunting for hookups?

But it was probably for the best Soren hadn't been around to hear the evidence of their extracurricular activities the night before. It was bad enough he might have heard them this morning, but Danny hadn't exactly been quiet while getting the fucking of a lifetime.

Danny fought a blush over the thought of it. He also fought down some resentment over being at the hospital instead of back in Roman's arms, working to convince the vampire that his fragile human body wasn't too sore for his cock after all.

Danny had been forced to make do with a disappointingly chaste kiss in the car when Roman dropped him off.

Yes, his vampire lover had sent him off to work with a peck on the lips like some sort of absurdly handsome househusband.

Again, a guy could really get used to it.

Except...surely Roman wouldn't be satisfied with this kind of routine for long, would he? Hanging around the house, waiting for Danny to get off work. Accompanying him on visits to the care home, using his magical vampire powers to help an old lady remember her son. Cooking food for the both of them that he didn't even need to eat.

It would grow old fast, right? Just like Danny would grow old fast.

Let's not go there, brain. Happy thoughts.

Or at least, less horribly depressing thoughts.

Danny was brought out of said horribly depressing thoughts by the sound of the nurse's station phone ringing, but his coworker Henry answered it before Danny could, nodding along to whoever was on the other end.

"Uh-huh. Yep. We'll be ready." The other nurse hung up and looked to Danny. "That was the transfer center."

Looked like break time would be brief.

"What's coming in?" Danny sighed, resigned to his fate.

"Thirty-five-year-old man with significant blood loss. Hypotensive and minimally responsive. They're about ten minutes out. I'll page the trauma doc and grab some fluids. Let the blood bank know?"

"I'm on it." They both leaped into action.

Danny's call to the hospital blood bank was brief, just a heads-up that they might be needing an emergent transfusion soon. He was just getting up to help Henry with the trauma bay setup when a shadow fell over his desk.

Looking up at the man standing in front of him, Danny had a strange sense of déjà vu, recalling his first meeting with Roman.

But the handsome man looming over him wasn't Danny's now familiar vampire lover. He had a shock of dark hair, lightly silvered at the temples. Not quite as tall as Roman but still much taller than Danny. He was well muscled, wearing a fashionable, formfitting black sweater and dark jeans.

And, Danny realized, his quick perusal returning to the man's face—his eyes were black.

Danny felt a pang of fear go through him but made himself take a deep breath. He'd been spending too much time around vampires. Maybe it was a trick of the light. Maybe this was just a guy—a regular human guy—with really dark-brown eyes.

Brown eyes without any whites around the edges. Sure.

Except even as he was thinking it, he knew it wasn't the case. He could feel it in the air, could see it in the man's gaze.

Danny was in the presence of a predator.

Had he really thought Roman creepy in their first encounter? He had nothing on the vibes this other man was giving off. Danny could sense the menace, the violence, just under the surface. Goose bumps erupted on his arms, and he suppressed a shiver.

"Daniel Kingman."

The man's voice was deep, gruffer than Roman's, with a hint of a French accent.

Lucien. It had to be.

"Yes." Danny forced himself to keep his voice steady. "How can I help you?"

"So very polite. I like it." The black-eyed man breathed in deeply. "And such a delicious scent of fear coming off you. I like that even more."

So the other vampire wasn't going to even pretend to be human. It seemed like they were starting off with all their cards on the table. "Well, you're a bit intimidating, Lucien," Danny reasoned.

"Ah." Lucien's black eyes gleamed. "So he's told you about me."

Danny nodded. "He has."

"I'm touched," the vampire said lightly, but there wasn't a hint of friendliness in his gaze.

"Can I ask what you're doing here? Roman isn't around, if you're looking for him." Danny didn't know what to do other than stall. He couldn't run. Lucien would catch him in an instant. And Henry would be back any minute, looking for Danny, hopefully with some other personnel in tow.

Would that be enough to deter the vampire from violence, or would Danny just be placing his coworkers in danger?

Lucien gave what Danny supposed could be considered a smile, had there been any hint of warmth in his eyes. And had there not been fangs poking out from between his lips. "I just wanted to see the human that has so fascinated my old friend." He leaned closer, peering at Danny. "Up close you're fairly stunning. Here I thought you were just a mousy little human." He hummed. "I suppose I can see the appeal."

"Do you mind putting those away?" Danny gestured at Lucien's mouth. The vampire only smiled wider, baring his sharp fangs more clearly.

"I'm afraid I'm not as tame as your little house vamp, Daniel. Mine don't get put away anymore."

"I wouldn't call him tame," Danny said tightly. "I'd call him controlled."

Lucien's fake smile dropped. "Then I'd say he has you fooled."

Danny didn't see this conversation going anywhere good. He should find a way to end it, and quickly. "Well, you've seen me. You can leave now. Unless you're planning to off me right here?"

He regretted the words as soon as they left his mouth. *Jesus, Danny, don't taunt the psycho vampire. Idiot.*

Lucien laughed, a terrifying sound. "Oh my, just what exactly has he been telling you about me?" He leaned even closer, and Danny couldn't help his cringe, half expecting the man to leap over the desk and sink his teeth into Danny's neck at any moment. "*He's* the killer, didn't you know?"

"And that body you left in the alleyway for us to find?" *Oh God, what was that about not taunting psychotic vampires again?* He couldn't seem to keep his mouth shut.

"That was a gift. Just cleaning up some of the trash around here."

"I see." Danny did not see. "So you're not a killer. And you're just here for a friendly visit. And then you'll be on your way?"

"Well, not exactly, Daniel." Lucien tutted. "I think I might be sticking around for a little while. I'm curious about you, you see. You know what he is. I presume you know some of what he's done. You're not afraid?"

"I'd be stupid to not be a *little* afraid. But not of him. Of the whole—" Danny used his hands to gesture vaguely around. "—situation."

"The situation..." Lucien seemed to be mulling over Danny's words. Understandable. It hadn't exactly been Danny's most eloquent moment.

He wasn't really sure what to make of the vampire in front of him.

Lucien was dangerous; that was clear. Danny could feel that much on an instinctual level. And Lucien was clearly not afraid of having his demon front and center. But he didn't seem *feral*, not in the way Soren and Roman had described it.

He clearly wasn't a mindless beast, with the way he was verbally poking at Danny.

Playing with his dinner, perhaps? Danny wasn't quite able to suppress his shiver this time around, and he could have sworn he saw Lucien's eyes light up at the sight.

Danny didn't want to give him the satisfaction. "They keep it very cold down here," he found himself saying haughtily.

Lucien just raised an eyebrow. "I wouldn't know. Vampire and all."

"But don't you...Roman feels..." Danny thought back to the heat of Roman's skin, of his mouth.

Lucien smirked at him. "Warm-blooded?"

Danny nodded. He knew he shouldn't be engaging the dangerous vampire in conversation, but he couldn't help his curiosity.

"We feel warm-blooded enough, if we're kept...fed." Lucien made the word sound salacious. "The only time we feel the elements is if we haven't been getting our steady supply of blood."

"I suppose saving on outerwear is one of the perks." What was Danny even saying anymore?

Lucien's black gaze narrowed. "And do you intend to explore these...perks...yourself?"

"Um..." Was the vampire asking what Danny thought he was asking?

"Will you *turn* for him?" Lucien's voice was harsh now, all hint of teasing gone.

Knowing Lucien's history, Danny felt that he was walking a very fine line, with death at this vampire's hands on either side of him.

But he couldn't tell which answer would set the vampire off. So Danny went with the honest one. "I don't...I don't know?"

"Don't you though?"

Before Danny could respond, his attention was caught by muted yelling coming down the hall, from the direction of the ambulance bay.

The trauma patient had arrived. The young man with significant blood loss.

A sudden thought occurred to Danny. He turned his eyes back to Lucien's. "Your work?"

The vampire gave Danny his first real smile, as far as Danny could tell. Not exactly a warm one but not mocking.

He really was devastatingly handsome, for a psychopathic monster.

"I'll be seeing you around, Daniel." He winked.

And then he was gone. Faster than Danny's eyes could even process.

After Danny had taken a few moments to tear himself from the stupor his strange meeting with Lucien had left him in, he ran down the hall to help with their new patient.

A patient that was possibly hurt because of Danny—because Danny's boyfriend was in Hyde Park, and that boyfriend's stalker was a literal monster.

The young man was covered in blood from the neck down, but his face was clear enough.

He could have been Danny's twin.

— ✺ —

The TV in the background was set on some reality show or another, but Danny kept his eyes on the phone in his lap. He was waiting in the staff break room for Roman to pick him up. He wasn't feeling brave enough to wait outside on his own, knowing Lucien could be around. He was feeling decidedly unbrave, as a matter of fact.

And possibly a bit shell-shocked.

Danny's doppelgänger hadn't made it. The man's heart had stopped despite the rapid blood transfusion they had started, and after a full half hour of CPR, the trauma doctor had called it. The mood at work had been somber after that.

Although, not quite as somber as it could have been. Because the staff had all heard something about the man from the police officers that had followed the ambulance. Something that had gotten Danny thinking...

His phone dinged, interrupting his thoughts. Roman had arrived.

Danny hadn't told Roman the reason he was waiting inside—hadn't told him about Lucien's visit yet. He'd been worried his vampire would barge into the hospital before Danny's shift was over and drag him away—possibly lock him in some panic room somewhere.

Still, Danny wasn't planning to keep it secret for long. He just wanted to be there in person to calm Roman down.

The vampire in question was outside, holding the door to the passenger seat open. Such a freaking gentleman, that one.

Danny gave him a hello and a quick kiss on the cheek and got into the car. Roman didn't immediately start the engine after rounding the car and settling in the driver's seat. Instead, he leaned over and kissed Danny thoroughly, leaving him breathless. He then proceeded to press additional kisses along Danny's jaw and down his neck. "I've missed you, little king."

Danny gave a half laugh even as his cock twitched in his scrubs, tilting his head back to give Roman better access. "It's only been twelve hours."

"Mm. Twelve long hours," Roman murmured, tugging the collar of Danny's scrubs down to lick and nip his way along Danny's collarbone. "Did you not miss me as well?"

The truth was Danny *had*, but that was a truth he might be afraid to admit even to himself, let alone to Roman.

How ridiculous was it to miss a man he'd only just met after twelve measly hours, fated mates or not?

He was feeling raw and anxious and overwhelmed. This couldn't last, could it? How would Danny cope when Roman walked away and left him to his boring, lonely life?

Would you turn for him? Luc's words echoed in Danny's mind. Would he?

But Roman hadn't asked him to, had very carefully not brought it up, even after discussing his past with Lucien and the woman Lucien had thought was his mate. The woman Lucien had desperately wanted to turn.

And now Danny was feeling jealous of a dead woman.

Roman noticed his sudden tenseness. "What's wrong, mon petit roi?"

Danny couldn't even begin to tell his vampire the whole jumble of anxieties filling up his brain at the moment, so he went with the most straightforward. "Lucien visited me at work tonight."

Roman immediately went rigid, looking at Danny with rapidly darkening eyes. "*What?*" he ground out.

"It's fine. I'm fine," Danny rushed to reassure him. "He just came to talk. To tease me a little, I think."

"To...tease you." Roman's fingers dug into Danny's upper arms.

Okay, maybe not the best choice of words. That sounded a little bad, actually.

This was not Danny's night for superb communication skills, that was for sure.

"Yes? He didn't hurt me. He'd already—already fed for the night, judging by the man who died in our trauma bay earlier." Danny very deliberately did not mention what—or more accurately, who—that man had looked like. No need to set Roman off in a nuclear way.

Roman's eyes softened slightly, and his fingers gentled. "Oh, mon pauvre petit, I am sorry. Sorry you had to bear witness to another of his victims."

Danny shrugged. "Not to be callous, but I've seen worse. And from what I heard, this guy wasn't such a nice guy. Not saying he deserved to die, but—it could have been worse is all."

"Yes. It could have been much worse." Roman's voice was low and harsh. "I should have known he would try to approach you in my absence. I thought the hospital would deter him. Luc may be relatively careless with his violence, but I still didn't believe he would risk anything with the security cameras. Getting caught on film can make life very tricky for someone who doesn't age or change appearance. I underestimated him. I should not have left you alone."

Danny resisted the urge to roll his eyes. He understood the sentiment, but he couldn't have an escort every hour of every day. It wasn't realistic. "I can't just not *work*, Roman."

"You can though, actually," Roman insisted, eyes intent on Danny's. "Like Soren said. I can provide for you. Be your...vampire sugar daddy, was it?" He tilted his head in question.

Don't laugh, don't laugh, don't laugh.

"No, you can't," Danny said firmly. "I won't stop what I do just because of one deranged loose cannon. We don't even know he wants to hurt me." Although, the dead doppelgänger might be a bit of a giveaway, but Danny wasn't about to tell Roman about that.

Not with him already all grr-y about a single visit with his old friend.

Roman just sighed, releasing Danny's arms to gently grab his hand, kissing Danny's knuckles lightly.

Oh. Well, that was sweet.

"Let me take you home, then, lovely."

Back at the house, Roman herded Danny over to the couch and wrapped him in a blanket, ordering him not to move. *Like I'm some sort of invalid.* But really, Danny wasn't complaining. It was kind of nice, being constantly pampered.

More than kind of nice, if he was being honest.

He looked up as a steaming mug was placed on the coffee table in front of him. "What is with you and tea?" he asked Roman with a grin.

Roman gave him an indignant look. "It is comforting to drink something warm, is it not? And I cannot give you coffee—humans cannot have caffeine too late, or they will not be able to sleep." He sounded oddly like he was quoting from something.

"How and why do you even know that? Aren't caffeine-related sleep studies a bit modern?" Danny questioned, taking a sip of his tea. *Mm. Chamomile with honey.*

"I read is how," Roman retorted, adjusting Danny's blanket. "And the why is obvious."

Did he mean because of Danny? To take care of Danny? Should Danny be flattered or offended thinking of Roman looking up tips on human habits?

How to Best Care for Your Human *by Some Vamp Dude.*

"You know, technically it's not *late*; it's the morning," Danny felt the need to say.

"Splitting hairs, little king. It is bedtime for you. Drink your tea."

Danny didn't obey right away, fingering the handle of the mug as Roman sat next to him on the couch. "You know, I've always been the caretaker. I mean, I guess not *always*. I remember Gabe taking care of me when I was a kid, after my dad died. When my mom was still grieving. But by the time I was in junior high, I felt like I was on my own. My mom was there, but we were less mother and son and more of a team, I guess? And then she...you know."

Roman wrapped an arm around his shoulders, pulling Danny into him. "I know, lovely."

There was a moment of silence, both of them in their thoughts.

"Do you not like it, then? My taking care of you?" Roman was clearly trying to keep his tone light, but Danny could sense the tension underneath.

Was his vampire afraid of rejection?

"No," Danny reassured. "I like it very much. Very, very much. Too much, maybe? I didn't even really know I had this side of me, this part of me that wants to be coddled like this. And now I feel like I'm getting addicted..."

Danny felt a lump forming in his throat, making it hard to bring the words up, but they had to be said. He was getting in too deep, standing out on a ledge, and he had to make sure he wasn't in it alone.

He made himself say it. "What happens when you leave? When I've become dependent on this and you walk away?"

"Walk away?" Roman sounded genuinely perplexed, but Danny couldn't bring himself to look into his vampire's eyes, to see what expression was on his face. "Why would I ever walk away?"

"Well, that's what people do, isn't it? They leave. One way or another. My dad, my mom, Gabe. It's just how life works. The people you lo—" Danny bit his lip. "—people leave."

Roman's fingers were on his chin then, pulling Danny's head gently to look him in the eyes.

"And that is what you think I will do one day? Leave you? Inevitably?"

Danny nodded ever so slightly.

Unexpectedly, Roman smiled then. Tender and a little sad, but genuine nonetheless. "Ohh, mon Dieu. My lovely mate. Life has not been fair to you." He gripped Danny's chin a little tighter. Not hard enough to hurt but enough to make sure Danny was paying attention. "Listen to me, Danny. I am not leaving. Not ever. Not unless you want me to, and even then, I can make no promises. You are mine. I am yours."

Danny swallowed hard. "But—"

"No buts, little king. I am realizing I have made an error. I have underestimated the trauma you hold. But if you need me to tell you every single day that I am staying, I will tell you. Gladly. Often. Always. That I am yours. Forever, if you will have me."

And then Danny was crying, and he wasn't even sure why. But it was as if the weight of the last decade of his life was crashing in on him, the loneliness and the stress and the worry. As if now that there was someone by his side to help shoulder the burden, he could finally process it.

He cried until there was nothing left, until he'd purged some of the doubt out of his system.

They didn't make it to Danny's room to sleep. Roman just covered them both with the blanket, tucking Danny to his side on the couch.

"You make me feel loved," Danny whispered right before sleep overtook him.

"You are." The words were whispered, but Danny could hear them clearly.

Thirteen

Roman

Roman knew he looked suspicious, prowling the alleys around the hospital in his dark coat, but he was hoping to lure another suspicious character out of the shadows.

Goddamn Luc.

Roman should have known the bastard would seek Danny out, even with the hospital security cameras. Roman had thought it would be enough—dropping Danny off and picking him up, keeping him from stepping out of the hospital alone—but it was too tempting for the psychopath, finally having someone Roman actually cared about to mess with.

To what end though? That was the question.

Roman wasn't quite sure exactly what Luc wanted with Danny. He hadn't attacked the boy last night, but that didn't mean he wouldn't.

Who knew how his mind worked anymore?

Roman could feel his demon itching to come out of his skin at the thought of Luc lurking around Danny with unclear intentions. It was restless, wanting to get back to their mate, to have him in their sights.

Me too, mon monstre. Me too.

Roman hadn't liked dropping Danny off at work that night. He had wanted to wrap himself around the boy and refuse to let him go. Roman had even asked Danny to take the night off, but his stubborn mate had refused, insisting he wasn't going to let "one puny, little threatening encounter" interfere with his duties.

"We're often short-staffed as it is. I'm not doing that to my coworkers," he'd argued.

And apparently Roman wandering the hospital halls for twelve hours would have security called in an instant, according to his mate. And Danny had worried a direct confrontation with Luc on hospital grounds would lead to patients getting hurt in the crossfire. So Roman was having to make do with circling the area around the hospital, lurking in the shadows.

That was Roman's lovely mate though. Caring for others at the expense of himself seemed to be deeply ingrained in his nature.

As were the insecurities he had confessed to Roman the night before.

Roman shook his head at his own obliviousness. He should have realized the scars that would have been left by his mate's past. Abandoned by his father to death, his mother to illness, his brother to denial. He needed more reassurances than Roman had been giving him, that was clear. Yes, Roman may have mentioned forever to the boy. But perhaps that simply sounded like platitudes when he had not specified what "forever" would mean.

Roman was afraid.

He was afraid to bring up the prospect of turning to his mate. He was afraid the very idea would horrify Danny, a man who valued human life so much.

And underneath that fear was the crippling doubt. The thought that Danny might turn and they would both find that the myth of fated mates was wrong. Roman hadn't even believed in mates until meeting Danny, and he'd never met a fated pair himself. What if he'd been right all along and his mate woke up with a demon that was not soothed by Roman's presence at all?

Maybe Roman would ruin Danny's life forever.

His sweet mate would become feral like Luc and be doomed to an eternity of violence and misery. Or maybe vampire Danny would realize the world was his for the taking and that he didn't need or want Roman after all.

Roman felt an ache in his chest at the very thought of it.

But what was the alternative? Allow his mate to grow old and die, sit by and watch while Danny slowly decayed each day?

Yes, Roman thought. If it came down to it, he would stay by Danny no matter what—vampire or human.

Danny was his mate, his person, for as long as they had, be it a few years or forever.

Had he not been making that clear enough?

It was ironic that the one person who could perhaps help Roman think through this dilemma, the one person who had experience in this arena, was the very same one intent on making Roman's life a misery.

———ele———

"You don't believe she's my mate, do you, Roman?"

Luc was lounging across from him in the bar's booth, all graceful ease and dapper elegance. Many eyes at the bar—both male and female—were on him, and Roman knew, despite his friend's apparent nonchalance, that he was not unaware. Luc's dark hair had been sprinkled with gray at the temples already when he was turned, but it did nothing to detract from his appeal. The man reveled in his own attractiveness and pushed Roman to do the same.

Luc knew the allure they had as a duo, tall and dark and predatory.

Roman gave his friend a smirk. "I do not believe in mates at all, Luc. I think they are a fairy tale, a myth you and Soren have taken to because it gives you hope." He cleared his throat. This was not a conversation he particularly wanted to have, but if Luc was going to push him to it, so be it. "I believe you are infatuated with your pretty human. You may even love her. She certainly has some sort of hold on you. But do I believe she is the magical solution to your fate?" Roman shook his head, taking a sip of his wine. "No. We are what we are. There is not some fated person who is coming to fix you. You are a vampire. A demon. Driven by blood and sex and violence. You have been since you were turned. As I have been since you turned me."

Roman watched the guilt flash across Luc's face. Perhaps Roman had gone too far, but he was tired of this obsession with mates. It was making his friend agitated, unstable. "I do not mean it as censure, mon ami," he consoled. "You saved my life. I am grateful. Turn her if you like. Create another monster like yourself to fuck and love and maybe even be happy with until you both lose yourselves to the demons inside you. But do not expect her to tame you."

Luc stared at him for a long moment, green eyes flashing in a way that made Roman think perhaps his friend would leap over the table to wring his neck. It wouldn't be the first time they'd come to blows. Two people couldn't have a friendship last as long as theirs without getting on each other's nerves every few decades.

The tension grew until, finally, Luc laughed. "You just don't like her, Rome."

Roman shrugged. "I like her fine. It is because I like her that I think she should go into this with eyes wide open, Luc. She is not like I was. She is not dying on some battlefield. Turn her and you are taking away her life. Her human life."

"Your self-loathing is showing again, mon ami."

"I'm not self-loathing. I'm realistic."

"And what is my other option, Rome?" Luc asked, eyes hard. "An eternity alone?"

Alone forever. It was Luc's biggest fear.

Roman leaned forward over the table, clasping his friend's hand. "You are not alone, Lucien. You have me. Always."

Roman knew it wasn't enough. Luc wanted a guarantee, a fated promise that he wouldn't end up a mindless beast, driven to madness by the creature inside him. Friendship wasn't enough for him anymore. He viewed Victoria as his salvation.

Luc gave a small sigh, eyeing Roman's hand on top of his. "To us, then." He raised his glass to Roman.

"To us." Roman took a sip, trying to ignore the feeling of dread building in his stomach.

Luc had said nothing more on the subject that night, but Roman knew afterward that the discussion had had an impact. It had been part of why Luc waited so long to try to turn Victoria.

Roman had thought Luc was grasping at straws. His friend had been a more pious man than Roman when he'd been human. Luc had struggled in the beginning, he had told Roman, with what they were, with the things they craved.

For most of the time Roman had known him, he had hidden it well under a guise of exuberant debauchery, but Roman knew underneath it all, Luc's conscience still plagued him.

And then they had met Soren, who had told them the hard truth—they didn't have an eternity after all. They only had as long as they could cling to their humanity, and who knew how long that would be. Unless, he had said, they found a soul to tether them...

Victoria had seemed like a lifeline to a drowning man.

Was Roman the same as Luc had been? Grasping at straws with Danny?

No, his demon growled.

Something deep within Roman recognized something deep within Danny. It was different from anything he had ever felt—Roman *knew* it was different. With every fiber of his being. What came next he might not be sure of, but he knew Danny and he belonged to each other, and that was not a thought Roman had ever expected to feel about another soul. Not when Roman wasn't even sure he had a soul left.

The thing was, he was still not sure he had been wrong about Luc and Victoria. That might be arrogant of him, to assume his situation with Danny was different—maybe a means to assuage his internal guilt—but Roman had been there when she'd died.

Her thoughts had not been of Luc. They had been of *fear*. Her fear of death, yes, but even more her fear of becoming like them. Roman had seen then for the first time what she truly thought about them, underneath the surface fascination and attraction, and it had been nothing good.

And how could someone feel that way about their fated mate?

Because as much as Roman might fear the thought of Danny not wanting to turn, he did not fear what Danny felt about what Roman *was*. He knew there was no contempt or disgust hiding underneath the surface. Roman had seen the way Danny had reacted to Roman's compulsion of his mother, all wonder and gratitude.

Danny *saw* him, both his human and demon side, and he liked what he saw, Roman was sure of it.

They needed time for their bond to strengthen, to better understand each other, yes, but it was there, the seed of something real and true. What they needed was a break from the drama and distraction.

They needed Luc gone.

Speak of the devil, and he will appear.

A familiar voice broke through Roman's thoughts. "Still here, mon ami? I thought you would have fled town by now. Must be a very special something keeping you here."

Lucien.

Roman should have been paying close attention to his surroundings, not losing himself in pointless reminiscences. Now Luc was standing at the mouth of the alleyway, blocking Roman's exit. He looked as elegant as ever, if one ignored the fangs and black eyes.

Well, Roman had wanted a confrontation. Here it was. "You already know why I'm here, Luc. Why are *you?*"

Luc took another step into the alleyway. "Oh, I think you know that too. Nice suit, by the way. Still trying to convince yourself and everyone else you're a civilized creature?"

Figured he wouldn't want to get straight to the point. Lucien had always loved to play with his food. Roman straightened his cuff. "You are the one that taught me looking respectable is half the battle in evading suspicion."

Luc laughed at that. "But evading suspicion from whom? Your human boy? Does he think you're a white hat, just one with an unfortunate blood-drinking habit?"

Roman's demon did *not* like Luc bringing up their mate. "He knows what I am."

"Does he really?"

"Really."

Luc seemed to take in the deeper meaning. He always had understood Roman easily, except regarding the one incident that had torn their lives apart. His black eyes narrowed on Roman. "Are you telling me you've shown your little boyfriend your demon side? You must be very serious about him. Is it possible that Roman, the *nonbeliever*, thinks he's actually found a mate?"

Roman said nothing. It was taking all his effort to keep his demon inside.

Luc carried on regardless. "Aren't you the one who told me this was it? Demons driven by blood and sex and violence—no magical solution, no human calming balm?"

For a semiferal monster, he had a good memory. "I was just saying what I thought," Roman defended. "I did not know any more than you did. You were hopeful; I was cautious."

"And now you're a true believer, are you?" Luc jeered.

"I could not tell you what I believe, Luc." He didn't *want* to tell Luc what he believed. He didn't want his relationship with Danny poisoned by past mistakes.

Lucien laughed then. It wasn't the exuberant laugh Roman had heard so often in the past. It was a harsh sound. Grating. "You doubt yourself, don't you? You doubted me, and now you doubt yourself. Always so consistent, Roman." He stalked closer. "Afraid you'll turn him and he'll be just another monster? A sadistic disappointment like me?"

Roman held his ground. "This is not something I feel the need to discuss with you, Luc. Why are you *here*?"

"Why am I here?" Luc smirked. "I thought that was the deal we made. You and me. Whither you go, so do I. Right, mon ami?"

"I think that deal was broken when you tried to kill me, Lucien."

"Psh," Luc scoffed, "what's a little disagreement between friends? You'd broken my heart. I wanted to break yours. I just took it a little more...literally. Besides, I haven't tried to kill you in decades. Over half a century."

It was true. Although, Roman hadn't been letting him get close enough to try.

Roman wasn't exactly sure what Luc wanted with him anymore. His old friend's goal in recent decades seemed to be to try and annoy Roman more than anything. Drive him out of town after town, either by his presence alone or by piling up the bodies and threatening to break Roman's cover.

Was his whole goal just to remind Roman of past sins, future madness?

Roman couldn't take that risk. Because if anything was going to set Luc off, break the armistice they'd found themselves in, it was going to be discovering that Roman had found himself a mate. The very thing Luc felt so sure that Roman had deprived him of.

Roman's hope now was that it was worth trying to talk it out. That perhaps his former friend could still be reached.

"Lucien," Roman breathed out. "About Victoria...I am sorry, all right? I tried to honor what she wanted."

Luc was by all appearances unmoved by the mention of his former love's name. "I see Soren's been sticking around," he announced in an abrupt change of subject.

Roman shrugged. "Yes. He comes around from time to time."

"Ah, but not just that," Luc contradicted. "Living together now, aren't you?"

That answered the question of whether Luc had been watching Danny's house. Roman felt his blood quicken and his demon seethe at the thought.

They needed Luc gone. They needed their mate safe.

Roman forced himself to focus. "We stay together for the time being. Not for long. He will move on soon. And you should do the same."

Luc glanced over his shoulder. "Is that right, Soren? Moving on soon?"

Roman started as his blond friend stepped out of the shadows at the edge of the alleyway. First he'd been too absorbed in memories to notice Luc's approach. Now he had been so distracted by his confrontation he hadn't even noticed Soren nearby.

Goddamn it.

It was sloppy. Inexcusable.

Soren said nothing in response to Luc's greeting. Just leaned against the wall at the end of the alley, hands in his pockets.

"So what's this?" Lucien questioned brightly. "The two of you are finally going to kill me? Put me down for my own good? The righteous Roman and his little sidekick."

Roman decided to try for reason one more time before violence broke out. "Victoria—"

"Fuck Victoria!" Luc roared, black eyes flashing and fangs gleaming. "This isn't *about* Victoria. It was supposed to be *us*! After all your promises, all your assurances, you *left* me. You *abandoned* me."

"You tried to kill me!" Roman protested.

Luc snarled at him. "I was *angry*!"

"And what was I supposed to do? Just let you end my existence?"

Luc was pulling at his hair with both hands, lost to his own anger. "You were supposed to *help* me."

Familiar guilt rushed through Roman. "I did not know *how*, Lucien! I did not know what to do with you. *For* you. How to reach you. Without-Without losing my own life in the process. The first time I thought it was your grief, but then you tried *again*. So tell me. Tell me how to help you."

As sudden as it came on, Lucien's rage seemed to evaporate. It was disconcerting, the rapidity of the change. "Oh, it's far too late for that," he whispered.

Two things happened at once then.

Roman heard police sirens, growing louder.

And footsteps sounded at the mouth of the alleyway. A passerby.

Faster than even Roman, with his heightened senses, could process, Luc had closed the distance between himself and the man walking by the alley. Black eyes on Roman, Luc bit into the man, draining him in large gulps before tossing the body at Soren and springing out of the alleyway.

Luc was gone in seconds, and Soren was left holding the drained body as two police cars blocked off the entrance, trapping Roman and Soren inside.

Merde.

Fourteen

Roman

Goddamn Luc.

The car was silent. Danny, normally so chatty, hadn't spoken a word since their initial greeting upon Roman picking him from work. Ever intuitive, he seemed to sense Roman's need to think and was instead holding Roman's nondriving hand quite firmly. The contact with his mate soothed the restless rage Roman's demon was stirring within him but just barely.

Goddamn Luc.

The police had apparently received a tip about some suspicious men loitering around the hospital. With the recent attacks in town, they'd taken the tip seriously, showing up in full force.

Soren and Roman had successfully compelled the police officers, convincing them the duo were just innocent bystanders. They had avoided being brought in for questioning and even avoided giving any contact information for follow-up. Roman was aware that, without Soren, he might have had a harder time doing so. He wasn't as skilled in compulsion as his older friend.

Luc hadn't killed the man after all. A small miracle.

Roman thought that perhaps he had not had time to drain the human thoroughly and still make a clean exit. He must have been wary of facing off against both Roman and Soren in one go.

An ambulance had arrived shortly after the police cars to take the unconscious man away. Roman just now realized his mate might have seen him being brought in to the hospital, might even have taken part in his care.

He looked over to the boy beside him—brown hair mussed and brown eyes tired, but just as lovely as ever—and considered asking him but in the end stayed silent. The bitten man wasn't his focus right now. That man was nothing.

But Danny. Danny was *everything*.

Luc had to have known his impromptu little trap wouldn't hold them for long, had probably been only looking to stall so he could make his getaway. Which still left the question of his bigger plans for them.

Roman parked the car in Danny's driveway, reluctantly releasing his mate's hand to exit the vehicle. Just that simple act of forgoing contact had his demon raging again.

As soon as Danny was out of the car, Roman rushed over to grab his hand again and pull him into the house, still without a word. He knew he was being a brute, but was hard-pressed to care. His demon was pulsing in him. Needing to touch. Needing to protect. Needing to claim.

Ours. Ours. Ours.

As he tugged Danny to the stairs, they passed Soren in the kitchen.

"Rome, we need to talk."

"Not. Now," Roman barked out. He continued forward, pulling his mate up the stairs, ignoring Soren's protests. Danny didn't argue, seeming for his part content to let Roman be as much of a beast as he needed to be.

In the bedroom, Roman pushed Danny down to sit at the edge of the bed. He found himself pacing in front of the boy, unable to stay still. "Luc paid me a visit," he managed to grit out.

"I see." Danny's voice was calm, gentle.

"I do not know what his end goal is."

"I'm not sure he does either."

That brought Roman up short. He paused his pacing. "What?"

Danny shrugged. "It's just the vibe I got from him when I saw him. He seemed...curious about me. Threatening, sure. But it didn't seem like he had some nefarious plan all figured out. He seemed a little...lost, maybe?"

"It does not make him any less dangerous," Roman snapped, hating himself as he did it. Mon Dieu. He'd tried to be so careful, so controlled around his human, but he could feel himself unraveling.

"No, it doesn't," Danny agreed. He didn't comment on Roman's tone, didn't censure him for his boorish behavior.

Roman moved with inhuman speed until he was only inches from Danny's face. His sweet mate blinked but didn't flinch.

Was the boy really so unafraid of him?

"I need…," Roman started to say, but was unable to finish the sentence. His own inadequacies were forefront in his mind. He was no gentle human lover, no docile boyfriend. He was a monster with monstrous appetites.

He didn't just want to touch Danny. He wanted to *consume* him.

Danny wet his lips with his tongue, and Roman found himself staring at the boy's mouth in a way he knew was predatory but could not help.

"You need…," Danny pressed him, voice a little hoarse.

"I—I don't know if I'm capable of being at all gentle right now, little king. I need you. I need to claim you." He watched in satisfaction as Danny's pupils dilated and his breaths quickened.

"Then claim me," Danny whispered. "I told you before: I don't need gentle."

It was all the encouragement Roman needed, all that his demon would allow him to wait for. He attacked the boy's mouth with his own, tearing at his clothes, enjoying the sound of the fabric of Danny's scrubs ripping under his hands.

His sweet mate was making little mewling sounds into Roman's mouth—sounds that went straight to his cock. Danny's hands were tugging at his clothes in turn, his movements matching Roman's in ferocity if not in strength.

His mate smelled so goddamn delicious. With him naked, his milk-and-honey scent intensified. Roman tore his mouth from the boy's lips, unable to help himself from licking and sucking his way down the smooth neck in front of him as Danny finished unbuckling Roman's belt.

This neck. He could hear the blood pulsing beneath Danny's skin, a current of ambrosia just waiting to be tasted.

But not quite yet.

"On your stomach," Roman growled.

Danny complied immediately, scrambling to lie facedown on the bed, and Roman's demon growled inside him in satisfaction at their mate's easy submission. He pushed his own pants the rest of the way off and prowled on top of the bed to blanket the boy's body with his own.

"So lovely. So sweet." He kissed his way down Danny's spine as he blindly reached into the bedside table drawer for lube. His demon was roaring at him now—*take, claim, own*—but Roman held on to just enough of a shred of his sanity to remember he didn't want to hurt his boy.

Or at least, didn't want to hurt him *too* badly.

A few bruises would only serve to enhance the loveliness of all the pale, creamy skin. He and his demon could agree on that.

Roman opened Danny up with rough, impatient fingers, placing blunt-toothed bites all along the boy's upper body, deeply satisfied with the marks he left behind. Danny was writhing and moaning underneath him. "Fuck. Oh fuck. Please, Roman. Fuck me."

His mate had such a dirty mouth when he was turned on.

As Roman pressed the blunt tip of his cock against Danny's hole, his mate arched up beneath him. "Yes. *Yes*. Please, Roman."

Oh, how he loved when his little king begged for him.

Roman pushed into Danny in one smooth glide. He didn't pause, didn't give the boy time to adjust. He knew he was going faster than he should, but his mate only keened in satisfaction, lifting his ass to meet him thrust for thrust.

Perfect boy. Perfect mate.

"You're mine," he growled, brute that he was.

Danny nodded frantically underneath him, panting out, "Yours."

"No one else can have you. No one else can take you. *Mine*."

Danny moaned into the pillow.

"Say it," Roman urged, pausing midthrust. Danny whined in protest, but Roman held himself still. He needed to hear the words.

"Fuck, Roman. Yes. Only you. No one else." Danny slapped the mattress. "Now fuck me. Please."

Roman obliged, pumping his hips with abandon, making sure to hit the one spot guaranteed to drive his boy crazy.

It somehow still wasn't enough.

"Bite!" Danny cried, his voice breathless but urgent. "Bite me."

Yes.

Roman let his fangs descend and bit down on Danny's neck, his mouth filling with the warm, sweet nectar of the gods.

Fuck. Nothing on this earth tasted as sweet as his mate's blood.

Danny cried out at the bite, pulsing around Roman's cock as he emptied himself onto the bed. "Come, Roman," he begged. "Come inside me. Please."

Jesus. Roman was powerless against his mate's command, his vision whiting out as his hips stuttered, pumping his seed into the boy.

Now they each had the other's essence inside them. His demon was purring at the thought.

Coming down from the high of his release, Roman licked lazily at the bite mark on Danny's neck and found himself wishing he didn't have to heal it. Wishing he could leave a permanent mark on his mate's milky skin. A sign of their bond. A sign of ownership.

Fuck, but he was a brute.

Something in Roman was snapping with Luc's murky threats on the horizon. His veneer of humanity was cracking, and Danny was going to be in the line of fire when the monster came out.

Instead of apologizing, he found himself growling out another promise. "Nothing is going to part you from me."

"Mm." Danny's beautiful brown eyes were barely open—his mate was drifting to sleep already. Danny was always like this after working all night, barely conscious long enough to get into bed. It only made the passion he'd matched Roman with just now that much more remarkable.

How had Roman found such a perfect mate? How would he manage if Danny was taken from him?

He couldn't take this fear, this vulnerability. Caring for Danny was like having his heart walking around outside his body, unprotected, mortal, fragile.

Roman needed to turn him. Soon. The human body was simply an inadequate vessel to house the most important soul in Roman's world.

Still, Roman's restlessness was momentarily soothed. The act of claiming the boy had eased something inside him, if only for a moment. He found the tightness in his chest loosening for the first time since his encounter with Luc.

Roman settled in to watch his precious mate sleep.

If he was going to be a brute, he might as well be a creep too.

~ ℓℓ ~

It had only been a few hours of peace when Roman's phone rang, breaking the silence. He rushed to pick it up where it had ended up on the bedroom floor before it could ring a second time and wake his mate.

Soren.

"Yes?" Roman whispered his greeting, knowing his friend would hear him regardless.

"I need you to come to the hospital." Soren's voice was sharp, lacking any of his usual teasing tones.

"What for? What are you doing in a human hospital?"

"Gabe was attacked."

Merde. Roman's eyes darted reflexively to Danny's sleeping form. "How bad is it?"

"He's okay. Relatively. He had a bite and some superficial wounds I was able to heal. But I had to bring him to the ER for a broken arm."

Not good. Not good at all. "Are you there with him now?"

Soren huffed into the phone. "He wouldn't let me stay in the room. Kept calling me a monster, kicked me out. I'm outside the hospital's emergency entrance."

"What did you do?" Roman accused, dressing as fast as his abilities allowed. Danny still hadn't stirred.

"I didn't *do* anything!" Soren sounded aggrieved. "I healed the dolt. But Luc wasn't exactly subtle when he attacked him, and my licking his wounds closed might have raised some additional questions about my own less-than-human condition. I kept him calm enough at the scene with a little compulsion, but whatever pain meds they gave him in the ER messed with it, and that's when he started panicking, yelling at me to leave."

Roman was gently shaking Danny awake as he listened to Soren's rant. It was unusual for his friend to get so worked up. Danny blinked up at him in sleepy confusion. "Gabriel was hurt," Roman whispered gently. "He is all right, but he is at the hospital. I need you to get dressed."

Roman watched as the blood drained out of his mate's face, but Danny only nodded, moving to grab his own clothes from the floor. Roman watched long enough to make sure Danny was steady on his feet before stepping out of the room, into the hallway, closing the door behind him.

He turned his attention back to the phone. "How did you even happen to be there? I thought you lost Luc's trail?"

There was a long pause on the other end. Then, "I picked it back up again."

Lying. His friend was lying to him, although Roman wasn't sure for what possible reason.

"We'll be there in five minutes," he snapped out.

"You know this could be a trap to lure Danny in."

"It could be." It was definitely a possibility. "But I am imagining the response if I tell Danny he cannot go see his injured brother, and I believe it would not be pretty."

"You're whipped."

"I do not know what that means."

There was a small, reluctant laugh at the other end of the line.

"Besides," Roman continued, "Danny works regularly at the hospital despite my protests. Luc does not need to injure his brother to lure him there."

Soren didn't sound convinced. "I'll stick around anyway. I can warn you off if Luc comes close."

"I owe you a debt, mon ami."

"Ugh, stop being so dramatic. You owe me nothing. Just get here."

Roman hung up, relieved to hear his friend's voice sounding slightly more normal.

The drive to the hospital was a mirror of their earlier drive to the house—tense and silent but for a few questions Danny asked about Gabe's condition. He clenched his jaw at hearing about the broken arm but said nothing more about it.

Roman wasn't sure if he should be grateful for the silence or worried.

They spotted Soren outside the hospital doors pacing back and forth in a way that reminded Roman of himself earlier that morning.

"A moment, sweet." Roman tugged at Danny's hand to attempt to halt the boy's entrance into the hospital.

"I need to see him, Roman." Danny's eyes were dry, but his voice broke at the words. He was clearly distressed at the thought of his brother hurt.

Roman hesitated. He was reluctant to let his mate out of his sight, but he trusted that Soren would have scouted for Luc's presence in the hospital, and they wouldn't be long outside. He had questions for Soren. And...perhaps it was better if Danny didn't hear any gruesome details of Gabe's attack.

"All right. I will be right behind you," Roman acquiesced, releasing Danny's hand.

Danny nodded at him and then at Soren in greeting before turning his back on them both and rushing inside the hospital entrance.

Roman turned to his friend. "No sign of him?"

"No." Soren looked terrible. His golden hair, usually perfectly coiffed, was standing in every direction, as if he'd been running his hands through it. His ridiculous fur coat had spatters of blood on the collar. Forced to stand still to talk to Roman, he was now biting at his nails, a nervous tic Roman had only seen him indulge in on a few occasions over the decades.

"He was out for breakfast with a woman. Some morning-after brunch affair with his latest bar hussy, I presume." Soren looked away as he said it, with a studied casualness that almost took the bite out of his words. Almost. "He was putting the lady in her car when Luc attacked. Broad daylight. Fucking bold."

Roman ignored the comments on Gabe's dating life, having no idea what to say to something so beside the point. "And you had picked up Luc's trail and followed him there?"

That hesitation again. "Yes."

"Soren, look at me."

Soren met Roman's eyes, a forced smile on his face. "Yes, Roman?"

"Were you following Gabe tonight? *Have* you been following Gabe?"

Soren said nothing. That was answer enough.

"Fuck," Roman swore. "Merde. I told you to leave him alone."

Soren huffed. "My being there might have saved his life."

"Your being there might be *why* Luc attacked him in the first place. You drew attention to him."

Soren's eyes narrowed. "I think Gabe being your presumed mate's *brother* is what drew Luc's attention, you cretin," he hissed. "You can't play house with your little human, ignoring the fact that an immortal psychopath is fixated on you and your love life, and not expect him and everyone else around him to be in danger!"

"I'm not *ignoring* it. I did not think Gabe would be a target. I do not know why I did not think that." Roman had been careless, too focused on Danny's person and not on the people his mate cared for, those Luc would see as weak spots.

"Because you're *not* thinking," Soren accused. "Being in love has made you stupid. It makes everyone so fucking stupid." He sounded so truly miserable, so defeated, that Roman's budding anger at his friend deflated in an instant.

He sighed, looking Soren over more closely. "Were you hurt? Fighting Luc off."

"What fighting?" Soren snorted bitterly. "I didn't have time. I was...lurking, I guess you could say, trying to keep my distance from the human, and then suddenly Luc was there. Biting. Tearing.

Breaking." Soren's voice cracked a bit at the last word. He cleared his throat. "And then he left just as suddenly. A fucking hurricane of destruction. He could have killed him if he wanted to. Snapped his neck in an instant. He's just toying with us. It has to stop, Rome."

"And you think killing him is the only way." It wasn't a question. Soren had made his feelings on the matter clear before.

"Were the ties of your friendship really so strong that you're still reluctant to, even after all he's done?" Soren sounded more curious than angry.

Roman didn't know how to answer that. Were they? He didn't feel like he had any love left for Luc. Too much had happened between them since their days spent as brothers. But Luc had been there, in some form or another, since the moment of Roman's transformation. He was a part of Roman, whether he liked it or not, and carving that part out would be painful.

"I am not fond of killing," was what Roman landed on. It sounded feeble even to him.

Soren scoffed. "You're a vampire. We're all fans of killing."

Roman shook his head. "You know that isn't true. You are being deliberately obtuse. I like violence; I will admit that much. Blood and fear and rage, like any other demon of our kind. But I have never really liked killing. Such a waste. Life is...precious."

"Depends on whose life you're talking about, if you ask me."

Roman shrugged but didn't argue. Maybe Soren had a point. Roman would protect Danny's life at the cost of his own without hesitation, but there wasn't really another person he could say the same for, except maybe Soren.

Roman didn't have his mate's love for all humanity, that need to heal and protect all those around him.

Soren's thoughts were on another track. "You're going to have trouble with that one now."

Roman raised an eyebrow. "Gabriel?"

"A different century and he would have a torch in one hand and a pitchfork in the other. He thinks we're monsters. Not everyone is as understanding as your little human love, it seems."

"He was attacked, Soren. He is in shock. Danny will get through to him."

"You think?" Soren's head was down, and he was scuffing his shoe against the sidewalk. He looked so...young. He wasn't—he was far older than even Roman—but there was a vulnerability there he still hadn't lost after centuries of living. Roman wondered, not for the first time, what it was that kept Soren running from place to place. He wondered if his friend would ever tell him.

So full of secrets, Roman's little friend.

"Gabe will not hate you forever, Soren."

Soren stopped his scuffing and glared at Roman. "He will if we let his little brother get killed."

Never. "Do not even jest about that."

"I'm not *jesting*. Figure out a plan, Roman. Stop letting Luc call all the shots or one of those shots is going to hit Danny."

There was no way Roman was letting that happen.

But his options were narrowing, and it seemed any path he took, he would be tearing out a piece of his heart to do it.

Fifteen

Danny

When Danny's dad had died, driving home from the airport after a red-eye flight, eight-year-old Danny had been woken in the middle of the night by his mom. "Your dad's been hurt," she'd whispered, shaking him gently. "We need to go to the hospital." There'd been no warning of how bad his crash had been, and nothing had prepared Danny for the fact that, by the time they'd gotten to the hospital, his father's heart had stopped.

Driving to see his brother—*Gabriel was hurt*—Roman hadn't pushed Danny for a reaction. He'd let him stay silent, and Danny was grateful for that. He hadn't realized how deeply entrenched the trauma of that night was until he'd felt it being repeated. Hadn't known how to process the fear Roman's whispered words had evoked.

Walking into Gabe's hospital room now, Danny only realized how truly numb he'd been since hearing the news of the attack when a painful mix of guilt and relief washed over him at the sight of his brother.

Gabe was hurt. Gabe was alive. Gabe would be okay.

His brother had already been moved out of the ER and was lying in a hospital bed with his splinted right arm resting on a stack of pillows. He was free from any obvious cuts or bruises—Soren's work, Roman had told him—and the only clear injury was the broken arm. His eyes looked vacant though, and his body was trembling slightly, almost imperceptibly. Even when he finally noted Danny's presence, almost a full minute after Danny had stepped into the room, the vacant look didn't leave his eyes. As if Danny wasn't really there.

"Gabe?" Danny kept his voice soft. Gabe's eyes, a more golden color than Danny's own, slowly focused from their empty stare and finally settled on Danny properly.

"Danny." Gabe's voice was hoarse.

"How-How are you feeling?"

His brother gave a slow shrug with the shoulder of his uninjured arm. "They've given me a good amount of pain meds, so..." It didn't really answer the question, but it seemed all he was willing to say on the matter.

"That's good," Danny said inadequately. "I'm glad—I'm glad you're not hurting. Are they going to keep you here overnight?"

Gabe stared at him dully. "It was an open fracture. They need to do surgery. I had eaten before—before all this happened, so they're waiting a few more hours."

An open fracture, meaning the skin had been broken, the bone having torn through it. Luc must have snapped Gabe's arm violently. Danny's stomach churned at the thought.

The silence became strained, but Danny didn't know where to begin. In the end, Gabe was the one who broke the it. "Where's your shadow?" His voice was bitter.

"My shadow?"

"That guy who's always around you lately. *Roman.*" Gabe said the name like a curse. That didn't bode well.

Danny cleared his throat. "I thought maybe you and I could use a moment alone."

Gabe nodded at that, but his mouth twisted. "That guy...except he's not a guy, is he? None of them are. Not him or that little blond one or the one—the one who did this to me." He raised his splinted arm in demonstration.

"What did he say to you? The one who did that."

"Not much. He was busy with...other stuff. Right before he snapped my arm, he told me to be a good brother and give his regards to Roman and his 'little human toy.' I'm assuming that's you?"

Jesus. "Not what I prefer to go by, but yeah, I guess so."

Gabe's stare went vacant again, the man lost in recollection. "He was so strong, Danny, so fast. I couldn't do a thing to defend myself. And his eyes...his teeth... He— He *bit* me. And it fucking *hurt*. Then suddenly he was gone, and Sor—that blond one was there, licking all my cuts and the bite, and then they were just—just gone?" Gabe's trembling had increased visibly, and the volume of his voice had risen until he was basically shouting. It was a miracle no one had come in to check on them. "Who the fuck are these people, Danny? *What* the fuck are they?"

Danny felt helpless and small in the face of Gabe's distress. It was one thing for his own world to be turned upside down in the span of a few days; it was a whole other thing for his brother's to be. For him to be hurt and scared and confused.

"Maybe now's not the best time—"

Gabe shook his head violently. "Tell me what's going on, Danny."

"You're in shock, Gabe."

"No shit." Gabe laughed humorously. "Tell. Me."

Danny went to sit on the edge of Gabe's bed, trying not to be hurt when his brother flinched at his closeness. "If I tell you, you have to promise to stay calm. No more yelling. Unless you want them to put you in a psych hold after your surgery."

Gabe nodded at him in agreement and said in much calmer, quieter voice, "Just tell me what's going on."

"Roman and Soren and Luc, the one who hurt you—you're right, they're the same. Well, not the *same*, exactly. Luc's gone kinda feral and grr-y, where the other two are generally pretty chill. Relatively. Mostly. Right. Well. Um. Well, they're all...vampires?" Was this how Roman had felt telling Danny the truth? Because Danny was feeling straight-up bananas saying it out loud to someone else.

"Vampires," Gabe deadpanned.

Danny bit his lip. "Yep. Uh-huh. They used to be human, and then they were turned—that's what they call it when they become a vampire—and now they don't age, and they drink blood, and they've got some other cool stuff going on like moving really fast or healing stuff with their saliva or like...mind control, I guess you'd call it?"

Gabe was staring at him, seemingly at a loss for words, so Danny figured he should just power through. In it to win it. Better for his brother to know it all if he was going to know any of it, right?

"So they all used to be friends, and then something tragic happened, and it loosened a few screws in Luc's brain, and he's had it out for Roman ever since. They've been playing this epic game of hide-and-seek for a few decades, but then Roman came here, and he saw me, and he thinks that maybe I'm his...destined vampire soulmate, I guess? Like, each vampire maybe has a person whose soul helps keep their inner demon thingy tame and not psychotic, and he thinks I'm that person for him?" Danny hated that all his statements were coming out as questions, but he'd never said any of that last part out loud to a non-Roman person, and he was aware that he sounded really, super, batshit crazy.

He tried to catch Gabe's eye to gauge his reaction, but his brother had taken to staring at the wall.

"Vampires," Gabe muttered a second time.

Danny giggled, to his own horror. "Kind of wild, right?"

"And that douchebag—"

"Hey!"

"—following you around... He's fixated on you as, like, his vampire bride or something?"

Danny couldn't help but roll his eyes at that. "Jeez, Gabe, offensive much? Vampire *husband*, if you please."

Wait, what?

Gabe was just nodding, eyes growing wild. "Okay. Okay, so...first step, we need to get you out of town. I can't go with you yet, surgery and all, but maybe one of my buddies..."

"Gabe."

"I've got a little saved up. Not nearly enough, but we can make it work. Do we need to change our names? How do you even go about changing your name, like, under the radar? Why didn't they teach us that in school?"

"Gabe!"

Gabe finally stopped his frantic muttering and looked at Danny.

"I'm not going anywhere." Danny enunciated each word clearly.

"If you're worried about leaving me here—"

"I don't *want* to leave, Gabe. Yes, Roman's fixated on me, but the fixation is...mutual. I like him. Maybe more than like. He's kind and thoughtful, and he *wants* me. No one's ever wanted me like this before. And I want him right back. I don't want to leave him."

Gabe nodded, but Danny's relief was short-lived.

"Mind control," Gabe said.

"Excuse me?"

"You said one of their powers was mind control."

Fuck. "Did I?" Danny definitely had.

Gabe was looking at him with something suspiciously like pity in his eyes. "Danny, if he's got his creepy vampire fingers in your brain, you can't be trusted to make your own decisions."

"He's not *mind-controlling* me, Gabe."

"How do you know?"

"I just—I just do! Besides, they only use it for simple, temporary stuff. They can't just make a person think they're in love with someone else long-term." At least, Danny didn't think so. He was sort of talking out of his ass at this point.

"In love." Gabe's voice was flat. "You're in *love* with this monster."

Had Danny really just accidentally confessed his love for Roman to his brother? Did he really mean it? *Not the time, Danny.* "He is *not* a monster, Gabe. Listen, you've been hurt, and you're angry, and I get it. But you're being very speciesist right now."

"*Speciesist?*" Gabe was now looking at him like he'd grown another head. This was going *very well*.

"Yes. Exactly. Assuming that simply because they're not human, they're evil monsters."

"It's the drinking blood and *breaking my arm* that has me convinced they're evil monsters, Danny."

"Humans do the same shit every day, Gabe! Well, maybe not the blood drinking," Danny conceded. "But how many injuries do we see on our patients that have been inflicted by other people? If vampires are evil because one hurt you, then the whole human race needs to be written off too. One bad banana doesn't mean you throw away the whole bunch."

"I think the phrase is 'bad apple.'"

"Whatever." Danny huffed. "Vampires are complicated creatures, just like any other species with any sort of intelligence. Learn a little more about them before you judge."

Gabe was looking at him now with an expression Danny couldn't quite place.

"*Well?*"

"Sometimes I forget how special you are, Danny." Gabe's voice had noticeably softened. "Ever since we were kids. You see the good in everyone. You want to *help* everyone. You're a good person."

It was maybe the nicest thing Gabe had said to Danny since he could remember.

It was probably the pain meds talking, but still.

Gabe brushed a hand through his dark hair. "I came back thinking that after so long away, I'd finally be in a position to help you out. Watch over you. I didn't really consider supernatural creatures as one of the things I'd need to look out for."

"Roman won't let Luc hurt me, Gabe. And now that we know you're a target, he won't let him hurt you either."

"You really trust him, don't you?" His brother looked floored by that fact.

"With my life," Danny confirmed. "Besides, I never needed watching over the way you thought, Gabe. I'm an adult. I've *been* an adult, fending for myself, for a long time now. I'm not always perfect at it, but I've been doing okay. I just needed someone to...I don't know...be there. I was lonely. Lonelier than I thought. And then Roman appeared, and he's just...here for me. I don't feel lonely. I feel *loved*. You don't need to worry."

Danny paused there, considering telling Gabe about what Roman had done for their mom, but it didn't feel like the right time. Particularly with Gabe so fixated on the whole mind-control aspect of things.

Gabe let out a deep breath. "I haven't been a very good older brother."

"Well, you're the only one I've got, so I guess I'll just have to love you anyway."

Gabe closed his eyes, leaning back against his pillows. He must be beyond exhausted. Danny should let him rest. "Which orthopedic surgeon is on call today?"

His brother answered without opening his eyes. "I didn't think to ask."

"I'll find out for you."

"Thanks."

Danny was on his way out the door when Gabe called out to him, "You know I love you too, right?"

Danny smiled. "I always have, silly. Get some rest."

Danny was on his way back down to the ER to find out who would be operating on Gabe when a strong hand grabbed his wrist and yanked him into a supply room he hadn't even noticed he was walking past.

He was pulled into a hard chest, his head pressed down at an angle that prevented him from seeing the man's face. He heard the door snick shut behind him.

"Hello again, Mr. Kingman."

Well, fuck, fuckity fuck, fuck. That was not the voice Danny wanted to be hearing right now.

Danny stepped back as far as the vampire's grip would let him—not nearly far enough, but at least he could see now—and looked up into familiar black eyes.

For a man that had just mauled Danny's brother, Luc was looking awfully refreshed, every strand of his salt-and-pepper hair perfectly in place, not a wrinkle to be seen on his... Was that an Armani sweater?

A mix of rage and fear bubbled up in Danny's chest, and he was speaking before he knew it. "You *asshole*. You hurt my brother."

Luc shrugged a broad shoulder carelessly. "Oops."

Oops? *Oops?*

Danny knew he was about to say something stupid, but he still couldn't stop the words from spilling out of his mouth. "Is that really all you have to say about it, you *fucking psychopath*?"

There it was. Stupid.

But Luc only smirked at him, black eyes glinting under the fluorescents. "My, aren't we feisty for someone I could kill faster than he could even blink."

"If you're gonna kill me either way, then it really doesn't matter what I say to you, does it?"

"True enough." Luc's face took on a mock-serious expression. "I *am* sorry about your brother. I really didn't intend to do any lasting damage. I just got so annoyed with little Soren sticking his nose in that I may have gotten a tad overzealous. Did you know he's been stalking your brother?"

Uh, what?

Luc raised a dark eyebrow at whatever he saw in Danny's expression, which must have reflected his surprise. "Ohh, you *didn't* know. Interesting. And here I thought maybe the four of you were planning to go on some sickeningly adorable double dates."

Danny would have to process the inappropriate stalking of his older brother at a later time. A time when he wasn't stuck in a tiny room with a killer.

A horrible thought occurred to him. "Where are Soren and Roman? Did you hurt them?" His gut clenched at the thought of Roman wounded.

Luc just smirked again, like the asshole he was. "Don't get yourself worked up, Daniel. I haven't touched them. Though, I admit it's cute how they're posted outside like little guard dogs. I arrived before they did. Surprised Soren didn't smell me out, actually, expert tracker that he is. Maybe he's not quite as sharp as he used to be. Dulled by the decades."

"Or maybe it's just hard to predict the movements of the truly unhinged." Why did Danny's mouth keep saying stupid things without his brain's permission?

Luc smiled at him then, all sharp teeth and dead black eyes. Danny was suddenly very aware of the strong grip on his arm, from a hand that had very recently snapped his brother's bones like a twig. "Too true. A bit hard to predict the movements of the lovestruck as well, it seems." Luc leaned in close, until they were nose to nose. "Tell me, Daniel, why hasn't Roman done the one thing that could *actually* protect you from me? Are you scared to turn? Afraid you'll become a monster like me?"

Danny tried to keep his expression blank, but clearly Luc read something in it anyway, because he started laughing, that terrifying sound again. "Ohh. Don't tell me. He hasn't even asked you yet. How interesting."

Danny was getting awfully tired of Luc finding everything about him "interesting."

"We've only known each other a few days," he gritted out through clenched teeth.

"Of course, of course." Luc's voice was a parody of sympathy. "But still, you love him already, don't you?"

What was it with everyone trying to pull love confessions from Danny today?

"He tends to have that effect on people," Luc continued. "And I'm sure he's very fond of you too. Staying here even with the big, bad wolf in town." He reached out with the hand not gripping Danny and pushed a piece of hair behind his ear, a horribly intimate gesture.

Danny suppressed a shudder. It felt wrong to be touched by this vampire. He only wanted to be touched by *his* vampire.

"Tell me," Luc crooned. "Has he made you promises? Vows to stay by your side forever?"

"I know where this is going. You're not going to make me doubt him."

Luc smiled again. "Wouldn't dream of it. But I think it's important to have all the facts when making big decisions like these, don't you? He promised me forever too, you know. Promised he'd stay by my side, through thick and thin. And at the first sign of difficulty, he was gone. Like I was *nothing*."

Danny wasn't sure trying to kill your best friend counted as just a "sign of difficulty," but regardless, there was real pain behind Luc's words. Danny could feel it. There would have to be, for Luc to be so fixated on Roman. And Danny knew what it felt like to be left behind by those you loved. He may not have murdered anyone about it, but still. "I don't understand why you two don't just talk it out."

"Oh, you sweet, naive little boy."

Rude, but okay.

Luc's grip on Danny tightened to the point of pain. He'd have bruises from the vampire's fingers. "Monsters like us don't just 'talk it out.' We *fight* it out. And mere mortals should be very careful about getting caught in the crosshairs."

"My brother wasn't *in* the crosshairs though, was he?"

Luc tutted. "You'll have to take that up with Soren. I apologized already, and I'm frankly a little bored talking about it. Now, when I let you out—graciously leaving you unharmed, I'd like to point out—I need you to tell Roman something for me."

Danny's irritation got the best of him. "What is this, grade school? Tell him yourself."

Luc hummed at that. "Well, see, I'm a little worried that after this morning, he might be in a bit of a 'punch first, ask questions later' kind of mood.'"

"Well then, wasn't that the whole point of attacking Gabe? Sending your message?"

"I told you," Luc gritted out. Apparently Danny wasn't the only one getting irritated by this exchange. "I got *annoyed*. Things didn't go quite as planned. Probably shouldn't have bothered at all, but it seemed convenient at the time."

Danny thought about the vacant look in his brother's eyes, the confusion and fear Gabe had shown him. The impending surgery and weeks of recovery ahead of his brother, all because Luc "got annoyed." Danny's blood boiled. A noise he'd never made before came out of him.

Luc just laughed, the absolute dick. "Did you just *growl* at me? Adorable. Tell your boyfriend I want him to keep his promises. A man should be held accountable for his words."

"That's it? That's the big message?" Honestly, Danny expected more maturity from centuries-old beings.

"That's it. I find simple is best with these things. " Luc released his grip on Danny. "Now run along before your white knight comes bursting in. You stink of human, and it's making me hungry."

Danny hated that he was shaking as he exited the supply room, walking down the hallway as fast as he could without it being technically considered running.

How was this his life right now?

He was getting awfully tired of being threatened and pushed around and just generally messed with. He may not have been physically strong enough to fight back when it came to Luc, but he wasn't willing to just sit around and play the victim either.

He may be a human, but he wasn't weak.

It was time for a conversation.

Sixteen

Roman

Roman was...alarmed.

He was sitting at Danny's kitchen table with Soren at his side, the both of them watching his mate rifle through the cabinets, mumbling something about needing alcohol.

It was barely past noon.

The boy had been vibrating with nervous energy since he'd met them in the hospital hallway, his brown eyes hard and his expression uncharacteristically unreadable. The only thing he'd said about his visit with Gabe was, "I told him everything." He'd been silent ever since, other than his current mutterings.

Roman had offered to make him something to eat when they got back to the house, but Danny had refused with a firm, "No. Sit. Both of you." Despite his demon's anger at being refused the opportunity to care for their mate, Roman had obeyed, and Soren, to Roman's surprise, had only raised an eyebrow before following suit. Another sign that Roman's friend was not himself—compliance wasn't usually his strong suit.

Roman raised his own eyebrow at what Danny finally pulled out when he found the right cabinet. "Whiskey?"

"Five o'clock somewhere, am I right?" Danny's voice was flat.

Something was definitely off with Roman's mate. Something other than the obvious fact of his injured brother.

"Let me make you—" Roman was cut off immediately, Danny shaking his head as he approached the table.

"No. No making. No cooking. No taking care of me right now. I don't need pampering. I need answers." He placed three shot glasses on the table and sat down across from the two vampires.

"Whiskey is mandatory for me but optional for you two." Danny downed his shot, swiveling his head to glare at Soren. "You. Have you been stalking my brother?"

Soren sighed and threw back his own whiskey, wincing. "Define 'stalking.'"

"Jesus Christ." Danny rubbed a hand over his face. "Is this like some genetic thing, then? Some Kingman family trait that makes us vampire catnip?"

Roman broke in, unwilling to let whatever was going on with Soren make Danny second-guess their own connection. "I don't think you can compare what Soren has been—"

"Luc told me you promised him forever," Danny cut him off, fixing him with a look.

Roman was out of his chair in an instant. "*What*? When did you see Luc again? How?"

"He was at the hospital. We had a...chat."

Soren swore. "I told you he might be luring the boy in."

Roman didn't need reminding. He had the brief urge to snap his friend's neck. "How did you not realize he was already there?" he ground out through gritted teeth.

"I was *distracted*."

"Doesn't matter." Danny waved a hand at both of them dismissively, taking another shot of whiskey. "Didn't hurt me. But he told me to tell you, *mate*"—Roman didn't like the bite with which Danny said that word—"that he expects you to keep your promises. And that was your promise, right? You and him by each other's sides? Forever?"

Fuck Luc and his big goddamn mouth. "I told you: it was never romantic between him and myself. We were brothers."

Danny laughed bitterly. It wounded wrong coming from Roman's sweet mate. "You think that's what I'm upset about? Romantic, platonic, I don't care. You promised to be by his side. Just like—like you've promised to stay by mine."

Roman tensed at the unspoken accusation: *You don't keep your promises.* He suppressed the urge to shout in frustration, keeping his voice as calm as he could manage. "There were—how should I put this?—extenuating circumstances. As you well know."

Danny poured more whiskey for himself, carefully avoiding Roman's gaze, a move Roman was finding infuriating. How could he reassure his mate if he wouldn't even look at him? "If you turned me and I turned out monstrous...became feral....would you abandon me like you abandoned him?"

Never.

"He tried to *kill* me, Danny. Twice. He kills humans regularly."

Danny went on as if he hadn't heard him. "Or do you not have any intention of turning me at all? Because you've never brought it up. A fact Luc really enjoyed shoving in my face."

Danny's gaze remained averted, but Roman could still see the glassiness of his eyes.

Merde. His mate was hurting. And it was his fault.

Roman vaguely registered Soren muttering something that sounded suspiciously like "told you so," but he kept his focus on Danny. He knew he should have brought up turning to him already. He shouldn't have let fear guide his actions when it came to his mate. Now he was left scrabbling to repair the damage.

"Danny, look at me."

Danny kept his eyes on his whiskey. "And you haven't put him down either. If you truly thought he was feral, with no sense of self left, wouldn't you have done him that mercy? You've just been...running away."

Roman was going to be forced to say it out loud, wasn't he? Admit his faults and weaknesses to the two people on this earth whose opinions mattered to him. "I have been...afraid. Afraid of how he's changed. Ashamed of my part in it. Facing that—that I did that to him. That I broke him."

Danny winced in sympathy before downing another shot. Roman frowned. The boy was going to keel over before the end of this conversation if he kept going at that rate. But Roman had a strong feeling his mate wouldn't appreciate that feedback at this time.

He kept his mouth shut.

He was rewarded when Danny's voice softened with his next words. "I'm not saying what happened to him is your fault. I don't think that. But he seems more pissed about the leaving than he does about Victoria. If you tried to talk it out. If you met with him. Could he kill you?"

The short answer was, of course, *yes*. Roman wasn't invincible. But that wasn't the reassurance his mate needed right now. "It's possible, of course," Roman hedged. "But very unlikely. He's strong, but so am I. And we are hard to kill. Putting one of us down tends to take quite a bit of effort. Or an ambush."

Danny had forgone staring at the whiskey to draw invisible patterns on the table with his fingertips. "I don't want to see you get hurt. And I couldn't bear it if you were killed. But I can't consider an eternity with you with this...person...lurking in the background. Looming over our shoulders. It needs to be fixed somehow."

Roman tried to ignore the warmth that filled his chest at his mate bringing up an eternity with him. Did Danny mean it? Would he be willing to put aside his humanity to be with Roman, to stay by his side? He forced himself to pay attention as Danny continued, oblivious of the effects of his words, "And I'm not so sure he deserves an execution."

Soren cut in, "Aren't you being awfully supportive of someone who just snapped your brother's arm like a goddamn twig? And in case you forgot—the psychopath *murders* humans."

Danny turned to Soren and raised a finger. "One—you do not get to talk about my brother. You are on a time-out from all things Gabe-related." He raised a second finger. "Two—what do you know about the people he's killed? Because I know of two in Hyde Park. One tried to mug me, and according to the police, it wasn't his first, and not all his victims were fortunate enough to live. The other that I know of...the police told us about him too. At the hospital. About some of the things he'd done. He wasn't a good guy, to say the least. And Luc said something that's been on my mind ever since, about taking out some of the 'trash' around here."

Soren scoffed. "You're telling us you think he's some kind of vampire vigilante?"

"I think in one night he lost the two things that made him hopeful about an eternity of living: the woman he loved and his brother. He's been full of rage and pain, letting his demon call the shots. But what if underneath that, he's still in there, mitigating the chaos by choosing his victims deliberately?" Danny sighed, losing some of his fire. "I'm not saying he's right, and I'm definitely not saying he's not dangerous. He's clearly hell-bent on some sort of revenge when it comes to Roman. But maybe he's doing what he can to not be a true monster."

Danny finally turned to Roman, his big eyes imploring. "And you're maybe the one person who has a chance of getting through to him. He's fixated on you, for better or worse."

"Clearly for worse," Soren muttered. "How do you expect Roman to do that without it turning into a giant bloodbath?"

"I don't know." Danny sounded frustrated. "You two know Luc better than I do."

They all fell into silence, contemplating the different paths in front of them. Roman was conflicted—could he really reach Luc? None of their recent interactions had been cause for any hope so far. But they had had very few actual conversations over the decades, and Roman certainly hadn't accomplished anything by running away, other than increasing Luc's ire.

But there was something else on Roman's mind, and it couldn't wait any longer. He cleared his throat, eyes on Danny. "Did you mean it? An eternity with me?"

Soren made an impatient sound and stood up from the table. "I'm leaving if we're getting into lovey-dovey talk. We can reconvene this doomed think tank tomorrow."

Danny reached out a hand to the blond vampire, and Roman did his best not to throw a fit and demand his mate's full attention. "Wait, please. What—what do you want with Gabe?"

Soren crossed his arms, the picture of petulance. "I don't know."

"Do you want to hurt him?"

Soren shook his head.

"Date him?"

Soren laughed, and Danny narrowed his eyes.

"All right then, Mr. Stubborn. Tell me this. Would you protect him if Luc came after him again?"

Soren paused long enough that Roman, in Danny's shoes, would have throttled him. But eventually Soren nodded slowly. Danny gave a little sigh of frustration, but his expression softened toward Roman's friend. "Can you please do me a favor and keep your distance? At least until Luc is dealt with. I don't want my brother to be a target."

Another nod from Soren. Roman had never seen his friend so taciturn. What the hell was going on with him?

Danny laid a hand on one of Soren's crossed arms, squeezing gently. "Thank you."

Soren gave a little cough. Was Roman imagining it or was Soren blushing ever so slightly? "Whatever," he huffed. "Just don't go forward with any insane, Luc-related plans without filling me in first, okay? I don't want your bleeding heart getting one of my best friends killed."

That was more like the Soren Roman knew. "I'm touched," Roman drawled.

"Shut it. Save the mush for your boyfriend." Soren walked out, and they listened to the sounds of his footsteps heading up the stairs, presumably to the guest bedroom.

Roman reached across the table to grab Danny's hand. He needed to be touching his mate. His demon was restless, frustrated with the distractions keeping them from getting answers. "So...forever."

That delicious flush stole across Danny's cheeks and down his neck as the boy fidgeted in his chair. "There's a lot to discuss before we even get to that. And—and you haven't even asked me, so..."

Roman turned Danny's hand over and placed a kiss on his palm. "Daniel Kingman. Lovely mate, my little king. Would you do me the honor of solidifying our mate bond, staying always by my side? Would you turn for me?"

Danny's flush deepened as he swallowed roughly. He was adorable in his embarrassment. "I'll think about it. We have other things to focus on right now. Also, I might be a little drunk."

Roman fought off his disappointment. It may not have been a resounding yes, but he knew his mate wasn't another Victoria. He wouldn't toy with Roman—wouldn't bring up eternity if he didn't have serious thoughts about following through.

"All right, little king. Although, there are...logistics we would need to consider, when you are up for the discussion."

"Like what?"

"It is often...difficult for a newly turned vampire, Danny. It can be hard to control your demon. They tend to wake up hungry, to take control more easily in the beginning, demanding to be fed. And families and friends tend to notice new changes like black eyes and fangs. You would most likely have to leave for a time, while you adjusted. And I know you have...responsibilities here."

He watched as Danny frowned in thought, swaying slightly in his chair. Definitely a little drunk.

"We can discuss it all another time. We should get you something to eat and put you to bed."

"It's not even nighttime." Danny's lower lip pushed out in a delicious pout.

"You barely slept at all today. You must be exhausted."

Danny nodded with a frown but grabbed at Roman's hand when he tried to free it to stand up from his chair. "Wait. I want you—I want you to promise me something. While I have the courage to ask." He took a deep breath before speaking again. "If I do turn out...monstrous. If I become feral. You'll put me down. You won't leave me to be a killer."

The very thought of it was like a sharp knife pressing into Roman's chest. His demon howled inside him at the thought, but Roman didn't let the sound out. He forced himself to stay calm. Danny didn't need his rage. He needed his reassurance. Even so. "I do not know if I can promise that, mon amour."

Danny squeezed his hand in understanding. "Please just think about it."

Roman found himself agreeing, but he already knew his answer.

He didn't know what it said about his own character, clearly nothing good, but if he had a choice between a monstrous Danny and a world without Danny at all, he would take the monster.

As far as Roman was concerned, the rest of the world was expendable. His mate was not.

Seventeen

Danny

"The whole thing," Roman said, tilting the water glass up so Danny was forced to finish its contents.

I mean, really, Danny thought. *I'm not a baby.*

But he didn't actually protest. Only stood there, blinking stupidly, as Roman took the glass away. Maybe whiskey on an empty stomach after only two hours of sleep had been a dumb idea after all, but Danny had been shaken by his separate encounters with Gabe and Luc. He'd needed something to steady his nerves, to give him courage to address the issue with the two vampires in his house.

Now he just needed something to steady his legs.

Roman had already made him eat some toast, and Danny had sobered up accordingly, but the exhaustion was catching up to him physically. Now his vampire was turning the bed down for him like some kind of manservant.

Some kind of *sexy* manservant. *Mm.*

"Come on," Roman urged. "Time for bed. Strip."

Danny smiled at him dopily, all his earlier irritation with overbearing vampires gone. What a cutie, taking care of Danny like this.

Roman stared at him for a minute. Danny was more than happy to gaze back at him in turn—he was so *handsome.* Roman broke it off when he sighed and moved forward to wrestle Danny's shirt off his head.

Right, he was supposed to be stripping.

As his shirt came off, the bruise Luc's hand had left on Danny's forearm came into view.

Roman tensed at the sight, eyes darkening. "Bastard," he growled.

"I like the bruises you leave on me much better," Danny said absently, tilting his head down and tracing one Roman had left on his collarbone with his fingers.

Roman's muscles remained tense, but his eyes flashed with heat. "I do too," he said, circling Danny to admire the marks he'd left the last time he'd claimed him. Because that was what sex with Roman always felt like to Danny—a claiming.

Danny shivered at the memory of their last time together. He'd always thought he was relatively vanilla when it came to sex, but something about being marked up and used by Roman ignited a fire in his belly. The bruises even felt like a form of care, in their own way. For Roman to be rough and wild but never seriously hurt Danny with his superior strength. It was passion and control at the same time.

Just like when he bit Danny, drank him in without taking too much, too fast.

So fucking hot.

"Will you still want me as much when you can't drink from me?" Danny hadn't known he was going to ask the question until he did. Danny was apparently loose-lipped in general today. And now that he'd brought up being turned by Roman, it seemed like his brain couldn't turn off thoughts about it.

Maybe he should be more scared of the idea of giving his humanity away, but he was choosing to have faith in Roman, in the truth of their theoretical mating bond. Danny knew his vampire hadn't always acted perfectly, Luc was proof of that, but Roman had admitted to his mistakes. He was willing to own up to his fear.

That alone meant a lot to Danny. He was so used to avoidance from the people he loved. His mom fighting him every step of the way leading up to her diagnosis. His brother bending over backward to care for Danny without actually *being there* for Danny. And here was Roman, answering his questions openly and honestly. Admitting to the bad along with the good.

And Danny knew from experience, both his own and what he'd seen as a nurse, that life couldn't always be counted on. He could choose his human life, choose dying peacefully of old age, and still get hit by a bus the next day.

He wanted to be brave for once in his life—to choose love and adventure and a chance to experience what the world had to offer.

But he didn't want anyone else to have to suffer for his decision. The thought of being killed didn't scare him nearly as much as the thought of killing someone else. Danny had to trust in Roman to be his safety net. Did he have that sort of trust left in him?

Danny was brought back to the moment by the feel of Roman's warm breath on his shoulder. The vampire had circled closer in his perusal of Danny's skin and was deftly unbuckling Danny's pants from behind.

"We'll have to make up for it, won't we? Get my fill of you in other ways." Roman pressed a soft kiss to the nape of Danny's neck as he relieved him of his pants and underwear. "And haven't I told you?" He straightened back up to whisper into Danny's ear, sending a shiver along his spine. "Every part of you is delicious. Not just your blood."

"Like, which parts?" Danny asked cheekily.

Roman huffed a laugh. "You know very well which parts."

"Show me." Danny commanded, tilting his head back against Roman's shoulder. "Erase Luc's touch. Help me remember I'm yours."

Roman complied immediately, dropping with a growl to his knees behind Danny, spreading his cheeks with both broad hands, and tonguing his hole with soft, wet strokes.

Ohh fuck. Danny was melting. A melty little popsicle. A puddle on the floor. Why did Roman's mouth feel so goddamn *good*? He'd thought he was too tired to get undressed, let alone get hard, but two seconds of Roman's magic tongue, and Danny's flushed cock was bobbing in front of his stomach, leaking generously from the tip.

Danny could feel the slight soreness left over from their last session abating. Ohh right, because Roman's tongue was *actually* magic. Healing Danny at the same time as he ate him out. Well, wasn't Danny just the luckiest duck?

That magic tongue penetrated him, and Danny couldn't help his long, drawn-out moan. He received a sharp nip on his ass in return. "Quiet," Roman scolded. "Soren is still here, and he is already in a mood."

"Don't care 'bout Soren," Danny slurred, losing his words as arousal fogged his brain. "No stop. More mouth, please."

He could feel Roman's lips curl in a smile against his ass, and then that tongue was back, licking and sucking and just generally making Danny lose his damn mind with pleasure.

He lifted his hand to grab his aching cock, groaning when Roman knocked it away and wrapped his own palm around Danny's shaft, stroking him fast and rough enough that Danny was coming in under a minute, keening as he emptied himself into Roman's hand.

Danny looked down and whimpered at the sight of his cum flowing over Roman's clenched fist.

"So hot," he whispered, his mind a pleasant, foggy haze.

His already weak knees gave up on him, and he started swaying in place, but a strong arm wrapped around his midsection, pulling his body back firmly against Roman's hard chest.

"So good for me, lovely," Roman purred, nibbling gently on Danny's ear.

Somewhere in the back of Danny's mind, he was aware of the wet tip of a hard cock grinding against his lower back and the rhythmic sounds of Roman stroking himself filling the air.

"Not gonna fuck me?" Danny asked.

"Do not tempt me. You are in no state for it." Roman grunted and gave him a light swat on the ass. "Now stay still for me. Almost there."

Danny liked the thought of Roman using Danny's body to get himself off. He hummed in pleasure a moment later when he felt the warm splatter of his vampire's cum on his back.

Roman nuzzled the back of Danny's neck. "I want to leave this here. Keep my scent on you."

Danny giggled. "You'd leave me all sticky, you caveman."

"I know." Roman sighed. "Let me get you a towel."

He led Danny over to the bed, where Danny flopped gracelessly onto the covers on his stomach. Oh sweet, sweet mattress. Blessed pillow.

Danny was on the verge of drifting off when he felt a warm, wet towel on his lower back. He gave a small sigh of pleasure. "That's nice."

"Why did you feel the need for whiskey for our conversation? Were you afraid to confront me about Luc?" Even in his hazy state, Danny could detect the hurt in Roman's voice.

"Maybe a little of it was 'cause of that, yeah. Also to confront Soren. I was worried he was going to literally rip my head off for asking about Gabe."

A rumbly chuckle from above him. "He would not do that. He likes you."

"Mm."

"You said 'a little of it' was that," Roman prompted.

Oh, right. Finishing his thoughts was good. "The other bit was just because I was shaken and...sad. It makes me sad. Imagining how it feels to be left all alone, losing your grip on your humanity. But also sad because...because I can't be totally sad for him, right? Because of what he's done. What he's doing."

Roman pressed a kiss to Danny's shoulder. "You are tenderhearted, sweet mate."

"I wish we could fix it."

Roman ran gentle fingers through Danny's hair. "You know it is not on you to fix, correct? I know your nature is to care for those around you. But I am here to care for *you*."

Danny frowned into his pillow. That wasn't right. "But I want to take care of you too. We're partners, aren't we?"

"Your presence alone has already helped me more than you can know, little king." Danny could hear the smile in Roman's voice. "I was lost before we met. The Luc situation is for me to fix."

Danny felt...feelings about that. He didn't want Roman to be alone for this. He cared about his vampire, this man with a demon inside him, who'd spent so long alone with his guilt and his fear.

The thought that Danny's existence in itself had helped Roman was a heady feeling. He knew what Roman meant too. Roman's scent, his warmth, his strength—Danny could feel them all healing the jagged little pieces of his heart, those pieces left sharp and broken from his life up until now.

And the fact that Roman needed Danny as much as Danny needed Roman? That was something he'd never had before.

It had always seemed so easy for people to leave him.

Danny had a partner now. For forever, it seemed, if he wanted it. Someone he loved. Because he *did* love Roman. Which, somehow, both Gage and fucking *Lucien* knew, but Roman still didn't.

Danny should tell him that, right? People deserved to know when they were loved.

But he was so tired he couldn't even make his mouth form the words.

He'd tell Roman tomorrow.

～ ee ～

It was well into the afternoon when Danny finally woke up—apparently his exhaustion had finally caught up with him—and he was a bit disgruntled not to find any sexy vampire lover cuddling with him in bed.

There was a full glass of water next to his bed, though, and a note taped to Danny's phone: *Drink this. I went to run some errands. There is also a quiche waiting for you in the refrigerator. Please eat. —Roman*

Danny found it ridiculous and maybe a little adorable that, instead of just texting, Roman had gone to the trouble of taping a physical piece of paper to Danny's phone. What a dork.

He brushed his teeth quickly and jogged downstairs, feeling refreshed after sleeping for practically an entire day. He found Soren at the kitchen counter, looking down at his own phone with a grim expression.

"Everything okay?" Danny asked.

Soren looked up, and Danny was mesmerized to see the switch when his familiar maniacal grin fell into place in less than an instant. The blond vampire must have been feeling more like himself, then.

"Everything's peachy, human."

"Roman's not back from his errands?" Danny went straight to the fridge to find this quiche he had been promised.

"Not quite. But I was instructed to take you to work and to make sure you were fed and watered beforehand."

Danny snorted at that. "Fed and watered? I'm not a horse."

Soren hummed. "Close enough, you high-maintenance mammal. But if you get a move on, I figured we could head to the hospital a few hours early and see your brother." At Danny's expression, he hurried on, "I won't go in. I'll just drop you off."

"Thank you, that's very...thoughtful."

Danny didn't know what to make of Soren apparently following his brother around. He wasn't exactly angry anymore, now that he'd had time to process. He knew that no matter what Luc had said about Soren being part of his reason for the attack, the psychopath still wouldn't have targeted Gabe if he hadn't been Danny's brother.

Still, it was a little...unsettling. Soren had been helping him and Roman out, and Danny liked the other vampire, even if he was a bit strange. There was an undercurrent of wildness to him—as if he played by his own chaotic rules of right and wrong. And while Danny knew Gabe was handsome—his brother always had both men and women at his heels—Soren was a knockout in his own right, all ethereal male beauty. Danny wasn't sure why he would be so fixated on Danny's straight-laced, all-American brother.

But Danny had decided he was going to focus on one thing at a time, in order to prevent his brain from exploding. And right now that thing was getting to work in time to visit with Gabe. Later, when Danny was done with work and Roman was back, that thing would be brainstorming ways to deal with Luc. So...priorities.

Danny crammed bites of quiche into his mouth—it still didn't seem fair that a vampire that didn't need to eat human food could cook so well—and hurried off to take a quick shower.

He had half expected Soren to try to sneak his way into the hospital after all, but after pulling up to the hospital entrance and booting Danny out, he only waved cheekily and sped off without a word.

Danny dropped his belongings off in the ER staff locker room, then rushed to the room where he'd found his brother the day before.

Gabe was sleeping in his hospital bed, with a new dressing on his arm and an antibiotic running through his IV. He'd had his surgery already, then. Nobody had called Danny to let him know. Was Danny even listed as Gabe's family contact?

He sat down in the chair next to his bed and studied his brother. Gabe looked so much softer than usual, sleeping like that.

"Hey, Gabe," he said when his brother's eyes finally opened. He found himself keeping his voice soft in that way people couldn't help when they were in a hospital room.

"Hey." Gabe's voice was thick with sleep. "You're okay?"

Danny laughed. "I'm supposed to be asking *you* that."

Gabe sat up with a little grimace. "Oh, I'm just dandy. They said I can go home tomorrow, after my rounds of antibiotics are done."

Danny grinned at the news. "I can take you home then. I'll get the night off tomorrow, take care of you."

Gabe frowned down at his arm. "You don't need to do that."

"Yes, I do. You'll need help while you're getting the hang of using just one arm. I bet you're not allowed to bear weight or lift with it, right?"

Gabe nodded reluctantly.

"You could even come home with me, if you think you can tolerate the presence of my monstrous boyfriend."

Gabe ran his hand through his hair. "I thought maybe I hallucinated that conversation."

The thought was tempting, to write the whole situation off as some kind of trauma-induced fever dream. This wasn't how Danny would have wanted to initiate his brother into his new world—with pain and anger and bloodshed. But it was too late for anything else. "No such luck, I'm afraid." He tried to keep his voice light.

Gabe studied Danny's face. Danny wasn't sure what his brother was looking for this time, but after a full minute of silence, Gabe sighed and said, "I can *maybe* give him a chance. For you. One chance."

Danny couldn't have contained his grin even if he tried. "How gracious of you."

"Mmph. Doesn't it—doesn't it gross you out though?"

"What?" Was his brother about to say something rude about gay sex? No, Danny knew for a fact Gabe had hooked up with more than one guy in the past.

"The whole drinking blood thing."

Oh, right. That thing.

"No. I mean, it doesn't hurt. They have this thing where they can make it feel really good actually, but—" Danny broke off when he saw the horrified look on Gabe's face. "Oh. Shit. You just meant, like, in general, didn't you?"

Gabe's face was turning an interesting shade of red. That kind of stress couldn't be good for healing. "You let him *drink* you? Your *blood*?"

Danny knew he shouldn't laugh, it was definitely not the time, but he just couldn't help it. "You really shouldn't get worked up in your condition. Your body needs to heal."

"That bastard!" Gabe shouted. It seemed they were back to yelling.

"Gabe," Danny placated, stifling his laughter. "I *asked* him to do it. I wanted to know how it feels. Blame my overcurious mind. And no, it doesn't gross me out. We see blood all the time. If I didn't have a strong stomach, I wouldn't be an ER nurse."

"There's a difference between seeing blood and drinking it, Danny." Gabe still looked horrified, but the volume of his voice dropped, at least. "You're being awfully blasé about this."

"Who's drinking blasé blood now?" A familiar feminine voice came from the doorway, and both brothers turned their heads to face the new guest.

"Chloe!" Danny was so happy to see his friend. He knew it hadn't been that long in reality, but with everything going on, it felt like it had been forever.

"Sorry to interrupt. Came by to see my favorite ICU doc. Heard you'd been in a fight. I didn't expect to walk in on such an...interesting...topic of conversation." She raised an eyebrow at Danny.

He grinned back at her. He figured she couldn't have heard much or she wouldn't be acting nearly so casual. "Oh, we were just discussing different fetish communities. Gabe's thinking of branching out."

Gabe glared at him, while Chloe gave a delighted laugh. "Dr. Kingman, I didn't think you had it in you."

"I hate you both," Gabe muttered, an impressive scowl on his face.

Chloe waltzed further into the room, raised a tinfoil-wrapped bundle, and shook it at him. "Even if I brought you homemade banana bread?"

Gabe's glower dropped immediately, and he reached out with his uninjured arm, making a "gimme" hand. Danny couldn't blame him. Chloe's husband was an amazing baker. All the staff lived for the days she brought in treats from him. She shook the bundle again at Gabe, keeping it just out of his reach. "Now, now. What do you say?"

"I hate you...less..." It sounded like even that much pained Gabe to say.

"There're those magic words." She handed the baked goods over to Gabe, who graciously allowed Danny to have a piece in exchange for unwrapping the bundle.

"Mm," Danny hummed around his bite. "Heaven."

Chloe looked pleased. "I'll tell Marcus you said so."

The three of them spent the next half hour chatting about various hospital gossip, but when Gabe began yawning atrociously, Chloe and Danny left him in peace to get coffee from the cafeteria before their shift started.

Danny hugged his brother goodbye, taking extra care not to bump his injured arm. "Text me when you're officially discharged. I'll come get you. No arguments!" He pulled Chloe out the door before Gabe could voice any more objections.

They grabbed their coffees—Chloe choosing, as usual, to put way more milk than should be legally allowed in hers—and found their favorite cafeteria booth empty.

"Danny, Danny, Danny." Chloe started tutting at him as soon as they sat down.

Danny froze with his coffee to his lips, racking his brain for any offenses. "What?"

"I've been getting complaints, you know?"

Danny's stomach dropped. Had his work been subpar? He knew he'd been a bit…distracted, but he didn't think it had been bad enough for his coworkers to notice.

Chloe nodded at him, her expression giving nothing away. "Yep. 'Fraid so. People are saying that Ol' Reliable Mr. Always Takes Your Shift is suddenly refusing everyone's requests for coverage."

Oh. *Oh*. It was true. Danny had been, for once, not taking every extra shift that came his way, focusing instead on spending time with Roman, enjoying real food and nights of full sleep and mind-blowing sex. But Chloe had always been telling him he was working himself to the bone. It wasn't like her to scold Danny about working too little.

"Um…"

Chloe pointed a finger at him. "Now, this might be considered forgivable, if this same person hadn't been guilty of giving me absolutely zero updates on a certain Mr. Handsome he recently bumped uglies with."

"Oh my God." Danny covered his face with his hands. "I'm sorry, I've been a bad friend." He peeked through his fingers to find Chloe smiling at him.

"So it's going good, huh? I get it. We've all been there. Sucked into the good dick vortex."

"Chloe!" Danny groaned in embarrassment.

"Alas," she sighed dramatically. "I miss those days."

Danny giggled. "Yeah, right. You and Marcus are sickeningly in love." It had made Danny feel beyond lonely more than once, watching the two of them together. But he didn't feel that way anymore. He removed his hands from his face. "It *is* good with him. More than good, really."

"But…?" Chloe prompted him, sensing he had more to say.

"He just has some…baggage…that's been getting in the way a little bit."

Chloe laughed not unkindly. "Who doesn't? You've definitely got your own. Is he being open and honest about it?"

"Yeah, he is. Although, I might have gotten tipsy last night and harassed him about handling it before we start thinking about a serious future together."

"Good for you, Danny Boy!" Chloe held her hand up for a high-five, one Danny couldn't help giving her. "You deserve the best, and sometimes you have to set boundaries to get it."

"Also...it's possible that at some point—not right away, maybe after my mom...um—well, I might be...leaving with him? For a while. Maybe a long while. He's traveled a bunch, and he wants to show me some of where he's been."

There, that sounded better than, *My boyfriend may at some point turn me into a newbie vampire who becomes crazy with blood lust and needs to leave the city to isolate from friends and family for a while*, right?

Chloe was giving him a look Danny couldn't quite read. "Oh, so it's *serious*, huh?"

Danny took a sip of his coffee, avoiding her eye. "It's getting there, maybe."

Chloe smiled broadly. "Well, I think that would be amazing."

"You do? You don't think it's crazy I just met him? You wouldn't be mad if I left?"

"Crazy, maybe, but who isn't when it comes to love. And *mad*? Daniel Kingman, in all the time I've known you, I've hardly ever seen you make a decision just for yourself. If your first one is to run off with your dream man for a while, I'm all for it. I can't say I won't miss you, but you *are* allowed to live your life."

He was, wasn't he? Danny could stay in town to see his mother through to the end, with Roman at his side, easing her mind as much as he could. And then he would get to actually *live his life*. His life with Roman.

Adventure and travel and mystery, all Danny's for the taking. He couldn't help but smile at the thought.

His happy daydreams kept Danny company his whole shift, and it wasn't until work was over and he saw Soren in the driver's seat of his car to pick Danny up that he realized something was wrong.

Where *was* Roman?

Eighteen

Roman

Roman fingered the sheets on the hotel bed and grimaced—the thread count was definitely not up to his usual standards. But it had been the best he could find in this tiny town, and he wasn't planning to stay long anyway.

Roman had been waiting in this hovel, only a few hours' drive from Hyde Park—not nearly far enough for Roman's taste—needing Soren's confirmation that Luc was actually following him before he could put any real miles between him and his mate. His mate who had looked so unbelievably lovely sleeping that Roman had barely found the strength within himself to leave the bed, let alone the city.

His mate who should have been in this bed with Roman now, whimpering while he rode Roman's cock. Not hours away and out of Roman's reach.

He had just received the text from Soren, and he was battling with his demon, trying to resist the urge to turn back the way they'd come. Roman's demon was never a fan of long-term planning over short-term gratification, especially now, when it came to their mate.

Roman's phone rang, and he answered it in an instant after confirming quickly that it was the call he'd been both dreading and longing for. "Little king?"

Roman had partly hoped Soren would be able to stall Danny a little longer, cover for Roman's absence, but maybe Danny had been feeling the pull of this separation the same way Roman had. Like an ache in his chest he couldn't seem to rid himself of.

"You *left*?! Without even telling me?" Danny's voice on the other end sounded just as angry and hurt as Roman had expected. Guilt surged through him.

"I am sorry, lovely. I thought it best this way. I was not sure I could go through with it otherwise." Already his demon had made it hell for him to leave, growling its protests and throwing itself at the bars of its internal cage, trying to take over control. *Wrong, wrong, wrong.* It only got more restless the further he strayed from Danny's side.

"You really thought leaving without any warning was the best way?"

"You know this is not me really leaving you. Not really, not for good." Oh God, did Danny know that? "Tell me you know that."

"I don't know what I know." Danny's voice had lowered from shouting to barely audible, but the hurt in it remained. This would not do. Roman needed his mate to understand.

"You were right, Danny. About Luc. About me needing to deal with him. And I would never forgive myself if you were hurt in the process. I needed to be far away from you to make any sort of move."

"How do you even know he'll follow you?"

"He has already. I had Soren make sure of it while you were working. Luc has left Hyde Park."

"But—but what will you do with him?"

"Talk with him, to start. Just him and myself. I have been running from it for far too long. Just as you said, little king."

Danny groaned in exasperation. "I was tipsy and spitballing ideas. I didn't think you'd leave *the very next day*. What if talking doesn't work?"

It was the same worry Roman had, but he didn't want to focus on potential failure. "Then I will have Soren come join me, and we will try to take him down."

"You could get hurt."

Roman's chest ached at the concern in his mate's voice. "I could. But my body can handle quite a lot. Yours cannot."

"Way to rub it in my face," Danny grumbled.

Roman chuckled. "There are many things I love about your body, sweet mate. Its fragility is not one of them."

"If I'd known you were leaving, I would have..." Danny's voice trailed off.

"What would you have done, mon amour?"

Danny made a strangled noise. "I mean, you could get really hurt, you know? What if Luc injures you or...or worse. And I never got a chance to say— Ugh, I'm really gonna have to say it over the phone, aren't I?"

"Say what, little king?"

"I love you, okay!" Danny was shouting again. "I love you and your dumb vampire face, and I really thought I'd get to tell you that in person."

Roman wanted to laugh. He wanted to cry. He wanted to do a million things, none of which he could do with his mate miles away and out of his reach. "You *will* tell me in person. Very soon. This is *not* goodbye."

"I don't like this."

"Neither do I. Neither I nor my demon have any interest in being away from the side of the person we love."

"You...love me too?" The hesitance in Danny's voice was like a knife to Roman's chest.

"Of course I do. My sweet, lovely, selfless little king. I could not ask fate for a better mate. You make me feel truly lucky, for the first time in I do not know how long."

There were conspicuous sniffles on the other end of the line. "Okay. That's—that's...really nice to hear. I wish I could kiss you for saying such nice things to me."

"I wish I could do more than kiss you, lovely mate." The little hitch in Danny's breath at Roman's words had his cock hardening.

"What would you do to me?" Danny's voice was husky.

"Ew." Roman sighed as Soren's voice cut in in the background. "No dirty talk in a hundred-foot radius of my person, please."

Danny giggled, and it was one of the sweetest sounds Roman had ever heard. "Oops. Sorry, I got carried away. Soren's driving me right now. I didn't want to wait until we were home to talk to you."

"I am glad you called. It is good to hear your voice. I am sorry to have left this way, but I need to handle my past so I can focus properly on my future. On you. I want to be the kind of man who deserves your forever."

"You already are that man."

Roman wasn't, but it warmed his heart that Danny thought so.

"Where are you?" Danny asked.

"Not nearly far enough. I have been trying to make sure Luc is able to follow me, so I am moving slower than usual. I am not used to *wanting* him on my tail."

"Please be careful," Danny said. "Very, very careful. I just got you. I'm not willing to lose you."

Roman smiled. His sweet, lovely mate. "If I had known all I needed was to leave town to get these declarations from you, I might have done it sooner, lovely."

"Come back to me in one piece and I'll give you all the declarations you want. Actually, wait." Danny's voice took on an indignant tone again. "I'm still mad at you for leaving without telling me. Am I? I think I am. I've got abandonment issues, you know."

Roman couldn't help his laugh. "How about when I return, I let you yell at me as much as you like. Then I give you as many orgasms as your body can handle. Then come the declarations."

Silence, then the sound of Danny clearing his throat. "That could work."

Was his little mate turned on? Roman wanted to explore this further—he'd never tried phone sex—but now was not the time. "Put Soren on the phone?" he requested.

"All right. You'll keep answering my calls, right? Reassure me I didn't dream you?"

"Always," Roman vowed.

"I do love you, you know?"

"I love you too, Daniel Kingman."

There was a shuffling noise, and then Soren's bright voice came on the line. "Are you going to be confessing your undying love for me too?"

"Perhaps another time. Everything is all right over there?"

"Everything's just dandy. I followed Luc a few hours out of town while Danny was working. He's definitely on your tail."

"I meant Danny. He seems...all right?"

"Jesus, what am I, his nanny?"

"Soren...," Roman chided.

"He seems okay. He was definitely pissed that you left. You called that one right. But talking to you seems to have calmed him down."

"I'm right *here*," Danny cut in. Roman could practically hear his pout over the phone. Adorable.

"He's picking his brother up in a few hours," Soren continued as if he hadn't heard Danny at all. "Now that Luc's out of town, he's going to bring him to stay at Chez Danny for a while."

"Danny must be pleased." Roman was glad his mate would have his brother there to keep him company in Roman's absence, even if Roman hadn't fully forgiven the man for not taking proper care of Danny over the years.

"Sure," Soren said lightly. "Though why anyone would be pleased to have that dull rock around, I'm not sure. He could've figured out that one-armed thing on his own."

Roman could hear Danny protesting again in the background, defending his brother. "Family is important to Danny. And now you will not have to go out of your way to follow Gabe."

"I'm *not* following him anymore." Soren's reply was indignant. "I just thought, for a minute, that he might be half-interesting. But I was wrong. He's straight and boring as dirt."

Roman had a feeling it was the "straight" part that was really upsetting Soren, but he let it slide. He had enough drama on his own without getting into Soren's.

"Take care of them for me?" Roman requested, hating that he was having to ask someone else to watch his mate for him.

"I will. Though I'd rather be kicking Luc's ass than be on babysitting duty. Call me if you need backup?"

"I will."

"Want me to kiss your mate goodbye for you?" Soren teased.

In the most even, pleasant voice he could muster, Roman replied, "Touch him and I rip your heart out of your chest, mon ami."

"Noted, you beast." Soren snorted.

"Put my mate back on the phone."

Roman and Danny said their goodbyes then, in terms that Soren only protested as being "too mushy" twice. Roman was loath to let the boy go, but he needed to continue moving.

He looked down at the last text he'd sent Luc.

You wanted me, come get me. Let us hash it out, old friend.

Roman could only hope he wouldn't be killed in the process.

Roman hadn't been driving long when the answering text from Luc dinged on his phone.

So dramatic, brother. Meet me in Islington, corner of First and Ash.

That was only a half hour away. Luc had definitely been catching up nicely, then. Unfortunately, it was back in the *other* direction, and Roman would be heading back toward Danny rather than further away.

The meeting would not be as far away from his mate as Roman would have liked. He would have preferred to have as much distance as possible between any Luc outbursts and his lovely human. Days away, even. But if this meeting went poorly, Roman would just continue heading south, pulling Luc along with him.

Further and further away.

Roman's chest ached at the thought.

South had been his original plan. Hyde Park had only been meant to be a stopping point. Of course, that had been before Roman had met Danny. It felt like a lifetime ago. Bizarre how much Roman's goals had changed since meeting the boy.

He had been aimless, hopeless, on the run—both from Luc and from the inevitable crumbling of Roman's hold on his own humanity. He and his demon had been at war with their urges. Now they had goals in common.

Protecting Danny. Possessing Danny. *Loving* Danny.

And Roman had faith, for the first time in forever, that he would not die alone, a monster.

———ele———

"*Your control is improving, Rome. Not enough for them to truly enjoy it yet, I don't think, but you'll get there.*"

Lucien was licking the blood off his own lips, looking pleased at his protégé. They were in plush armchairs by the fire in his bedroom, across from Roman's own in their shared apartment. It was grander than anywhere Roman had lived before. Their human guests, if one could call them that, had just left, compelled into confusion, a trick the older vampire had been teaching Roman over the past few weeks.

The weeks since Roman's family had driven him away, their faces full of fear and confusion and hatred.

Lucien had told Roman not to return to his home, but he hadn't been able to listen. Had been convinced his family would be able to see he was still the man from before. Convinced he could play the part of human.

He'd been very wrong.

But the other vampire hadn't chastised Roman when he'd returned, crushed and defeated. He had sat by Roman's side while he sobbed out his despair, had stood by his side while Roman broke furniture in his rage, and when Roman was spent and exhausted, had taken him by the hand and told him it was time to learn the ways of his new existence.

They had settled in Paris, with plenty of dark alleys and dubious neighborhoods to find their victims—or "partners," as Lucien called them—for the night.

Roman had been stunned when, tonight, Lucien had chosen a man to feed on, and had done more than just bite him. Luc had touched him, kissed him, crooned sweetly at him. Roman had seen him do the same with his female partners, it came with the territory of the pleasure they could give humans during a bite, but never a man before.

At his shocked face, Lucien had just smirked at him. "Our old rules do not apply anymore, mon ami. We take what we want now. Men. Women. Either or both. If you like them, have them. We can't be damned more than we are already."

The thought never seemed to be far from Lucien's mind. Their damnation.

Roman had never heard the term bisexual—*wouldn't hear it until many years later—but it was the first time he'd been given permission to give in to cravings he'd known his whole life. Cravings he'd pushed into the back of his mind and locked away. Cravings that had only gotten stronger with this new demon inside him, this voice that called for him to give in to every temptation.*

It took time for Roman to adjust, but it wouldn't be long until he followed Luc's example and chose whoever appealed to him most to be his partner for the night, regardless of gender.

"Who taught you all this?" he asked Lucien now, his hunger sated and that voice that called for blood pleasantly quiet. "Compulsions and control?" He knew Lucien had been turned a decade before he had found Roman, but the other vampire never spoke of any other of their kind.

"The one who turned me taught me," Luc replied, the pleased look falling off his face.

"Where is he now?"

Lucien shrugged in that careless way he had, but something pained passed over his face. "He left," he answered shortly.

"Why?" Roman knew he was prying, but his desire to know more overrode any thoughts of propriety.

Lucien sighed, leaning his head against the back of his chair. "I don't think he was ever looking for a long-term companion. He was...strange. Monstrous." A small smirk. "More monstrous even than us, I mean. He barely seemed human sometimes. I think he turned me for the fun of it. He had eaten his fill already, saw me there dying, thought it would be fun, maybe? He stuck around long enough to teach me the basics, but that was it."

Roman felt a surge of disquiet run through him. "And that is what you plan to do? Leave me after I have mastered...all this?" He gestured vaguely.

Lucien lifted his head and smiled at him then, and there was still hints of blood at the corners of his mouth. "No. I'm not leaving." He stretched forward in his chair, leaning over toward Roman. "You know, I wasn't planning to turn anyone. I felt like I would be...dooming...whoever I chose. But then I saw you dying, and you looked so hopeful at the offer of a second chance. And you reminded me of me. I hadn't wanted to die either. And I'm glad to still be alive, even as a monster. But I never wanted to be alone."

"A monster," Roman mused. "So you really think we are both damned, then?"

Lucien shook his head. "I don't know. My maker told me we won't age and that we are very hard to kill." He grinned slyly. "Let's just live forever, never die, and never have to find out one way or another."

He was such a conundrum, this man. One part doom and gloom, the other part sly mischief. Roman wondered which part was real and which was the front.

And forever was such a long, long time to consider. Roman didn't know what to do with the thought of it, the weight of it.

Lucien reached out a hand and placed it on top of Roman's. "I mean it. I don't want to be alone forever. I wanted a family before. We can't have children, and we can't go back to our old families now that we're monsters. So we'll be each other's family, yes? Brothers."

Roman felt some of the weight of that "forever" ease in his chest. It wasn't the life he'd thought he'd have, but Lucien was right—Roman hadn't wanted to die on that battlefield. And he didn't want to be alone either.

Roman nodded at his friend, his maker. "Brothers, then."

Roman swallowed against the lump in his throat as he pulled into the parking lot on the corner of First and Ash. Luc had never wanted to be alone, and now he had been, for decades. And it hadn't been serving the older vampire well at all.

Roman spotted the man of the hour leaning against the hood of a black car, arms crossed but posture otherwise relaxed. He was wearing a leather jacket and dark jeans, sunglasses protecting his demon's eyes from the sunlight.

Roman parked in the lot, keeping a healthy amount of space between Luc's car and his own. There was a large building, one that had clearly seen better days, with a For Lease sign in the window, behind them. The neighborhood was noticeably quiet for so early in the morning.

Roman stepped out of his car, making his way over to the front to lean against it as well, imitating Luc's stance. Luc eyed him all the while, any thoughts hidden behind his dark shades.

"You wanted to see me?" Luc's voice was mild, but Roman wasn't fooled into any false sense of comfort.

"I did." Roman kept his voice equally calm. "Our last conversation ended a bit...abruptly."

Luc smirked at him then.

Roman continued, "You've been trying to get my attention for an awfully long time, Luc. What do you want from me, really? Do you even know?"

Luc tilted his head. "And you felt you had to lure me out to the middle of bumfuck nowhere to have this conversation why?"

"You know why." Roman tried his best to keep the growl out of his voice. "I don't want you anywhere near my mate."

"Ah, yes." Luc's smirk grew, fangs glinting from between his lips. "Your precious little mate. What a lovely choice you've made. He's so...cute. So breakable."

It took all Roman's self-control to keep his muscles from tensing and his demon from growling. He knew Luc was trying to rile him up, set him off. For someone who'd been trying to get Roman's attention for decades, the man couldn't seem to resist antagonizing him once he got it.

"I know you aren't really feral," Roman bit out, trying to move the subject off Danny. "Your actions have always been too deliberate, too calculated. So are you really just a run-of-the-mill violent psychopath now or is there actually something you want from me?"

Luc straightened from his slouch, uncrossing his arms and sliding his hands into his pockets. Roman did tense then, preparing himself to be rushed, possibly with a hidden weapon, but the other vampire didn't make any move toward him. "You know," Luc mused, "for the longest time, after the dust settled and my rage died down a little, I wanted you back. My friend. My brother. But you kept running away. Wouldn't let me get close."

Familiar guilt tugged at Roman. Past failures, past cowardice. He wished suddenly that he could see Luc's eyes.

Luc carried on, "I figured I was too wild for you now. Too aggressive, too violent. You were clinging with both hands to your own humanity, and I was a risk to that." He began stepping closer, but Roman held his ground. "So I started thinking. If you were just a little more like me, we could be brothers again. If you weren't so caught up in your own control. So focused on your own sanity."

Roman tried to make sense of what he was hearing. "You were, what, trying to push me into becoming feral?"

Luc shrugged, halting his forward progress a few feet from Roman. "I wouldn't go that far. I just wanted you a little...untethered. Thought maybe if you had to cut ties with humanity for a bit, had to keep moving, you might welcome your old friend back."

"You were murdering people just to keep me on the move and push me back into your brotherly arms? A little extreme, do you not think?"

"I never killed anyone who didn't deserve it. Mostly."

So Danny had been right—Luc was choosing his victims deliberately. Not completely lost, then.

Roman took his own step forward, remaining just out of Luc's reach. "And if I were to have you back in my life, how could I be assured Danny would be safe?"

Luc laughed then. It wasn't the old, carefree laugh Roman had loved to hear from his friend once upon a time. It was cold. Bitter. "I think you misunderstand. I *wanted* you back. Past tense, mon ami. Things have changed—for the both of us, I think."

Roman wasn't exactly surprised. He couldn't see the pair of them picking up where they had left off either. "And what do you want now, Luc?"

"Before I answer that, I want to know something."

Roman nodded for him to continue.

"What made you a believer? Why are you so certain, now, that you've found your mate?"

Even with the sunglasses, Roman could feel the intensity of Luc's gaze as he asked the question. Roman considered not answering, considered pushing the conversation away from Danny again, but if some honesty was required to end this toxic chase, Roman needed to provide it. "I could just feel it. When I met him. My demon...calmed. My mind cleared. I just...wanted him. *Want* him. I can already feel him tethering me, and he hasn't even turned yet."

Roman watched as Luc's face tightened and his lips twitched. "Fascinating," the other vampire murmured.

"Is that how you felt about Victoria?"

"You know what I want now?" Luc asked, ignoring Roman's question. "I want to *know*." Luc took off his sunglasses, tucking them into his jacket pocket. Black eyes settled on Roman's. "You said—even your little mate has said—that Victoria couldn't have been my mate, seeing as how she chose to die rather than be with me. I would think it goes to say, then, that *your* mate, choosing between death or turning...he would choose you, right? I want to *know*, Roman."

There was a sinking feeling in Roman's stomach. "You will not touch him," he growled.

Roman barely saw Luc move. Roman's reflexes were accelerated even in his human form but not as much as they would have been with his demon out. And Luc's demon was always out.

Before he knew it, Roman found himself on his stomach on the asphalt, his arm pulled back at a painful angle and Luc's knee digging into his back.

Roman heard the crunch and felt the white-hot heat of his arm breaking. He stifled his groan. "What is this, your go-to move now?"

He had been so stupid. He should have had his demon out the whole conversation. He should have been on higher alert. He stupidly hadn't wanted to antagonize Luc, had wanted their meeting to be friendly. *Friendly.*

"Don't worry," Luc was saying. "I won't kill you, mon ami." Roman felt the tug of Luc digging into Roman's back pocket, and then there was another crunch, this time the sound of metal and plastic splintering into pieces. Roman's cell phone. "Just don't want you giving away the game before it starts," Luc explained.

The older vampire shifted his weight, and he whispered in Roman's ear. "You see, I've thought about this. If it's really fated, you'll get there in time, won't you? You'll manage to turn him before I kill him. I want to see it. I want to *know*."

Roman felt both Luc's hands on his head then and had only a half second to register the sound of his own neck snapping before the world went dark.

—*ele*—

"Are you okay?"

Roman blinked slowly, and the silhouette of a man's head against a bright sky came into focus. Roman snapped his arm out—the one that didn't feel like it was on fire—and the man's resulting scream was cut off as Roman squeezed his neck firmly.

He held the man there in his line of sight, but it took Roman a minute to make out the details. Young face. Reddish hair. Terrified eyes.

Not Luc.

Merde. How long had he been out?

"I need your phone." Roman's voice came out hoarse. Not surprising after a broken neck.

The man whimpered, eyes wide.

"Give me your phone," Roman repeated. He put the weight of compulsion behind his words this time and watched dispassionately as the man fumbled a phone out of his back pocket and handed it over, Roman's hand firmly circling his neck all the while.

"Stay," Roman ordered, releasing the man from his grip in order to dial. He tried Danny's number first. No answer. Merde.

Roman kept his message brief. "Danny. Stay with Soren. Both of you run if you can. Luc is coming."

He tried Soren's number next, swore again in frustration, and left another message, brief and to the point. He didn't have time for anything else. He needed to get moving.

Roman stretched his neck carefully—tender but otherwise all right. He could tell his arm was still knitting itself back together, but that would take longer—it had been a messier break. He was relieved to see his car, at least, was still behind him.

Fucking Luc. He was a dead vampire walking.

"I'm taking this with me." Roman raised the phone to the stupefied man.

In a matter of minutes, he was back on the road, heading toward Danny as fast as he could make the useless hunk of metal move.

Roman had been so stupid. To think Luc cared more about their broken friendship than his obsession with fated mates. Luc been a man possessed from the beginning, from the very moment he'd heard about them, long before he'd even met Victoria.

Roman and Luc hadn't realized until they'd met Soren, over a century after Roman had been turned, what a disservice they had been done by Luc's maker leaving the way he had. They had been isolated, with Luc just a baby vampire himself. They had known next to nothing about other vampires, about themselves. They had thought they really had forever.

It was Soren who had told them about the eventual erosion of their humanity, and it had been a horrifying revelation for the both of them. That they wouldn't be able, after all, to outlast death and any repercussions. They would be damned, just as Luc had feared.

But then Soren had told them about fated mates, about tethering their humanity and grounding their demons with a connection to another soul.

Eternal life. Eternal love.

Roman had been skeptical, but Lucien had been hopeful.

So hopeful.

Someone to keep him sane, someone to prevent damnation, someone who wouldn't leave.

And then those hopes had been dashed to bits when Victoria had died, leaving him mateless, with their bond as brothers broken.

It was heartbreaking, but Roman couldn't find any pity for his friend when now the psychopath was going to use Danny as a fucking test subject.

Roman had to get there in time. Losing Danny was not an option he would accept.

For the first time since he had been shunned by his family as a monster, Roman prayed.

Nineteen

Danny

Danny was in pain.

Roman's absence was an ever-present ache in his chest, which was ridiculous—his vampire had barely been gone a day. But nonetheless, there it was. Pain.

Danny couldn't help but fear that their goodbyes over the phone were the last they'd say to each other.

From across the kitchen counter, Soren rolled his pale eyes at him.

"What?" Danny snapped. "I didn't even say anything."

"No," Soren drawled. "You've just sighed approximately five hundred times in the past ten minutes."

A blatant exaggeration.

Soren rolled his eyes again. Danny hoped they got stuck that way if the blond vampire kept it up. "He'll be fine, human."

Danny fiddled with his now empty coffee cup. He'd for some reason decided caffeine was the solution to missing Roman, but so far it had just added an elevated heart rate to his sad-sack symptoms. "You don't think Luc will hurt him?"

Soren made a noncommittal noise. "Hurt him, maybe. Kill him though? Probably not."

"*Probably* not?" Would Roman forgive him if Danny stabbed his annoying friend with a spoon?

Soren grinned that maniacal grin, but his eyes weren't unkind. "I wouldn't have let him go if I thought he'd get himself killed, human. There are very few people I actually like in this world. He's one of them."

"But what if...even then..." Danny forced himself to voice his fears out loud. "What if he decides to just keep moving? That's it not safe enough...or worth it...to come back."

Soren shook his head at Danny, exasperation in his voice. "He's not going to stay away from you forever. He *can't*."

"How do you know that though?"

"Because I believe you're mates. Real fated mates." Soren's grin dropped, and he looked at Danny seriously. "I've been around a long time, little human. And I wasn't always as isolated from the vampire world as I am now. I've seen mated pairs. I've talked to a few. And they all described a...pull to that other person. One that's stronger than anything they've felt, one that might not even make sense. I see that pull between you and Roman."

Danny didn't think he was imagining the wistful look in Soren's eyes. "And you've never felt that pull yourself?"

"You don't see me with a mate, do you?" Soren asked harshly.

"Sorry." Danny should really stop prying into other people's love lives.

"It's fine." Soren waved a hand at him, his mood turning in an instant, as it often did. "Go pick up your boring brother."

Danny huffed. "Will you stop calling him that? Just because he didn't entertain his stalker doesn't make him boring."

"No, his being boring makes him boring."

Danny wasn't so sure. He'd heard Soren talking to Roman earlier. He was pretty sure "boring" was Soren's code for "straight." Danny could have told Soren that his brother was bi and that Danny knew he'd been with men in the past.

But that wasn't Danny's truth to tell.

He kept his mouth shut about his brother. "I'll be back soon. Don't have any blood orgies while I'm gone."

"What's a blood orgy?" Soren sounded disturbingly intrigued.

"I don't know, it just sounds like something you'd do."

Soren's grin flashed again, more unhinged than ever. "It does, doesn't it?"

See? Disturbing.

Danny ignored an incoming call from an unknown number on the way to his car. Always with the spam phone calls.

He was feeling relieved and a little more hopeful as he drove to the hospital to pick up Gabe. Danny knew there were risks. He knew Roman wasn't out of danger, but there was a certain relief in hearing Soren validate what Danny felt on the inside—that he and Roman were connected. They were *mates*.

Danny was feeling that relief right up until the moment his car was run off the road.

⁓ℓℓℓ⁓

Danny blinked slowly, warm wetness running into his eyes. He wasn't sure if he'd actually lost consciousness or was just stunned.

Everything hurt.

He closed his eyes and tried to take mental stock of his injuries. His left shoulder and chest were agony—probably from where the seat belt had held him in when the car crashed. And he must have some sort of head injury, because that definitely wasn't rain dripping down off his forehead. He wasn't crushed into smithereens, though, so that was a plus. The other car must have hit the back end of his?

Danny hadn't even seen it coming. There hadn't been any cars around at all when he was passing through the intersection. The other driver must have been going at practically highway speeds.

An itchy panic was building under Danny's skin. He started to reach over to pull at the handle of his door with his right hand, but his healthcare training kicked in. He shouldn't be twisting or moving his neck at all. What if he had a spinal cord injury? Danny needed to keep still and wait for the paramedics.

Wait, had anyone even called the paramedics? Fuck, was the other car okay?

Danny was considering reaching blindly into his back pocket for his phone to call 911 when he heard the screeching sound of tearing metal. His door was being torn open.

No, not open. *Off.* Torn completely off its hinges.

Danny resisted the urge to turn his head to look at whoever was currently opening his car like a tin can. He was not going to paralyze himself out of curiosity. "Roman?" he asked hopefully.

He heard a murmured "how sweet" in response, but the ringing Danny was just now noticing in his ears made it hard to distinguish the voice. It wasn't Roman though. Danny would know *his* voice, even through the ringing.

"Soren?" he asked. *Please be Soren.*

"I'm afraid not." Strong hands ripped Danny's seat belt into pieces and grabbed him by the shoulders. Danny whimpered and shut his eyes tight as white heat ran through his left shoulder at the rough touch.

A feeling of dread came over him, followed immediately by grief and terror. Danny knew that voice now. And if Luc was here, what had happened to Roman?

"Tell—tell me. Is...alive?" Danny tried to get the words out clearly, but his mouth was having trouble following instructions. He managed a sort of slurred whisper. Hopefully it was good enough.

He must have made some sort of sense, because the rough hands paused in pulling him out of the car. Danny didn't exactly see because he was refusing to open his eyes at the moment. If he couldn't see what was happening, it wasn't happening. Right?

"Ohh, little human. You're covered in blood. You smell delicious, by the way. Probably have some internal hemorrhaging as well. Definitely a fractured clavicle here on the left. Overall, you must be in excruciating pain, and you're asking after the welfare of your beloved?" There was taunting in Luc's voice, but also...envy? Danny's stomach churned as he was lifted abruptly into strong arms. "You should worry about yourself now, Daniel."

Danny was definitely worrying about himself, but he didn't feel like telling Luc that. The fact was if Luc was here and Roman was...gone...then it was more than likely Danny was going to die very, very soon.

He found himself swimming in and out of consciousness as he was carried away. They seemed to be walking some distance, at least as far as Danny could tell with his eyes closed and his brain only aware half the time.

A memory surfaced. Some stranger-danger presentation in junior high, where a police officer had warned Danny's class their chances of surviving a kidnapping dropped exponentially if they were ever brought to a secondary location by the kidnapper. Did those statistics hold true for vampire kidnappings?

Danny almost giggled at the thought, which considering his most likely imminent death, did not bode well for his mental state. Maybe he had a concussion. Or a brain bleed.

When he surfaced again, Danny was being placed with more gentleness than he would have expected onto a hard, cold floor. He opened his eyes fully for the first time since his car door had been ripped off. Gray concrete. Lots of exposed beams. Danny was in some kind of...abandoned warehouse?

How cliché.

Danny heard the rustling of clothing as Luc settled in beside him, and he decided to finally stop being a baby and face the vampire. He even turned his head to look because, hey, spinal precautions probably weren't important at this point anymore, right?

Luc was looking completely untouched by the accident, the asshole. Barely a hair out of place. Maybe he hadn't even been in the car. Maybe he'd just, like, tossed an SUV at Danny. How strong exactly were vampires? It felt like something Danny needed to know right about now. Why hadn't he asked Roman more specifics?

Luc smirked down at him. "How are you feeling?"

"I hurt." Danny's voice might have sounded a little petulant, but it was warranted as far as he was concerned.

"Yes, well, sorry about that. I thought maybe the crash would kill you, but I suppose vehicular homicide isn't my specialty."

"Why do you want to kill me anyway?" Danny was relieved that he seemed to be capable of normal speech again. Maybe he didn't have a brain bleed after all. "Does Roman finding love really make you that angry?"

Luc's smirk dropped, and he stared at Danny for a long moment. The vampire didn't look angry exactly. More...contemplative. "I thought that was it, at first. When I realized what he thought he'd found with you. I'll admit there's a part of me that goes a little crazy at the thought of Roman finding eternal happiness after sabotaging mine."

"He didn't sabotage—"

Luc shushed Danny. "Don't start. I don't want to talk about Victoria. And I don't think you want to piss me off right now, hm?"

Right. Because there was a difference between a quick, relatively painless death and a slow, very painful death. Call him crazy, but Danny had never been much into the idea of being tortured.

Luc nodded approvingly at his silence. "Tell me about how he made you feel. Your mate," he demanded.

Made. Past tense. Danny couldn't let himself dwell on that, couldn't let himself think that maybe Roman hadn't made it. If Danny was leaving this world, he wanted to leave believing Roman was still in it.

"Why would I tell you?" There it was, petulance again.

"Because I want to know."

Danny considered refusing to answer out of spite. But maybe if Danny stalled, Soren would still be able to find them. Assuming Soren was even okay. "He makes me feel...safe."

There was a pause. Luc seemed to be waiting for Danny to say more. Then, "That's it? That's your description of your *fated mate?* Safety? That's just a glorified bodyguard."

Danny snorted, which ended up being kind of gross because it felt like maybe some blood bubbled out of his nose when he did it. Ew. "You're so centered on violence you don't even know what I mean."

"Enlighten me."

"Before I met him, I was so...lonely. And tired. And afraid. Afraid of living my life. Of letting anyone in. When I met him, he was clearly dangerous. But even so, I felt...safe. I knew he wouldn't hurt me." Danny narrowed his eyes at Luc. "Beyond the physical. I knew he'd hold on to my heart. That he'd protect it. Even when my mind was trying to scare me with my own insecurities, it was like my soul knew it. *Knows* it."

Danny was panting for breath by the end of his explanation. Speechifying was exhausting when your body was broken, turned out. Now would probably be a good time to go to the hospital.

Except, right, he'd been kidnapped by a psychotic vampire with a thirst for vengeance. No hospital for Danny.

"Victoria never felt safe with me," Luc mused. "No matter how wild, how joyful she seemed. There was always an undercurrent of fear. I could smell it. Taste it. Always."

I don't fucking blame her, was the thought Danny sagely decided not to voice out loud.

"You really don't fear him?" Luc asked.

"Never."

Luc hummed. "He's not dead, you know. He's on his way to you now. Your knight in fucking shining armor."

The relief was so overwhelming that Danny found it hard to breathe. Or maybe he just had a punctured lung. Luc was watching his reaction with interest.

"So what's the plan?" Danny asked between gasps. "You're going to kill me before he can get here? Force him to live with the same rage and guilt you've been living with?"

Luc shrugged a shoulder. "Possibly. I wanted to see. Special fated mates, he should get here in time, right?"

That didn't really add up to Danny. "If you want to take free will out of the equation entirely, I guess?"

Luc ignored him after that.

Danny waited for what felt like forever for the attack, but it didn't come. Luc never made a move.

Danny had a realization. "You *want* him to get here in time, don't you?"

Luc smiled down at him, but it didn't reach his black eyes. "Why would I want that? You think I care about your pitiful life that much?"

"Not me. You want to know if fated mates are real. You *want* them to be real. Victoria's death rocked your faith in them, and you've been living a life of misery and loneliness ever since."

"Watch yourself," Luc chided mildly.

"Am I wrong?" Danny was on a roll now. "You want to know if your person could still be out there. I get it. But if you kill me before Roman gets here, he'll kill you, and you'll never find out for sure."

"If I kill you, and it turns out they're not real, I'll be glad to let him." Luc said the words so quietly Danny almost didn't catch them.

And there it was. Luc was still desperate for a mate.

"If you let yourself go completely, become feral, it won't matter if they're real. You'll be lost before you ever find yours. Is vengeance really worth that?"

Luc cocked his head, but maybe he heard something outside the warehouse, because he only seemed half-focused on Danny. "You've got a point there." He paused a beat longer, listening to something Danny couldn't hear. Then he smiled, fangs glinting, and focused back on Danny. "Still, I should give Roman one last little gift, hm?"

Then Luc was on him, and the world around Danny blurred. A sharp sting, and then Danny felt like his blood was boiling. Like he was being burned alive from the inside out. He tried to scream, but all he could manage was a whimper.

The last thing he heard before the world turned to black was a cry of rage.

It sounded like heartbreak.

Twenty

Danny

Fear. Worry. Guilt. Worry. Rage. Worry.

Danny opened his eyes. He stared at the ceiling above him slowly coming into focus, much lower than the one from the warehouse. And he was no longer on a hard cement floor but in a comfortable bed. His own bed—he could smell the familiar scent of his detergent, as well as hints of himself and Roman.

Danny felt...different. He was having a hard time coming back to himself. How had he gotten here? He tried to remember.

Danny could remember...pain. First the sharp pain of traumatic wounds from the crash. Right, he'd been in a car crash. That was coming back to him. But that earlier pain was overshadowed by the last moments he remembered, after Luc had pounced.

"Danny." Roman's voice, husky and strained, broke through Danny's remembrances.

Roman was here.

Danny sat up quicker than he should have been able to, turning to look to the side. Roman had a chair pulled up to the edge of the bed and was leaning forward, hands clasped tightly together on his knees. Looking at his vampire, Danny realized he had never seen Roman look truly miserable before. The vampire's normally pristine suit was wrinkled and covered in dirt and other sketchy bits that looked suspiciously like dried blood. His straight dark hair was mussed, and his blue eyes were rimmed in red.

Had Danny's vampire been crying?

"Hi," Danny greeted a little lamely. He'd expected his voice to come out as a croak, but he didn't sound even the slightest bit hoarse. Danny sounded...refreshed. Taking mental stock, he *felt* refreshed. Which was odd. His whole body should have been one big ache. He should have been in the hospital, especially after Luc had...had...

Luc had *bitten* him.

Asshole.

Danny lifted a hand to his throat, pressing his fingers along the side, but he couldn't feel anything unusual there—no gaping wound, no tender, bruised skin.

"Where is he?" Danny asked.

"He's...contained. You're safe." Roman didn't have to ask who Danny meant by "he."

Danny eyed Roman, trying to see any obvious injuries, resisting the urge to leap out of bed and into his lover's arms. Roman sounded worried. He looked worried. He *felt* worried. The demon inside him was restless, concerned about his mate—concerned about Danny.

Hold up.

Danny really could *feel* Roman's worry. He closed his eyes and focused on the strange sensation, a part of Danny but also not. Worry. Anger. And love. So much love for Danny that it was overwhelming in its intensity.

Danny opened his eyes in time to see Roman looking momentarily stunned by the wide grin Danny suddenly couldn't help. "I can feel you," Danny explained, awe in his voice.

Roman nodded, and there was a spike of another emotion—shame, maybe?—flaring up through their connection. "I can feel you too, little king. It's an effect of the mate bond, I think. Now that it's been...solidified."

Danny pondered that for a second. Their mate bond had been solidified? Had there been some sort of ceremony Danny had missed out on while he'd been unconscious?

"You must be hungry," Roman said, his tone strangely cautious.

Danny was, in fact. Hungry in a way he hadn't really felt before. It wasn't the gnawing feeling in the pit of his stomach he was used to feeling at the end of a long shift without a chance for a lunch break. Or rather, that was there, but there was also a...buzzing under Danny's skin. Like an internal itch that needed to be scratched.

And then the pieces were coming together. Danny had been bitten, drained to the point of death. His body, which should be broken, was feeling shiny and new. His mate bond was properly in place. And he was hungry for something other than food.

Danny focused inward, not on his connection with Roman but on himself. Danny could feel it, pulsing under his skin, now that he was paying attention. There was a whole new presence there. It was hungry, definitely—animalistic, even—like all Danny's baser instincts given their own voice inside his head, their own entity inside his body.

But the new presence wasn't raging or feral or any of the other things Danny had been warned about a new vampire feeling. It was relatively...calm. Soothed by Roman at their side. Danny could even feel that new part of him calling out to Roman's restless demon, trying to calm him in turn.

"I'm a vampire." He said it out loud, needing to hear it.

Luc hadn't killed Danny. But he'd turned him.

Danny wasn't human anymore.

He looked back to Roman, understanding the worry in his vampire's eyes now. It wasn't about Danny's injuries. It was about Danny's *reaction*.

"I'm sorry." Roman's voice was barely above a whisper.

"Why?" Danny asked. "You didn't turn me." A troubling thought came to him. "Did you—did you not want me to turn after all? Were you hoping I would stay human?"

Roman was shaking his head before the words were fully out of Danny's mouth. "He took away your choice, Danny. You were not yet ready. You needed more time, and he took that away from you."

"He did." Danny nodded. "That was very rude of him."

Roman's bark of laughter in response to Danny's blasé reply seemed to surprise even him, but his expression immediately shifted back to concern. "I am so sorry, mon amour. I did not get to you in time. I did not protect you as I should have. I failed you."

Overwhelmed by the depth of Roman's self-blame, Danny reached out and grabbed his hand, pulling the vampire out of his chair and into the bed beside him. "Shh. Shh. None of that. You're not going to hold yourself responsible for Luc's actions. We're just...not going to do that."

Roman grunted in response, unconvinced, but he let Danny arrange him so he was lying on the bed next to Danny, close enough that their sides were touching and Danny was able to rest his head on his vampire's shoulder.

Holy hell, his mate smelled good. So good. Danny could make out so many nuances to Roman's scent that he hadn't been able to before—each spice its own distinct note.

Vampire senses, hell yeah.

Danny's hearing was heightened too. He could make out Gabe and Soren whispering together downstairs. Someone must have picked up Gabe from the hospital after all, then. That was good. Danny pushed down thoughts of his brother's possible reaction to Danny's less-than-human state. Now was not the time. Danny focused on his other senses instead. Everything *looked* sharper too. The sunlight coming through the window was even causing a bit of an ache behind his eyes, though nothing unbearable.

He wondered if his taste would be sharpened too. Which made him think of tasting the yummy-smelling vampire sitting right next to him. Would Roman let Danny lick him all over and compare the difference?

No, not the time. Focus, he told himself.

Danny cleared his throat. "I feel pretty good. Considering." That was putting it mildly. The fatigue Danny had been feeling for—well, basically for years now—was fully gone for the first time. He hadn't even realized how foggy it had made his head until it was gone.

Would this clearheadedness last though? "Am I going to get worse than this?" he asked. "I'm hungry, but I'm—I'm okay. I don't feel like Mr. Demon is going to take over and get all snarly or anything."

"No, you should not worsen," Roman answered gently. He had started nuzzling his chin against the top of Danny's head, as if once he'd gotten permission to touch him, the vampire couldn't get enough. Danny could *feel* the satisfaction his mate's demon was getting from the physical contact. So cool. "New vampires usually wake up feeling already out of their minds. They then gradually improve and settle. They eventually devolve again, but that can take centuries. I think it may be the bond. I have never met a bonded pair, but I think maybe having been turned when you had already found your tethered soul... There must be benefits we had not considered."

"So cool." Danny said it out loud this time.

"You think so?" Roman's voice was hesitant, almost shy.

"Duh," Danny answered. "I'm a freaking magical creature, Roman. How is that not cool?"

Roman huffed a small laugh into Danny's hair. "I thought maybe you would be a bit more...put out?...having your choice taken away."

Danny considered that point. "Well," he reasoned, "maybe not ideal circumstances. I didn't enjoy the car crash part *at all*. But I thought I was going to die, and I really didn't want to, and now here I am, feeling good as new. Besides, my main worries were about hurting people, being out of control, having to leave my mom because I couldn't pull off pretending to be human. But if I'm all chill and tethered and whatnot, I don't have to worry about all that."

Danny could feel the rush of Roman's immense relief as the vampire pulled Danny onto his lap, holding him tight—tighter than he ever would have held Danny's human body. "I was so scared, lovely. When I found you, you looked—you—I thought—"

He'd thought Danny had died.

Danny could feel the grief Roman had gone through and decided to try something. He focused on pumping all the love and reassurance he could muster through their bond. He was rewarded with a small gasp from Roman, who leaned back enough to look into Danny's eyes. "I can feel that, little king."

Danny wriggled in Roman's lap, immensely pleased with himself. He was such a good vampire mate already. He was going to be fucking amazing at this.

And now Danny was feeling...something else. A telltale bulge under his ass. Danny hummed, wriggling himself a little more deliberately now.

"Stop that," Roman chided, tightening his arms to try and still Danny's body.

"Why?" Danny pouted. "I think my demon wants to come out and play with your demon. And by play, I mean fu—"

Roman's hand covered Danny's mouth. Spoilsport. Now that Danny had started thinking about sex, his demon was taking a real serious interest in the matter. He still had that buzzing sensation under his skin that he now recognized as a hunger for blood, but now it was hungry for Roman too. Smart demon. They could definitely both agree on that.

Danny tried to tell Roman all this with his eyes, but Roman just shook his head at him.

"There are things we need to deal with first."

***

There was a vampire chained in Danny's garage. Huh.

It was a strange contrast, seeing someone looking like the captured snitch in a mafia movie right next to Danny's washer-dryer unit.

Luc had definitely seen better days. His face was a bruised, bloody mess, and Danny couldn't begin to imagine how bad his initial injuries must have been for them not to have healed with his accelerated vampire healing yet.

Danny stepped closer, mindful of keeping a decent distance between them. He'd asked Roman to stay inside the house. Danny could feel how anxious and upset Roman was to be left out of the room, but he couldn't imagine holding this conversation with his overprotective mate growling in the corner.

Luc smirked up at him. "Oh, look. It's the new and improved Daniel." His voice was hoarse and rusty, like maybe his vocal cords were recovering from being squeezed in a choke hold.

Danny was having a hard time feeling bad about that.

"Why didn't you run?" he asked the restrained vampire. "I'm sure Roman was sufficiently distracted by my, you know, apparent death to get you a clean getaway."

"Oh, he was." Luc looked unrepentant. "You should have seen the poor guy's face."

"Then why didn't you?"

Luc looked up at Danny, his smirk gone and his eyes hungry. "I told you: I wanted to know. Well?" he asked, urgency in his voice.

Danny knew what Luc was asking, and he had a choice to make. He could choose cruelty. He could punish Luc, never letting him know for certain whether fated mates really existed, whether there was any hope out there for him.

It was very, very tempting.

Danny sighed. He wasn't vicious enough for that. Maybe that made him a fool, and a bad vampire candidate, but he could understand Luc's pain all too well. He could understand the loneliness and rage that had driven him to be the way he was. To do the things he had done. Danny didn't like any of it, but he could understand it.

"We've mated," he said. "I'm sure of it. I can feel a connection to him now, to his feelings, to his demon."

Luc took a deep breath and let it out slowly. "I'm glad to know. Even if I never—even if this is it. Thank you for telling me." He pointed with his chin at the stairs. "You can go tell your mate I'm ready for him to finish the job now, if you like."

Danny shook his head, not understanding the request. "What?"

A grim smile took over Luc's face. "You don't really think he's going to let me live after all I've done to you, do you?"

"I don't...I mean..." Fuck. Was that really why Roman had kept Luc here? For Danny to gloat over him and then have Roman turn around and kill him?

It would be hard to argue that the world wouldn't be safer with Luc gone. Except...

"Tell me something," said Danny. "Why do you kill the people you kill?"

Luc laughed without humor. "Because I'm a monster, obviously."

Danny shook his head, frustrated. "Why do you kill the *specific* people that you choose to kill?"

They had a bit of a standoff then, Luc staring at Danny, searching for something in his face. After a few more moments of this, the vampire gave a defeated sigh. "After what happened...with Victoria...something in me snapped. I could feel it happen. My monster was taking over, demanding more. More blood, more violence. But I didn't want to—I wasn't ready to lose myself completely to damnation. I found a way to temper the cravings. Finding despicable people, those who hurt others, those who don't deserve the lives they have. I thought maybe if I fed my monster's wants, without giving in completely to chaos, I could put off the inevitable. Keep from turning completely feral."

Luc was such a strange conundrum. Violent and cruel, vengeful and sadistic. But he hadn't killed Danny when he'd had the opportunity. Even if it had been for his own selfish reasons, he'd instead given Danny a chance at forever. A chance at eternity with the one he loved.

"You know," Danny said slowly. "If you hadn't been chasing Roman these past few decades, he never would have ended up here, in this town, at this time, with me."

"And?"

Danny shrugged. "I never gave much thought to fate. Life just seems too cruel sometimes to think there's any higher purpose. But maybe some things do happen for a reason. And maybe your mate is still out there and everything up until now will bring you closer to finding them."

The hope that appeared on Luc's face was painful to witness in its intensity. Danny took a few steps closer to the bound vampire, bending slightly so they were eye to eye. "If we let you go, are you going to rampage around, murdering innocents? Will we find out you've gone feral a few weeks from now, that you've let go of your humanity completely...or will you hold on?"

Luc's black eyes met Danny's. "I can hold on." The sincerity in his voice was unmistakable.

Danny straightened. "Let me see what I can do."

Danny left the broken vampire behind him, heading back into the house. Roman was waiting on the other side of the garage door, clearly on the verge of heading there himself.

One look at Danny's face, and Roman was shaking his head. "No. Absolutely not."

Danny blew out a breath. "We can't just murder him in cold blood, Roman."

"What do you even mean, cold blood?" Roman's voice was harsh. "He is a *killer*. He hurt your brother. He almost *killed* you."

Fair, fair, and fair. But still. "He didn't though."

"And what if he comes right back?" Roman drew a hand roughly through his hair, his aggravation clear. "I will not lose you. I refuse to let him loose, knowing you will be at risk the moment he decides vengeance is worth more than a truce."

"He won't come back." Danny didn't know why, but he was certain of it. "He just proved to himself that mates are real. He has *hope* again, Roman. He's not going to jeopardize that just to mess with us for funsies."

"You think that monster has a *mate* out there?" Roman was staring at Danny in disbelief.

"People marry serial killers in prison all the time. A lid for every pot, right?"

Roman's expression hadn't changed, but Danny could feel his mate's resolve wavering.

He pushed. "Why didn't you kill him right away? Just to torture him?" Roman said nothing, and Danny pressed on mercilessly. "I don't think you really want him dead. Trust me. Please. If he comes back, if he threatens us in any way, I'll let you put him down. I'll *help* you put him down."

Danny stepped closer to his mate, winding his arms around Roman's neck, pressing his whole body flush against Roman's, head to toe. "Please. Let's get him out of here. The sooner he's gone, the sooner we can be alone and the sooner you can be inside me."

It was amazing, feeling the bolt of lust from Roman through their connection. Lust that reflected Danny's own. He knew he was employing a bit of a cheap trick, but he was also being honest. It felt like it had been years since he'd had his mate inside him, and Danny needed it now.

He needed to be claimed and to claim in turn. He could feel the baby demon inside him yearning, and it only magnified his own want.

Jesus, Danny felt like a teenage boy again. A restless ball of horny hormones. He was already hard, and he couldn't help thrusting himself against Roman slightly, trying to get some friction. And then, to his astonishment, he could feel his fangs popping out.

Did he just pop the vampire version of a boner?

There was a strange internal shift as, for the first time, Danny could feel his demon coming to the forefront of his consciousness. Danny was still there, still had some control over his body and his thoughts, but it was like letting a different part of his subconscious take the wheel.

"Please, Roman," he heard himself purr. He actually *purred*.

Roman's eyes had gone black, likely mirroring Danny's own, and his voice took on that huskier growl it did when his demon was starting to take charge. "So you are a new vampire in some ways after all, little king. Are you getting restless in there? Do you need my hands on you? My cock inside you?"

Danny nodded frantically, finding words a little difficult now. Roman bent his head and nuzzled into Danny's neck, sighing against Danny's skin. "Fine. We'll let him go."

Danny was starting to get a little fuzzy about what they were even talking about, his hunger for his mate overwhelming his senses—why weren't they in a bed yet?—but he nodded anyway.

"But," Roman added, lifting his head, "we are having Soren drop him off somewhere. I am done with it all. And you, my little mate, are coming with me."

With that, he threw Danny over his shoulder, heading toward the stairs up to Danny's bedroom.

Twenty-one

Roman

Roman gave a light slap to the pert, denim-clad ass hanging over his shoulder, gratified when Danny gave a little yelp in response.

Roman still had his doubts about letting Luc go free, but Danny's ploy had worked all too well. Roman could think of nothing now but claiming his mate. Add that to the fact that he had never relished the idea of killing his old friend, and Roman was a lost cause.

It had all been too much: the mind-numbing grief of thinking he'd lost Danny, the shock of the mating bond snapping into place, the frustration in being made to stand back while his mate faced Luc one last time.

Roman needed tactile assurance that Danny was okay, that Danny was *his*.

Ours, his demon growled.

Ours, Roman agreed.

He managed to gather his thoughts enough to call out to Soren in the kitchen on the way up the stairs, "Drop Luc out of town somewhere."

He ignored Soren's squawking protest in response. He knew Soren would do as he asked. The blond vampire was feeling guilty enough having left Danny out of his sights, allowing Luc to get to him.

Roman didn't actually blame his friend for that—they had both thought Luc was out of town and Danny safe—but he would use that guilt in his favor for this last Luc-related task.

Entering Danny's bedroom, Roman tossed his mate onto the bed before slamming the door shut. Danny bounced once on the mattress, but in the blink of an eye, he was upright again, kneeling at the edge of the bed, black eyes on Roman.

Roman was momentarily stunned to see his mate move so fast, but he recovered quickly. "Take off your clothes," Roman growled, unbuttoning his own shirt.

"No." Danny grinned at him cheekily, and Roman raised one eyebrow, his fingers stilling on his last button.

"I thought you wanted me inside you, lovely."

"I do," Danny agreed, tilting his head to the side. "But I want to do this my own way."

He launched himself at Roman, twisting them in the last moment so the momentum landed Roman on his back on the bed, with Danny straddled over his hips.

Roman was a little impressed.

He smirked up at his lovely mate, whose eyes had returned to their usual deep brown, pupils dilated. Apparently Danny was finally losing a little of that unnatural control he had over his demon, if he was shifting back and forth like this.

Roman couldn't help but feel pleased it was Danny's desire for him that was the cause.

"Are you wanting to play, little king?" Roman crooned, tracing his fingers over Danny's jawline.

Danny nodded, but it was an absent gesture. He was more focused on eyeing Roman's body like it was his next meal.

"I want to see what you taste like now," Danny murmured before ripping the rest of Roman's clothes right off him. He hummed in satisfaction when the fabric tore easily under his fingers.

Roman was enchanted by Danny's delight in his own strength. This was a whole new side to his mate, and Roman loved every bit of it.

He had been so worried Danny would be grieving the loss of his humanity, the loss of his own choice in his transition, when he awoke, but his mate was clearly reveling in his newfound abilities. Perhaps that would change when the shock wore off, but if Danny wanted to play in this way with his new senses, Roman was more than willing to be his mate's guinea pig.

"You can do whatever you want to me, little king, " he purred. "I am at your mercy, as usual."

Danny smiled sweetly at him before leaning to kiss Roman deeply, pushing his tongue into Roman's mouth with a new aggression that sent all the blood rushing straight to Roman's cock.

"I know you are," Danny whispered when he was done with his plundering.

Cocky little thing.

Roman knew he wasn't, really. Even after Danny's transition, he could still easily overpower the smaller vampire. But he'd let it slide for now. Although, there was potential there. Roman could easily imagine a night of battling for dominance in the bedroom. The thought made him growl in arousal.

His mate was already moving down Roman's body, licking and nibbling at all the skin along the way. He stopped at Roman's cock, engulfing it in his hot mouth in one deep swallow.

Roman's back arched off the bed, and he almost lost it completely when Danny hummed around his length, only saved the embarrassment by the relief of Danny popping off him to lick the precum off his lips, muttering, seemingly to himself, "Fucking delicious."

His mate was going to kill him at this rate.

Danny began ripping off his own clothes, and his weight disappeared briefly from Roman's hips before he was back in an instant, brandishing lube.

Roman reached out a hand in demand. "Let me."

"No." Danny smacked his hand away with another cheeky grin. "This is my rodeo."

Roman could only watch in helpless desire as Danny reached behind himself with lubed fingers to open himself up for Roman's cock.

It was one of the sexiest sights he'd ever laid eyes on. Danny's head thrown back, eyes closed, full mouth slack with pleasure. Roman was pleased to see his mate's whole upper body still apparently flushed a rosy pink when he was turned on, even after the change.

It was Roman's favorite color.

He could feel his nails ripping through the sheets and into Danny's mattress with the effort to keep his hands to himself, but Roman kept himself under control, allowing his mate to take the lead. For now.

After what felt like an eternity, Danny lowered himself onto Roman's cock with single-minded determination.

Roman moaned low, closing his eyes at the full-body pleasure he felt as Danny's tight heat gripped him. This was where Roman belonged. Inside his mate.

Danny didn't wait any time at all to adjust to Roman's size, immediately snapping his hips forward, riding Roman with abandon. Any attempts Roman made to grab onto his hips, to lead the pace, were met with snarls, his hands immediately slapped away.

Roman had no choice but to relax back and allow his mate to use his body as he wanted.

When Danny was on the verge of coming, his body tensing and losing its rhythm, he stilled completely.

"Move," Roman growled. He was so close. They both were.

Danny ignored his request. "Can I? Do vampires ever...?" He was eyeing Roman's neck, and heat swirled in Roman's belly as he realized what his mate was asking.

"They do," he answered. "You won't get any sustenance from it. But it is a form of...intimacy...for our kind."

Danny's eyes turned black, his fangs dropped, and he bit into Roman's neck without any further warning. Roman relished the sharp sting, even more so when Danny started to move his hips again.

Roman's mate drank deeply, growling in a way that Roman found positively adorable.

Roman grabbed Danny's ass with both hands, finally pulling his mate's hips into the fast, ruthless pace he'd been craving. This time Danny let him without protest.

It took only a few of those fast, deep thrusts before Danny released Roman's neck with a groan. Warm wetness hit Roman's chest as his mate found his release.

Roman growled, lifting his hands from Danny's hips to the boy's shoulders, flipping them both so he could fold his mate in half and drive into him properly, chasing his own release.

Sex with Danny had always been mind-blowing, but now, not having to hold himself back anymore for fear of hurting the boy, it was at another level. Roman felt like a mindless, rutting beast, using his mate's body for his own pleasure.

Danny seemed happy to take it, his cock rallying, growing hard and flushed again against Roman's stomach. He was babbling in the way he did when he was overwhelmed and turned on. "Fuck. Yes, yes. Please. Fuck, Rome."

Roman's sack was full and tight against his body, his release imminent, but he held on until his mate came a second time, coating both their stomachs in sticky cum.

Yes.

Pleasure shot throughout his own body, his demon roaring in triumph as he emptied himself into their mate.

Roman and Danny both spent long moments catching their breath. Roman didn't want to move at all. He was content, his weight resting on his mate. Keeping Danny where he belonged—in their bed.

Roman lifted his head. "Show me."

Danny didn't have to ask what he meant. He flushed slightly, embarrassed by the request, but then his eyes shifted to black, and his fangs dropped again.

Roman took it in, the sight of his sweet, formerly human mate shifted. The differences were so slight yet life-altering.

"Am I...am I okay like this?" Roman heard it, the almost imperceptible difference in Danny's voice when his demon was at the forefront. Unlike Roman's, which turned even deeper, almost gravelly, Danny's voice took on a more melodic tone.

Roman smiled at his mate in wonder. "Your demon is as lovely as you are."

Danny smiled, relief lighting up his eyes as they shifted back to brown. "He really likes you," he whispered shyly. "My demon."

"That is fortunate," Roman laughed. "Because I am afraid he is going to have to keep me. I am not going anywhere."

Danny's answering smile was one of the sweetest things Roman had ever seen.

⸻

Roman eyed the candy thermometer sticking out of the copper pot in front of him. A few more minutes, and it would be ready.

He could hear Danny's stomach growling from across the kitchen. Roman hadn't even known vampire stomachs *could* growl, but he supposed he'd never seen a vampire go hungry for long enough to find out. Self-control wasn't normally their strong suit.

As it was, he'd had to forcibly remove Danny from their bed once Roman had realized the shadows under his mate's eyes—the ones being turned had mercifully gotten rid of—were reappearing.

It turned out that, while a newly turned vampire with a bonded mate may have more control over their blood lust than normal, they were insatiable little creatures when it came to *actual* lust. They'd already had sex twice more after Danny's initial claiming of him, and Danny had been ready for another go. But the boy needed sustenance.

It was amazing Danny had gone this many hours already without drinking any blood. Any *human* blood, that was. Roman suppressed a smirk at the memories of his fierce little mate drinking from his neck while riding him. He'd later claimed Roman tasted like "the best candy in the world, sprinkled with crack on top or something."

Roman figured the description was meant to be flattering, if a little disturbing. Was crack-sprinkled candy considered a good thing?

"What's that face for?" Danny asked, watching Roman from the kitchen counter as he heated blood on the stove. Roman had asked Soren to snag a few blood bags from the hospital, much to Danny's dismay.

"Those are for *patients*, Roman," he'd gasped in outrage.

Truly, his little king was too sweet for this world.

But Roman's mate came before all others. He needed blood, and Roman would give it to him. He'd convinced Danny with the argument that it was better than Danny overdoing it on his first feeding and accidentally killing someone.

A new vampire wasn't normally even controlled enough for blood bags—they needed the aggression of a live hunt—but Danny was sitting more or less patiently, waiting for his takeout, as he'd called it, once he'd acquiesced to the idea of a little hospital theft.

Roman hummed to himself as he stirred, not bothering to answer his mate's earlier question. He didn't want to bring up the bite, for fear any mention of sexual activities would lead to Danny jumping Roman again before he could get any blood into his boy.

Although, he supposed there were worse things.

They had already kicked Soren and Gabe out of the kitchen. Gabe because he'd looked visibly ill at the thought of his little brother drinking blood, and Danny didn't need that kind of judgment right now, and Soren because he'd looked *too* delighted at the prospect, and Danny likewise didn't need to feel like a zoo animal.

"Tell me again why we can't just nuke it?" Danny asked. Roman turned to him in horror, and Danny laughed out loud at whatever expression was on Roman's face. "Oh my God, Rome. Is the aversion to microwaves a French thing or an ancient thing?"

"It is a matter of *taste* thing, little heathen."

Danny snorted at him but kept his mouth otherwise shut.

The candy thermometer—Danny had been shocked to find he even had one in his kitchen—hit ninety-eight degrees, and Roman removed the pan from the stove before pouring the heated blood into a mug with a cartoon picture of a fat orange cat on it. He placed the hideous mug in front of Danny, who looked at it a little apprehensively but nonetheless pulled it closer, his eyes turning black and fangs popping out with the motion.

"Drink," Roman urged.

He tried not to give the impression that this was some kind of moment of truth, but in a way it was. It was one thing for Danny to find pleasure in his newfound strength and enhanced senses and quite another for him to face the reality of drinking human blood for an eternity. A bloodthirsty new vampire was usually too keyed up to really think about the implications, but Danny was far too cognizant for that blessed ignorance.

Roman watched as his mate winced slightly, then lifted the mug and threw his head back, draining the blood in one go.

Roman blinked. Well, that was one way to do it.

He waited with bated breath for Danny to gag or declare the blood disgusting, but Roman's mate just looked thoughtful as he licked his lips, placing the mug gently back on the counter.

"Well?" Roman couldn't help but push for a verdict.

"I like yours better."

"You what?" That was not the answer Roman had been expecting.

Danny nodded. "Yep. I mean, I can feel this filling me up properly, which I guess yours doesn't, but your blood is still tastier. Like, this is eggs and toast, but yours is a margarita. Is that a mate thing?"

"Um. I do not know." Roman could feel his mouth gaping a little in his astonishment, but his demon was gloating, feeling *immensely* smug that Danny preferred them to the taste of human blood.

"You are not...grossed out though?" he pressed.

"I mean, I don't love the thought that I'm on a liquid diet for the rest of my life, but you'll still make me French toast sometimes, right?" Danny looked up at him with hopeful eyes.

Drinking human blood for the first time and his first concern is for the possibility of future French toast.

Roman couldn't help himself. He burst out laughing, so long and so deep that he had tears in his eyes by the end of it. Danny cocked his head, a bemused smile playing across his lips. "Is that a no to the French toast?"

Roman walked around the counter to step between his mate's legs. He cupped Danny's lovely face with his hands, his thumbs stroking gently along the boy's cheekbones. "You can have all the French toast you desire, little king. I just...I love you so. I do not know what I ever did to deserve this, but I promise I will cherish it—cherish *you*—always."

"Good." Danny was studying him with eyes that had returned to their lovely deep brown. "Because, like you said, I'm not going anywhere. You're stuck with me. Pretty sure this baby demon in me would hunt you down if you tried to get away."

Danny said it like it was a threat rather than the sweetest promise Roman had ever heard.

"Just your demon?" he found himself asking, echoing the question Danny had once posed to him.

"Of course not, silly." Danny giggled lightly, but there was nothing but trust and adoration in his gaze. "I love you too, Roman. More than I ever thought was possible. You've made my life something magical. And I don't just mean the vampire business. I mean *you*. Everything you are. Magical."

Roman pressed a kiss to Danny's lips, at a loss for words to describe the joy he felt at Danny's declaration. "Should we go tell those two your first feeding was a success?"

Danny crinkled his nose. "First feeding? You make me sound like an infant."

"You are the one who calls it your 'baby demon,' not me. Shall we?"

"Uh-uh." Danny shook his head, a sly smile on his face. "No time for that. I think we need to go back upstairs. My demon and I are hungry for...other things...again." He dipped a hand into Roman's waistband, indicating the direction his mind was headed. "Plus, I want to see if my blood still tastes as good to you, now that I'm all vamptastic and everything."

Jesus.

Roman's cock filled at the thought of sinking his teeth into his mate once more. It had been too long since he'd had his fill of that particular nectar.

"Think you can handle that?" Danny teased, squealing when Roman scooped him up from the kitchen chair, gripping the backs of Danny's thighs and urging his little mate to wrap those legs around his waist.

"I can handle it, little king."

Roman felt like he could handle anything with his mate by his side.

Life was good and the future full of possibility.

Epilogue

Danny

Danny hurried down the hall of the care home, careful to keep his speed human appropriate. He was running behind, but he'd promised to stay until the end of the western he and his mom had been watching, and he never broke his promises to her.

Mary was waiting for him at the front desk, smiling warmly. "Seems like she had a pretty good day again."

Danny grinned at her. "She did. It was lovely."

It had been. Danny hadn't been able to compel her into remembering exactly who he was—those days were getting fewer and farther between, as her illness inevitably progressed—but he'd been able to keep her calm and happy. They'd watched TV together and discussed the different birds they could see through her window.

He would be forever grateful for this extra time with her. Even Gabe had started visiting regularly, although the days she didn't know him still seemed to take a lot out of Danny's brother. He was trying though, and that was more than he'd been doing before.

"When is your hubby coming next? The ladies have been asking about him." Mary winked, and Danny found himself blushing.

"He'll be here with me tomorrow."

His *husband*.

Danny grinned down at the simple gold band glinting on his left hand. He and Roman had been married at City Hall a few months after Danny had turned. Weirdly enough, it had been

Roman's idea. "Your human friends do not understand the concept of mates," he'd said in all seriousness. "We have to show them in some other way that you are mine. *Permanently* mine," he'd emphasized.

Sweet, possessive vampire.

They tried to visit Danny's mother together regularly, but sometimes they switched off their visits so someone would be there to soothe her on any given day. Danny was only working part-time now, as Roman had paid off his mother's place at the home for the next five years. Danny still wasn't sure how much money his vampire was hoarding, but it didn't seem like they'd get to the bottom of it anytime soon.

In his extra time, Danny had been discovering hobbies—he still hated cooking, but it turned out he was pretty good at baking, and he was learning French—and spending time with friends. He had friends now, besides just Chloe. Other coworkers and a few new faces he'd met at a book club he was now a part of.

Ironic that a vampire coming into his world had finally given Danny the full, human life he'd always longed for: family, friends, leisure time. He'd been worried Roman would get bored with small-town existence, but his mate seemed to be reveling in being able to settle into a place for the first time in decades. The little old ladies at the home adored him, as did Danny's coworkers.

Even Soren had stuck around.

After saying his goodbyes to Mary, Danny rushed home. Roman was waiting for him in the kitchen, chopping vegetables at the counter. Gabe would be coming over for dinner later.

"Bonsoir, mon amour," Danny greeted, coming up behind his mate to wrap his arms around Roman's waist, nuzzling the back of his neck. Roman's scent was still Danny's favorite smell in the whole world.

"Bonsoir, mon petit roi," Roman replied, tilting his head back for a kiss. "Have you decided our destination after dinner?"

"The Hideaway, I'm thinking."

They were going out tonight. Danny had put his foot down on stealing more blood bags once they realized he had the control to feed normally, but he didn't like the idea of drinking from people in his town he was going to see day after day. So they'd decided tourists were fair game. He and Roman went to the downtown bars on the weekends. They fed together these days. At first they'd done it to make sure Danny didn't slip and lose control, but they'd continued because drinking blood made Danny's demon pretty frisky and Roman took pleasure in catering to those needs as soon as possible.

More than one alley in town had been witness to their postfeeding indiscretion.

Roman nodded, moving Danny's arms off his waist and stepping back from the kitchen counter. He stepped over to Danny's laptop, which Danny was just noticing lay open on the kitchen table. "There is something we need to address prior to dinner."

Uh-oh.

So far Luc had been true to his word, and they hadn't heard anything of him for the past year. Had that changed?

Roman beckoned Danny to the laptop, where a web browser was open with multiple tabs that he began clicking through. They were all different photos of gorgeous locales: mountains, deserts, tropical beaches.

"Pick one," Roman ordered.

"Huh?"

"Our honeymoon, little king. It is overdue. Pick one."

Danny understood now. He had been avoiding choosing a honeymoon destination. He'd never been anywhere, never left the country. How could he pick just one place? It felt...monumental.

Roman must have intuited the source of Danny's hesitation through their bond, because he brushed his fingers gently along the back of Danny's neck. "There will be more travels, little king. An eternity's worth. This is only the first of many."

Danny took a deep breath and pointed to one of the photos.

Roman gave his waist a squeeze in approval. "Bali. Good choice, mon amour. I will book the tickets. We are taking three weeks."

"Three whole

weeks?" Danny had never had a vacation for that long.

"Mm. Yes. I have been graciously sharing you this past year, but it is my turn to have you all to myself. How do you feel about naked swims in the moonlight?"

Danny thought he was past the point of blushing, but apparently he was wrong. "You spoil me."

"I would spoil you even more, if you would let me."

It was true. Roman delighted in giving Danny everything he asked for.

Danny turned and wrapped his arms around Roman's neck. "How much time do we have before Gabe gets here?"

Danny wasn't quite as insatiable as he had been a year ago, when they'd hardly left his bedroom for a week, but he still couldn't get enough of his mate. Touching him. Tasting him. There was nothing better.

"We have enough." Roman grinned at him. "Come, little king. Show me who you belong to."

Danny scoffed. "You mean who *you* belong to."

He'd meant it to be teasing, but Roman nodded at him, his expression serious. "Yes, I do. For always."

For always.

Nothing had ever sounded better.

The End

Author's Note

Thank you so much for reading Roman! I hope you enjoyed Danny and Roman's story even half as much as I enjoyed writing it.

This was my debut novel, and I couldn't resist centering it around my first paranormal obsession: our fanged friends. I love stories where the paranormal meets the completely mundane, so it started with my brain fixating on the idea: "A vampire walks into a hospital..." and then immediately conjuring up the sweet, slightly sassy nurse who'd be questioning exactly what this rando creature of the night was doing in his hospital.

What's Next?

Soren and Gabe! The stubborn brother and the bratty vamp. I'm working on their story now, and these two together make me giggle and swoon almost as much as they make me bang my head against the table.

If you want to stay in the know, you can sign up for my newsletter for updates and news on upcoming releases. And I can always be reached by email if you just want to say howdy:

graebryanauthor@gmail.com

If you enjoyed Roman, please consider leaving a review on Amazon or Goodreads. I'd love to know what you thought, and as an indie author, reviews are crucial, like, um...blood to a vampire :)

Thank you and happy reading!

About the Author

Grae Bryan has been reading romance since she was far too young to know any better. Her love for love stories spans all genres, and while her current series is of the paranormal variety, she knows she'll be exploring other worlds further down the line.

She lives in Arizona with her husband, who graciously shares space with all the imaginary men in her head. When not writing, she can generally be found reading more than is healthy, walking her monster-dog, or cuddling her demon-cat.

Find her online: graebryan.com

Facebook: @GraeBryanAuthor

Sign up for her Newsletter